After Me

The Unfinished Series
Book 1

Joyce Scarbrough

Copyright 2014 by Joyce Scarbrough

All rights reserved. No part of this book may be reproduced, transmitted, downloaded, decompiled, reverse engineered, or stored in or introduced into any information storage and retrieval system, in any form or by any means, whether electronic or mechanical, now known or hereinafter invented, without the express written permission of the copyright owner, except for "fair use" as attributed quotations in reviews of the book.

All characters in this book are fictional. Any likeness to persons or situations are entirely coincidental.

Original cover design by Malena Lott
Paperback cover design by Treasure Scarbrough
Paperback Edition

ISBN-13:978-1500740221
ISBN-10:1500740225

For Tony S.—my Superhero

Acknowledgments

Thanks as always to the people who support me in everything I do—my husband Tony, my children TJ, Tia and Treasure, and my best friend Lee Ann Ward. Thanks also to my wonderful writing buddies, Carrie Cox, Sandi Buford, Stephanie Lawton, Israel Parker, Chris Cox and Brenda Barry, and to my awesome editor Mari Farthing for all your help in bringing a dead girl to life. I also want to thank my son-in-law Curtis Vickery for reading my manuscript on a Greyhound bus and texting me with 147 helpful comments. And I have to thank Henry Snow for letting us stay at his family's beach house in Gulf Shores and making me fall in love with that swing at the end of the pier.

After Me

Chapter One

When I heard the car doors unlock at the first red light I came to, I knew I'd made a fatal mistake. For a second I thought I'd accidentally hit the button, then I heard the Ferrari's trunk pop open and looked in the rearview mirror just in time to see a man running around to the passenger side, a black bandana covering the bottom of his face.

"Drive!" He got in and jammed the nose of a freakishly big pistol into my ribs. "Go to the intersection and make a U-turn. Keep going until you get back to where you picked up the car."

If I'd still felt emotions like normal girls, I probably would've been scared shitless, but the best I could manage was irritation that he'd tricked me.

"Look, you don't need the gun," I said. "I'll do whatever you say."

"You sure as hell will."

Even more than his words, the laugh that came from behind the bandana was the second thing that told me I wouldn't live to see nineteen. Dang, I'd need my fake ID for all eternity. And it wasn't even a good picture.

I drove until I reached the spot where Courtney had dropped me off half an hour earlier. He told me to keep going over a small bridge and pull off on the dirt road just past. I figured it must've been used by people who fished in the lake, but nobody would be there this late at night.

"Pull between those trees," he said. "Cut the engine and lights."

I did as he ordered, wondering if I should try to open the door and make a run for it as soon as the car stopped. Before I could decide whether or not I wanted to risk it, I felt the gun dig deeper into my side.

"Don't even think about trying to run," he said in my ear. "The door locks are programmed, and I got the only remote."

He snatched the keys from the ignition and put them in his pocket, then he pressed the gun into my neck.

"Now we're gonna do all those things you liked telling me about so much in your messages. You know, all those naughty things you and your girlfriends like to do with the boys and the men teachers at school."

I tried to swallow, but the gun was pressed too hard against my throat. "Hey, you know none of that stuff was true, right? I made it all up because you said you liked that kinda sh—"

"I *know* you made it up! I'm not a *fool*, you little tramp!" The nose of the pistol slammed against my cheekbone and set off fireworks behind my eyes. "I'm sure you had yourselves a good laugh over the way you kept feeding me your nasty little stories to get me all worked up. Well I bet your friends won't think it's so funny when they find out what it got you. And you sure as hell won't be laughing at anybody ever again!"

The side of my face throbbed like a toothache and I still couldn't see straight, but I heard the doors unlock.

"Get out!" He reached across me and opened the driver's side door. "And remember what I said about trying to run. I'll shoot you before you take a step!"

2

I stumbled out of the car and immediately tried to run anyway, but my legs had turned into cooked spaghetti. I fell to my knees on the bank, and before I had a chance to yell for help, a kick to the middle of my back knocked all the wind out of me. Gasping for air on the ground like a dying goldfish, all I got was a mouthful of sand.

"Get up!" He yanked me to my knees by the hair. "Take off your clothes, then get in the back seat!"

"No, listen—"

"Shut up and do what I tell you!" The gun smashed against my other cheekbone and knocked me sideways. "I'm the one in charge, not *you*."

I knew I was close to blacking out and didn't really care, and that gave me an idea. If I made him mad enough to hit me again, maybe it would knock me out so I wouldn't have to know what he did to me before he killed me. I struggled to my hands and knees and managed to lift my head so I could say something that would piss him off for sure.

"You're right, you know. I did laugh at you, you pathetic bastard. The only way you'd *ever* get laid is at gunpoint!"

After a brief flash of pain when the butt of the gun smashed into my skull, I welcomed the darkness.

But my oblivion didn't last long.

When I opened my eyes again, I was sitting on an upholstered chair in a room that almost looked like the guidance counselor's office at Tallahassee Premier Academy where I was a senior. But here everything was painted such a bright white that it almost hurt my eyes, and the sign on the door to my left leading into the inner office was lettered in some kind of glowing gold paint.

When I got up to read the sign, I realized I was wearing some kind of weird white dress. Where had that come from? Had somebody found me and taken me to a hospital?

I knew that wasn't the case when I read the sign on the door: AFTERLIFE ADMISSIONS OFFICE.

"Oh, crap. I'm dead."

Chapter Two

The door was locked, so I turned to go back to my chair and saw another sign on the wall behind it.

TAKE A SEAT AND WAIT TO BE CALLED. NO TALKING.

"Great. I'm in Death Detention."

I sat down with a sigh, then I noticed a magazine rack next to me that held *Eternity Fair, Deadbook, Spirits Illustrated.* Yeah, no thanks.

Could this place be for real, or was it some kind of purgatorial joke? And if I was really dead, why hadn't there been any bright lights or sense of floating or any of the other out-of-body stuff I'd always heard about? All I remembered was getting cracked in the head.

I still didn't feel scared or nervous at all, but that was nothing new. I hadn't really felt anything since Mommie Dearest had found me in the tub of bloody bath water with my wrist slit and she put me on happy pills.

After who knows how long—apparently there were no clocks or watches in the hereafter—I was about to give in and read one of the magazines when the door to the inner office opened and a man in a white suit came out.

"Jada Celeste Gayle," he said, reading from a silver tablet in his hands. "You're next. Follow me."

What choice did I have? I got up and followed him.

The inner office was the same blinding white as the waiting area, but it was filled with cubicles separated by stained glass walls painted with angels and cherubs. At the far end of the room I could see two large doors with a glowing EXIT sign above them. One door looked like it was solid gold and the other had red and yellow flames painted on it. I had some pajamas with the same fiery logo, but I was pretty sure there was no slumber party going on behind that door.

Each of the cubicles contained a pair of white-clad people facing each other across a counter that held a computer with the monitor turned so they could both see the display. I couldn't read the screens except for the heading across the top of each one: LIFESCORE 6.2 ®

Tablet Guy stopped at an empty cubicle about halfway down the aisle and turned to look at me. "Have a seat here. Someone will be with you momentarily. Don't touch anything."

I gave him a salute. "Gotcha. No hacking into God's e-mail while I wait."

He frowned and took a silver stylus from his jacket pocket to enter something on the tablet. "Impudence doesn't help your case any, young lady. If anyone in this department had a sense of humor, we wouldn't be assigned to this office."

After he walked away, I tried to hear what the people in the next cubicle were saying, but everything was drowned out by the god-awful elevator music coming from the speakers on top of the cubicle walls. The best I could tell, it sounded like the Muzak version of *Hannah Montana in Concert*, making me wonder if I was already in the first level of Hell.

A blonde woman wearing a white suit identical to Tablet Guy's sat down across from me and started typing on the keyboard. "Hello, Miss Gayle. I'm Florence, your Afterlife Advisor."

"Florence, huh?" I said. "Doesn't sound very angelic to me."

"Since I'm not an angel, that's really not an issue." She gave me a look without a trace of humor. "I'd think your recent unfortunate experiences would have at least taught you not to be so quick to make assumptions." She went back to typing. "Let's take a look at your account, shall we?"

"My *account*?" I almost laughed. "You mean I was supposed to be saving money to bribe my way in here or something?"

"No. It's your Afterlife Account, and it's what determines whether or not you're admitted and where you'll be assigned."

"Oh, jeez." I leaned back in my chair and looked at the ceiling. More angels. With harps. "If you're gonna put me someplace like this, I'd rather just burn for eternity."

"No, this department is reserved for people who had no sense of humor when they were alive," she said. "For the most part, we're staffed by IRS agents and high school English teachers."

I did laugh at that. "Okay, so what's my assignment? Scrubbing floors for being a slob while I was alive? No—I got it. Washing all this white gear for being a fashion freak."

Florence sighed and looked at the monitor. "I'm afraid you won't be staying with us at all, Miss Gayle. There's an administrative hold on your account."

"A *hold*? Who put it there?"

One of her eyebrows went up. "It's an *administrative* hold. Do you really need an answer to that question?"

"Okay, fine. So what does it mean exactly?"

"It means, Miss Gayle, that in order to clear your account, you'll have to serve time as a Transdead Trustee back on Earth." She typed something else. "I'll print out your instructions and answer any questions you may have before you're sent back."

"Sent back?" I sat up in my chair and leaned forward. "I get to stay alive?"

"Not exactly. You'll be among the living and will appear to be one of them, but you won't be alive, *per se*." Printing sounds came from under the counter, and she bent over to collect a stack of papers. "Here are the details of your specific assignment along with some general guidelines for Trustees. I'll explain anything you don't understand after you read it."

I took the papers and scanned the one on top, then I looked at her as if she were crazy. "I have to track down predators until I find the one who killed me? Are you kidding me?"

"Another pointless question, Miss Gayle."

I threw the papers down on the counter. "Okay, then here's a question for you. Why do I have to go back as some kind of psycho zombie chick as punishment for what that sicko did? He's the one who should have to pay for it, not me!"

"Oh, he will. Make no mistake about that. Your job is to bring him to justice sooner than he expects, possibly putting others like him out of commission along the way." She pointed to a yellow box of text at the bottom of my

8

assignment page. "And you're not being punished, you're paying an early termination fee. As are all Transdead Trustees, you're being sent back to complete what was left unfinished in your life."

"That's a load of crap!" I slapped my hands on the counter. "Just send me to burn and be done with it."

"I'm afraid that's not an option. You had a verbal contract with us that must be honored."

"What contract?"

She typed something then looked at the monitor. "This one."

I watched the screen go black, then I saw myself when I was thirteen, kneeling on the floor next to my bed with my eyes turned heavenward. Florence turned up the volume on the monitor, and I heard myself promising that I would do *anything* to keep my best friend Cassie from dying of leukemia.

"But that's not fair," I said. "Yeah, Cassie went into remission, but look what happened to her later. I shouldn't have to keep a promise for *that*."

"I'm sorry, but we don't argue semantics here. You said you would do anything, and now it's time to pay up."

Chapter Three

After Florence left me to read the rest of the papers, I sat stewing over the unfairness of it all, but I didn't figure it would do me any good to complain. The verdict had obviously come down from the CEO's office, and I didn't suppose there was an appeals committee where I could file a protest.

According to what I read in the "General Rules and Regulations for Transdead Trustees," I would be returning to Earth in a transitional state that wasn't quite dead or alive. I would appear alive to everyone around me, but I wouldn't have to rely on normal body functions like breathing, eating, or sleeping. Any injuries I got would disappear after a short time, and I obviously couldn't be killed.

By the time Florence came back, I was starting to think it all sounded kinda interesting, but I sure wasn't gonna admit that to Ms. No Nonsense.

"Okay, I got some more questions for you," I said. "Where will I be living when I go back? My mother thinks I'm dead, right?"

She typed something then pointed to a list of names on the screen. "You'll be given a new identity and sent to a location far enough away from your mother's home that there will be no risk of your running into someone you know. We have a comprehensive database of artificially generated identities that we use for these purposes."

"Will I still look like myself, or will I be inhabiting a new body too?" The thought made me shudder.

She frowned at me. "This isn't a horror flick, Miss Gayle. Of course you'll keep your own body. We'll simply give you all the necessary paperwork you'll need to assume your new identity, which will be that of a homeless teen with no family ties. You'll need to turn yourself in to a juvenile facility, proclaim that you can't take living on the streets any longer, and request assignment to a foster or group home."

I supposed that could work, but it sure didn't sound like any fun.

"Okay, so after I've assumed a new identity, how do I go about finding the perverts? And what do I do to them exactly? Kill them or just cut off their winkies?"

"All that depends on you, Miss Gayle. But from what I read in the account of how you came to be here through your online dalliances, I'm sure you won't have any trouble finding the men you're after by using the Internet. As to what you do to them, that's completely up to you."

"Wait, won't I automatically get sent to the hot place if I kill somebody? What's the use in clearing my account if I'm gonna end up frying anyway?"

I could tell from her expression that she didn't approve of my terminology. "The usual restrictions on killing do not apply to these creatures. Once they make the choice to become a child predator—even when the child is as old as you—they forfeit their rights as a human creation."

"Sweet," I said. "That's the first thing I've heard in

11

a long time that makes sense."

"Do you have any other questions, or are you ready to assume your first identity?"

"What do you mean my *first* identity? Why will I need more than one?"

"Think about it, Miss Gayle. After you've found and disposed of one of your targets, unless he is the one who killed you, you'll remain among the living and may need to change your identity and location in order to avoid attracting the attention of the authorities. Trustees must always be diligent about protecting their anonymity."

That got my attention. "You mean there'll be others like me down there? Will I know who they are? Can I meet them?"

She sighed again. "Transdead Trustees are not a social club. If you happen to encounter one of the others who are fulfilling their obligations, you would be well advised not to acknowledge them and to stay focused on your own mission."

"So I *will* be able to recognize them," I said. "How can I tell they're one of the undead like me?"

"*Trans*dead, Miss Gayle. Once again, I would remind you that this is not a Stephen King novel. You will also refrain from using terms like zombies, body snatchers and pod people."

"Okay, whatever," I said. "Just tell me how I can recognize other dead kids."

She pressed her lips together while she decided whether or not to answer, then she sighed again. "You'll know them by their eyes. The transdead have black eyes that aren't visible to the living." She reached under the counter for a compact that she handed to me. "See for

12

yourself."

I opened it and looked in the mirror. My green eyes—the one thing I'd gotten from my mother that I'd appreciated—were now solid black orbs where my eyeballs used to be. From what I could tell in the small mirror, the rest of my looks were the same. Blonde supermodel hair and a face that had always been my ticket to anything I wanted. Yay, lucky me.

I handed the compact back to Florence. "Okay, so do I get like heavenly brownie points for all the perverts I take out, or does none of it count until I find the one who killed me?"

"Your prime directive is to find and eliminate the man who murdered you," she said. "However, all of your actions while there will be duly noted in your account. Commendable acts will certainly not hurt your case."

"So what happens after I get rid of the right scumbag? Do I melt or turn into dust, or do I just go up in a puff of smoke?"

She shook her head. "Nothing quite so theatrical. You'll simply disappear and return to this department. Since the identity you'll assume will be that of a girl with a history of running away, your disappearance will be attributed to that once again."

"I guess that makes sense. Okay, let's get this over with. Tell me who I have to be and send me back."

"Wait, there are a few more things you need to know. Under no circumstances are you to contact anyone you knew from your former life. Doing so could possibly jeopardize your mission beyond recovery."

"What happens if I do? Will I get to quit and go on

13

to wherever I'm gonna end up?"

"I'm afraid not, Miss Gayle. If your mission fails because of inappropriate contact, you may have to remain transdead indefinitely."

"Man, that's cold," I said. "Good thing I don't give a damn about anybody from my previous life, huh?"

"Yes, I suppose your emotional detachment is quite fortuitous in this case."

"Okay, so what's my new name?" I turned the screen toward me. "Do I get to pick who I want to be?"

"Of course not." She turned the monitor back around and typed something. "Your new name is Gwen Stewart. You're seventeen years old and have been living on the streets of Miami for the past year after your mother died of a drug overdose a few months ago, and you never knew your father. Along with your new identification papers, I'll print out your complete character profile in case you're asked specific details by the authorities."

I read the highlighted text on the computer screen. "Gwen Diane Stewart. Okay, I guess I can live with that name for a while. What else do I need to know?"

"In order to maintain contact with us here, you'll need access to a computer so you can log in to a blog accessible only to Trustees by using a special password. You are to enter a journal record there of your activities as often as possible. If your foster home doesn't have a computer you can use, you can always go to the library."

"The *library*? I've never been to one of those in my life."

"Considering that life as you knew it is now over, you shouldn't be hampered by past prejudices."

I rolled my eyes. "Fine. So how do I access this

14

blog, and what's the password?"

She hit the ENTER key and the printer went off again. "I'm printing out everything you'll need."

I took the papers from her and noticed that the URL domain for the blog was *blueyonder.net*. I almost cracked up at the idea of a heavenly Internet with wayward nerds doing tech support for eternity.

I stood up to leave, then a thought occurred to me. "Hey, is this what happens to everybody who dies as a teenager? Do they all have to be a Transdead Trustee?"

"That's private information, Miss Gayle. But not everyone has a contract to honor. Unfortunately, some of your peers never had any communication with us whatsoever in their lives, so they never made any promises."

"Lucky for them, huh?"

"I don't think they'd consider it lucky. The alternative is . . . how did you put it earlier? The 'hot place.' I'm sure they'd be happy to trade places with you."

"Oh, yeah. Who wouldn't want to be me?" I said. "The world's newest superhero, Zombie Girl. Pathetic foster kid by day, perv-whacker extraordinaire by night."

Florence folded her hands in front of her and sighed once again. "Although I can't appreciate your humor, Miss Gayle, I hope it will assist you in completing your mission. Perhaps you can incapacitate your targets with laughter."

"Uh-oh," I said. "They might be transferring you out of here soon, Flo. That was almost a joke."

Chapter Four

After dumping the tramp's body in the lake, Julian drove the Ferrari back to the McCarthy mansion in Jacksonville's San Marco neighborhood and parked it with the other cars waiting to be cleaned and serviced. No one had seen him take it from the garage, and no one was around to see him bring it back either. He'd made sure the security camera aimed at this area was turned off before he left for the day, and he knew the security crew was goofing off the way they always did when Morris McCarthy was away on one of his "business" trips to Vegas.

Julian's own archaic Ford Pinto was parked in the staff parking lot where he'd left it. He got in and locked the doors, pausing to slam his hands and forehead against the steering wheel a few times and let out a stream of obscenities before starting the engine.

How could he have been so stupid and let her goad him into bashing in her skull before he got the chance to make her do the things he'd wanted her to do? He was supposed to be the one calling the shots, not *her*. That's what the gun was for. It always turned them into sniveling little girls begging for mercy, willing to do anything he said if he wouldn't kill them.

But this time he'd been cheated. The little whore had pushed his buttons and made him lose his temper. Sure, it had felt good to turn that pretty face of hers into hamburger meat, but not as good as the things he'd been planning to make her do. Now he would have to go downtown and find a hooker, and it was getting hard to find one who hadn't heard through the grapevine that he liked to knock them around as foreplay.

His fury eased a little as he pulled out of the McCarthy grounds and passed the other mansions on his way out of San Marco. He loved pretending he was house shopping and would someday own one of the huge riverside estates instead of working as a personal assistant to the wealthy men who owned them.

By the time he reached the Interstate on-ramp that would take him downtown, he had consoled himself with plans to amp up the online relationship he'd been fostering with a naughty little thing who called herself WETNWILD16. She'd been dropping hints in her messages that sparkly things really turned her on, and Vera McCarthy had a more than ample supply of what she called "disposable" jewelry—complimentary trinkets from upstart jewelers trying to get exposure. She never missed the things Julian pilfered to send to his online sugar babies.

Yes, he'd start this one out with something sparkly, then he'd reel her in with something sporty and fast. And this time he would make sure she stayed alive long enough to repay him for his generosity.

Chapter Five

PAYING IT UPWARD Blog
Saturday, October 5, 2013

Okay, so here's my first week as Jada The Pervert Slayer.

I woke up in an old warehouse somewhere in Miami, surrounded by empty Thunderbird bottles, syringes and used condoms. I couldn't resist testing what Flo had told me, so I broke one of the bottles and stuck the jagged edge into my palm. Nothing—no blood, no pain, and the cuts started to close up almost immediately. It would've been kinda cool if not for the whole being dead part.

I found a purse beside me (a hideous pink sequined thing) that held my new ID cards but no money. The character profile for Gwen said I had been living on the streets and prostituting myself to pay for my meth habit, and once I got outside in the sunlight, (which neither fried me nor made me sparkle) I realized they'd dressed me in my work clothes—a black shirt tied in a knot between my boobs, hot pink booty shorts and silver stilettos. Actually, the purse matched the shorts perfectly. Gwen was color coordinated at least.

I figured I'd just start walking and hope the cops would pick me up. At least that would save me from having to locate the nearest police station to give them my sob story about wanting help to get off the streets. But when I came out of the alley onto the sidewalk, I realized the clothes I had on made me pretty much inconspicuous in that neighborhood.

I found an ancient phone book in a convenience store and looked up the police precincts, but since I'd never been to Miami before and didn't know my way around, the addresses meant nothing to me. While I was trying to think of my next move as I walked out of the store, I saw the old geezer behind the counter watching me like he thought I was gonna steal something. Bingo! Problem solved. I turned down the next aisle and stuffed a box of Mike and Ike and some Combos into my top where they would be obvious, then I headed toward the door.

Long story short, I shoplifted in three different stores and got three offers to trade sex or a blow job for the crap I was trying to steal. Even after I turned them all down and tried to run, none of them called the cops. Finally, I went into Kripke's Package Store and was happy to see a scowling old woman working the counter. I figured she'd either shoot me or call the cops for sure. I tucked a bottle of Mad Dog 20/20 under my arm, and the old babushka didn't disappoint me.

Thirty minutes later, I was in the back of a Miami patrol car, sobbing my poor misguided little heart out. I guess the two cops felt a little sorry for me, although that didn't keep one of them from feeling me up when he searched me before putting me in the car. Anyway, they took me to the juvie center, and after convincing my case worker that I'd had enough of life on the streets, I got sent to a group home while I waited for a foster family to take me in.

I'll skip the sordid details of the group home except to point out that if I'd been there any longer, I'm sure a couple of the male workers would've been my first victims. And I couldn't help feeling bad for real girls like Gwen who had to live on the street or in places like that. My life before had really sucked, but this was a lot worse.

Luckily, after only three days in the group home, I got the good news that a family who was willing to take a teenaged girl had contacted the agency. The next day I met the Shermans, my new foster family. Brad, Karen and twelve-year-old Nathan. Yuppies with a heart of gold, determined to save the world, one teenaged delinquent at a time. Gwen's a lucky girl for sure.

At least there's a computer in my room here so I won't have to hit the library. More later.

I logged off the blog and opened my FaceSpace page to check for new friend requests. With a name like Cherry Licious and a profile picture of legs clad in lacy thigh highs, I'd been getting plenty of requests and private messages from guys of all ages, but none of their names or personal info sounded like the one I was looking for: BOSSMAN. What a joke. I bet that pathetic loser wasn't the boss of anything but his favorite video game.

I shut down the browser and lay across the bed. I still wasn't used to all the things that were different about me now, and I only had a day and a half before I started school on Monday. Like the Transdead Trustee guidelines had said, I hadn't felt any emotions since I came back, but at least I could still appreciate a good joke. Flo probably hated that.

Still, I definitely saw things a lot different now. Take my new foster brother for example. Nathan was a nerdy little kid who would've gotten on my last nerve when I was Jada, but I kinda liked him as Gwen. He had a great sense of humor that I'm sure most of the kids at school totally didn't get, and he was really smart. He was always looking at me like I was Wonder Woman, but even that didn't bug me too much.

Karen and Brad were both pretty okay too. Sometimes they pushed too much for me to "open up" and talk about my past life, but I managed to convince them it was just too upsetting and I wanted to forget it all and start over. Their house in Coconut Grove was nice. Nothing fancy, but they had plenty of space and all the necessities. I even liked my room with its lack of stupid girly decorations. Not a ruffle or pink lampshade in sight, which made me like Karen even more.

The whole transdead thing was weird, but it wasn't as bad as I'd thought at first. At least I wasn't grief-stricken from missing anybody. Jada and Gwen probably had that in common if nothing else. I'd never had another real friend after what happened to Cassie, and the guys I'd dated had only been something to keep me from being bored out of my mind. As for my mother, unless her assistant had programmed a reminder into her iPhone, I wasn't sure she even realized I was gone.

A knock on the door interrupted my fond memories, so I got up and opened it to Nathan's adoring face.

"Hey, Gwen," he said. "Can I ask you about something?"

I waved him in. "Sure, Nate. What's up?"

He sat in my computer chair and swept his bangs out of his eyes the way he did a thousand times a day. "Why don't girls care if a guy's a jerk if he's a jock or he looks like Taylor Lautner?"

Oh, the poor kid. I did my best to answer him seriously.

"Only stupid girls are like that, Nate. You don't want a stupid girl, do you?"

He shook his head and stared at his hands in his lap. "No, but I know a couple who seemed smart up until this year."

"Anybody in particular?"

He didn't look up. "No. Well . . . maybe."

"Look, Nateman." I knelt on the floor in front of him and held his hands. "If this girl really is smart, she'll get over her temporary stupidity in a year or so. And if she doesn't, you're better off without her. Just be yourself and

22

don't worry about what anybody thinks. As hard as it is for you to believe, nothing that happens in middle school or high school is gonna matter after you graduate. Right now it might seem like it's all a big deal, but trust me, it won't mean a damn thing later on."

"Really?" He looked up at me hopefully.

"Yep."

"How do you know that already, Gwen? You're still in high school."

I walked over to look out the window. "Yeah, but I've seen enough of the real world to know what a joke all the high school cliques and clubs and crowns are." I turned to wink at him. "You think I care if anybody's gonna like me when I go to school on Monday? I'll probably never see any of them again after high school. Unless I eat at McDonald's or watch 'Cops.'"

He laughed. "Yeah, they've probably got a hair net with Kirk Simpson's name on it right now."

"Let me guess. Quarterback?"

He shook his head. "Way too dumb for that. Offensive lineman."

"Oh, jeez." I rolled my eyes. "Does this Kirk dude give you a hard time, or do you just want a building to fall on him because the girls drool over his muscles?"

He picked at a hole in the knee of his jeans. "He's been making my life miserable since second grade, but now he does it in front of Lauren Ross every chance he gets."

"What does she do when he acts that way?"

He shrugged. "She doesn't laugh or anything like some of the girls. She usually just looks disgusted and walks away."

"Sounds like she thinks he's a jerk too."

"Then why is she going to the Winter Formal with him?"

"Probably because all her friends *oohed* and *ahhed* when he asked her." I walked over and put a hand on his shoulder. "Look, Nate. If she's got any brains like you thought, she'll find out real quick that he's nothing but a bully and kick him to the curb."

He kept his eyes downcast and sighed. "I won't be holding my breath until that happens."

"Then she's as dumb as he is. And I know a smart kid like you would be bored to tears with a dumb girl, no matter how cute she is. Wouldn't you?"

"Yeah, probably." He looked up at me with a little smile. "But maybe I wouldn't care how boring she was as long as I got to see her in that red skirt."

I pretended to be shocked. "Here I was thinking you were one of the good guys, and you turn out to be a little creeper." I pulled him to his feet and pushed him toward the door with a laugh. "Get out of my room, you disgusting male."

* * *

Monday morning I stepped off the bus at Bay Harbor High School and checked out all the clichéd groups gathered in the parking lot outside the main building—popular kids, druggies, emo kids, nerds, and the outcasts who didn't fit in anywhere. Well, all but one boy who was just sprinting back and forth across the parking lot for no apparent reason, although the look on his face made it clear that he was determined to be on time for *something*.

Like I'd told Nathan, I'd never cared what anybody thought about me when I was alive, so I sure didn't now

24

that I was dead. But my Barbie doll looks and my mother's bank balance had always guaranteed me a spot at the top of the high school food chain, and I'd never considered hanging out anywhere else, mainly because it hadn't been worth the effort. Now that I was free to be part of any group I wanted, why not have some fun?

I ignored the looks I was getting from the A-List crowd and walked toward a group of boys who were all wearing T-shirts featuring comic book heroes or video games. Surely one of them was a computer whiz who might be able to help me track down BOSSMAN.

"Hi, I'm Gwen," I said to nobody in particular. "Today's my first day. Can one of you guys help me find my way around?" They stared at me with their mouths literally hanging open, so I snapped my fingers in front of a couple of faces. "Hello? Anybody in there?"

The boy closest to me—a short little dude with dark curly hair—recovered first and grinned at me. "I'll help you. My name's Sidney—Sidney Ambrose."

"Great, thanks." I pulled my schedule from my purse. "I've got Algebra II and Trig first period. Guess I ought to at least show up, even though it's pretty much pointless."

"Hey, I'm in that class too!" Sidney's brown eyes were huge with excitement. "Don't worry, I can help you pass, no problem."

I smiled and put an arm across his shoulders. "I knew I liked you, Sid."

A tall boy with glasses and a ponytail tapped me on the shoulder. "He gets mad if anybody calls him Sid."

"Mind your own business, Justin." Sidney glared at

him. "She can call me anything she wants."

Justin pushed his glasses up on his nose with an indignant sniff. The rest of the group looked at Sidney with either jealousy or awe marring their acne-ravaged little faces, and I knew he would probably commit grand theft auto for me if I asked.

Out of the corner of my eye, I saw a guy wearing a football jersey walking toward us with a *hey-baby-you-must-be-new-so-I'm-gonna-do-you-a-favor-and-let-you-meet-me* look on his face. Luckily, the bell rang before he reached us.

"Let's go, Sid. We don't want to be late for first period." I linked my arm with his and didn't slow down until we were inside the building and I was sure Mr. Jockstrap wasn't following us.

"I need to stop by my locker first," Sidney said. "Do you know where yours is?"

I stopped and reached in my pocket. "No, but here's the number."

"Wow, it's only four down from mine. What luck, huh?"

I hiked my eyebrows at him. "It must be destiny. Lead the way." While we walked I said, "Hey, you know anything about computers?"

"A little. Enough to keep mine running for our . . . uh, club meetings."

Weekly gaming sessions, no doubt.

"Think you could help me find somebody's IP address?"

"Um, maybe," he said, his face saying *probably not.* "But I know somebody who can for sure. My friend Lew could hack into the Pentagon if he wanted to."

26

My interest meter spiked. "Great. When can I meet him?"

"I don't have any classes with him, but he'll be at practice today after school. If you can hang around, I'll introduce you then."

"Practice for what? Don't tell me he's a jock."

"No, I meant chess team practice." He flushed a little. "Lew's our star player."

"Oh, okay." I did my best not to laugh. "And I bet you're pretty good too."

He shrugged again as we went into one of the classrooms. "I'm just an alternate. Chess isn't really my game."

"Oh, yeah? What is?"

"*World of Warcraft*." His eyes lit up as he said it. "Ever played?"

"Um, no," I said. "Hey, I'd better go get my transfer slip signed and see where he wants me to sit. I'll talk to you after class, okay?"

When the bell rang for the next period, Sidney looked at my schedule card and was heartbroken because we didn't have any other classes together, but he cheered up when he saw that we ate on the same lunch wave. I promised to meet him in the cafeteria, and he left wearing a big smile.

I got looks from several guys in my next two classes, but since I just yawned at them in return, they left me alone. I know it was pretty bitchy of me, but I had no interest in playing their stupid little games. I thought I'd dodged all the pretty-boy bullets until I got to the cafeteria foyer and ran smack into Mr. Jockstrap.

"Whoa, where's the fire, baby?" He stepped in front of me and put his hands on my shoulders. "I promise there's nothing in the lunchroom worth going that fast."

I tried to look as bored as possible. "Nothing out here either."

"You'll change your mind about that after you get to know me," he said. "My name's Matt Winston. What's yours?"

I removed his hands from my shoulders. "First name *Not*, last name *Interested*."

His arrogant look changed to irritation. "What's your problem, babe? You know how many girls would kill to be in your place?"

"Then I guess I'm saving lives by vacating my spot voluntarily, huh? Tell the other girls hi for me."

I walked around him and went into the cafeteria, ignoring the stares I was getting from several of the murderous girls I'd just heard about. I looked around for Sidney and spotted him with a couple of the boys he'd been standing with that morning and one blond guy I didn't remember seeing before.

"Hey, guys," I said. "Can I sit with you?"

"Sure, Gwen!" Sidney slid over to make room for me and almost pushed Justin off the end of the bench. "Here's a spot by me."

I laughed as I sat down. "Thanks, Sid. I knew I could count on you to look out for me."

"Aren't you gonna get a lunch tray?" he asked.

Eating was one of the hardest things for me to get used to. It wasn't disgusting, even though the texture of some things really grossed me out. It was just that I couldn't remember to do it. If I wasn't careful, Karen and

Brad would think I had an eating disorder.

I looked at Sid's tray and made a face. "No offense, guys, but I'm not wasting my lunch money on mystery meat and crap delight. I'll grab a sandwich when I get home from school."

A red-haired boy with braces said, "Here, you can have my apple. I can't eat them unless they're cut up."

Sidney added, "Yeah, by his *mommy*."

"Thanks, uh . . ." I took the apple and tried to remember the redheaded boy's name. "Leonard, right?"

"Right." He gave Sidney a smug grin. "Leonard Webster. But you can call me Leo if you want to."

Justin put down his fork with an offended sigh. "You told us not to ever shorten it because you were named for Leonard Nimoy."

Leonard glared at him. "You really do need to mind your own business, Justin."

I tried my best not to laugh, then I noticed the blond guy at the other end of the table was looking at me like I was wearing *eau de garbage.*

"Hey, Sid," I whispered. "What's with that guy?"

He followed my gaze. "That's Lew Stanton. I told you about him this morning."

"Oh, yeah. The hacker and chess champ. So why's he looking at me like I kicked his dog or something?"

"I don't know," Sidney said. "You want me to introduce you to him?"

Before I could answer, Matt and a coed group of A-Listers walked up to the table.

"Hey look, guys," Matt said. "The geek squad's got a new member." He bent over and put an arm across

29

Leonard's shoulder then pointed at me. "That type of humanoid is called a *girl*. Can you say *girl*, geekboy?"

God, I hated bullies.

"At least he can spell *girl*," I said. "Why aren't you eating, Matt? Haven't mastered the whole opposable thumb thing yet?"

Sidney and his friends snickered, but the look on Matt's face made it clear that he didn't get the reference and also didn't like being laughed at by a bunch of nerds. He smacked Leonard on the back of the head and probably would have done more if one of the teachers hadn't walked over just then.

"Either get in line for a tray or vacate the cafeteria, Winston," the man said. "How many times do I have to tell you and your groupies that?"

"We were just leaving, Mr. Kopelecki." Matt elbowed Sidney as he walked past him.

I hoped I hadn't made things worse for Sid and his friends because of my smartass remarks. I probably should've just kept my mouth shut instead of yanking Matt's chain, and when I saw Lew glaring at me even more, I could tell he was thinking the same thing. Oh, well. So much for getting him to help me with the computer stuff, but there were plenty more nerds to choose from. No biggie.

So why did it bother me so much that this one seemed to hate me?

Chapter Six

By the time the last period arrived, I couldn't wait to get it over with and go back to Brad and Karen's. School had been hard enough to tolerate when I was Jada and needed a diploma for later in life. Gwen sure didn't have any use for one.

When I walked into the room for my chemistry class sixth period, I saw Gwen's name taped to one of the two-person tables and sat down. A second later, I heard a sigh and looked up to see Lew Stanton scowling as he took the seat beside me.

"Yeah, nice to meet you too," I said. "What exactly is your problem anyway?"

He opened his chemistry book and didn't look at me. "Guess I'm just not as impressed by you as Sidney and the other guys. Hope that doesn't screw up your plans or anything."

My plans? Did he know about me? Was he a Transdead Trustee too? I didn't know why I felt so excited at the possibility, but I got up and moved around in front of him to get a closer look at his eyes. They weren't black like mine though. They were blue—an amazing, pale shade of blue that made me catch my breath even though I didn't breathe anymore.

Wait, what?

He scowled at me even more. "What are you looking at?"

"Nothing." I shrugged and tried to act like I hadn't just fangirled over his eyes. "I just want to know what kind of plans you think I've got."

He scoffed and looked at his book again. "Never mind. Just don't include me in any of them."

"Fine with me."

"Fine with me too."

"Glad we agree on something." I sat down and wondered when I had reverted into a third grader.

The bell rang and everyone stopped talking while Mr. Forrester called roll. When he got to Matt Winston's name at the end of the list, I looked around and realized he was sitting at the table behind me. Great. I was surrounded by jerks.

I tried to pay attention to what Mr. Forrester was saying about the chapter we were about to start, mostly to keep myself from looking sideways at Lew, but it didn't work. I couldn't resist checking out his short blond hair with its razor-sharp part, the way his blue Oxford was buttoned all the way up to his neck, the ring on his left hand with the strange black stone, and the almost manicured look of his fingernails. And instead of wanting to laugh at any of it, I found it all weirdly appealing.

What the crap was going on?

At one point, while I was trying to figure out what the weird numbers and symbols on his watch meant, he looked up from his note taking and said, "What are you staring at?"

"What kind of crazy watch is that?"

He glanced at it and sighed. "They're square roots." When I just looked at him, he pointed at one of the numbers. "Instead of twelve, it has the square root of 144.

They're the same thing."

"Yeah, I'll have to take your word for it on that," I said. "Guess that's a math thing or something, huh?"

He rolled his eyes and went back to taking notes. Once Mr. Forrester finished going over the formulas in the chapter, he said he had to go to the office for something and told us to read the chapter in our textbooks. I made it almost to the end of the first sentence before I lost interest. I turned sideways in my seat to face Lew.

"So I hear from Sid you're the star player on the chess team."

He didn't look up from his reading. "I'm the captain."

"Pretty cool," I said, utterly amazed that the words had come out of my mouth. What was with me around this guy?

He closed his book with another sigh. "Look, I don't know why you're pretending to be interested in anything I do, but you're not fooling anybody. I know it's just an act. Like I already told you, I'm not awestruck by you like Sidney and the other guys, so if you think you're gonna sucker me into doing your work for you in this class or something like that, you can forget it."

I could tell my face was flushed, something I couldn't remember happening to me since—oh, I don't know—*ever*, and I felt my throat getting tight like I was about to freaking *cry*. What the hell? There was definitely a glitch somewhere in the Transdead Trustee software, and Flo had a lot of explaining to do. I swallowed the lump in my throat and poked Lew in his buttoned-up chest.

"For your information, Mr. Personality, I care even

33

less about my grade in this class than I do about what impresses you. And just so you know, if I wanted somebody to do my work for me, I could probably get the teacher to do it."

"Wow. Your parents must be so proud of you for that." He opened his book again and turned away.

"Hey, give her a break, Stanton," Matt said loudly from behind us. "She's a foster kid fresh off the streets and doesn't even have parents. She can't help it if she's used to turning tricks for whatever she needs." He looked around to make sure he had everyone's attention. "My girl Lisa checked her out in the office for me last period."

I actually felt kinda relieved, because at least Matt's announcement chased away all the stupid emotions I'd been feeling a second earlier. But before I could give Matt the verbal butt-kicking he deserved, Lew stood up and turned around to face him.

"Shut up, Matt. You don't have room to be putting *anybody* down, and unless you want me to elaborate on why, you'd better shut your mouth."

Everyone in the room except Matt gaped at Lew in total surprise, and if my heart had still worked, it would've been pounding in my chest because he was taking up for me. But even in my enthralled state, I didn't miss the fear that flashed across Matt's face at Lew's threat. He replaced it quickly with anger, but not before I saw it. Yep, Lew had something on him that Matt clearly didn't want anybody to know about.

"Bad move, Stanton." Matt got up and started around the table until he saw Mr. Forrester coming back in the room.

"What's going on here? Mr. Stanton, Mr.

34

Winston—is there a problem?"

Lew and Matt both sat down and shook their heads.

"Good, then I'd suggest you finish the reading I assigned. And I think maybe we need to have a quiz on it tomorrow."

Groans echoed throughout the room. I opened my book and pretended to read, but I didn't even see the words on the page. All I saw was Lew's face when he'd told Matt to shut up. I glanced sideways at him and could tell he wasn't reading either.

"Hey, thanks for that," I whispered.

"Forget it," he replied. "It had more to do with him than it did with you."

"Well, thanks anyway. And if he can't stand you either, I guess we have something in common after all."

He shook his head, but I could see the hint of a smile hiding at the corners of his mouth, and it set off a flock of zombie butterflies in my stomach.

Yeah, Flo had a buttload of explaining to do.

* * *

I got plenty of curious stares from people on the school bus who must've heard about me from Matt and his crowd, but it was easy to ignore them because all I could think about was the crazy way I felt around Lew Stanton. I wasn't supposed to be feeling *anything*, let alone some kind of stupid, giggly infatuation over a guy I wouldn't have ever spoken to while I was alive.

When I stepped off the bus, a guy who hadn't been at the stop with me that morning got off too, and I managed to quit daydreaming about Lew long enough to get suspicious. When he followed me down the sidewalk toward Karen and Brad's house, I stopped and turned around.

"Hey, you lost or something?" I said. "You don't live on this street."

He looked me up and down and laughed. "Just trying to make up my mind how much to offer you."

"Give it up, jerkwad," I said with my hands on my hips. "You wouldn't have enough if you robbed Bill Gates *and* won the Nigerian lottery."

His face lost its smirk, and his hand shot out to grab my wrist. "Don't get uppity with me, you little tramp!"

Maybe it was because it was the same thing BOSSMAN had called me on the night I died, but his words echoed in my head like they were being broadcast from a loud speaker. It suddenly seemed as though I were looking through some kind of red film or at a TV with the tint turned completely to red. I snatched my arm free and pushed him in the middle of his chest with both my hands, and he went flying backward at least ten feet to thud against a sycamore tree in the yard behind him.

Wait, what?

I stared at my hands in amazement. "*Sweet.* Super zombie strength."

Both my rage and the red filter over my vision dissolved quickly as I wondered what other cool things I could do. Fat boy had lost consciousness when he hit the tree, and I didn't care enough to wait around and see if he ever came to. I wasn't worried about consequences, at least not Earthly ones. What was he gonna do? Tell the cops a hundred-pound girl threw him into a tree?

When I got home, Nathan was eating microwave pizza rolls at the kitchen bar while he did his homework. I sneaked one off his plate and popped it into my mouth, even though it was like chewing a mouthful of minced cardboard.

"Hey, get your own," he said. "There's another box."

Karen poked her head out of the utility room. "So you do eat occasionally, Gwen. I was beginning to worry that you had anorexia."

"Nah, and I don't have that barfing one either." I got the other box of pizza rolls from the freezer. "I just can't eat a lot at one time. I guess it's from not eating much while I was on the street."

I turned to put the pizza rolls on a plate and stick them in the microwave, smiling at my double score—I'd remembered to eat and polished my homeless waif storyline a little more at the same time. I didn't have to see it to know that Karen and Nathan were exchanging sad looks about my heartbreaking life on the street, and I knew Karen wouldn't bug me about eating from now on.

I took the pizza rolls upstairs to my room, then I logged onto the blog and posted in all caps for Flo to contact me ASAP because I had some questions for her. A few minutes later, the theme music from *Dexter* announced that I had a new e-mail message.

FROM: florence@blueyonder.net
TO: dead_girls_do_it_better@gmail.com
SUBJECT: Contact Request

Dear Miss Gayle:

You may reply to this message with your

questions.

Regards,
Florence

P.S. Change your e-mail address to
something more appropriate.

A knock on my door interrupted me before I could
type my message to Flo. I minimized my e-mail and called,
"Come in."

Karen opened the door and poked in her head. "Just
wanted to see how your first day at school went."

I shrugged. "Fine. Pretty much the same as the last
school I went to."

She came in and sat on the end of the bed. "Make
any friends?"

"Yeah, I met a guy named Sid and some of his
buddies. They're all pretty nerdy, but I like 'em."

"What about girlfriends?"

I scoffed. "Girls don't like me. They usually think
I'm after their boyfriends or something stupid like that. It's
okay. I've never been one for the BFF thing anyway." I'd
answered from Jada's experience, but I figured it probably
fit Gwen's profile too since I couldn't imagine many girls
being okay with having a hooker for a friend.

Karen covered my hand with hers and sighed.
"Well, everybody needs a friend they can talk to and
confide in. If you don't find one your own age, I'm always
willing to listen if you want to talk."

Wow, so this was what it was like to have a mom.

I smiled and squeezed her hand. "Okay, thanks. I
might take you up on that."

38

After Karen left, I finished my message to Flo and sent it.

> FROM: dead_girls_do_it_better@gmail.com
> TO: florence@blueyonder.net
> SUBJECT: What the hell?
>
> I thought you told me Transdead Trustees don't feel any emotions, so why did I just spend my first day at school mooning over some guy like a love struck sixth grader? And if that's not bad enough, he's a total geek and hates my guts. Somebody's got some explaining to do!
>
> Jada

While I waited for her reply, I checked FaceSpace but still didn't think any of the men trying to hook up with me were the perv I was looking for, and I didn't see anyone who might be him on their list of friends either. I wasn't really sure how I'd recognize him, I just knew I would. I accepted a few friend requests just to broaden my search.

Of course, the best way to find him was to go back to one of the Sugar Daddy chat rooms where I'd found him in the first place, but I didn't want to do that. The last time had gotten me a bunch of disgusting porn sent by e-mail, and I didn't want that happening again.

I lay across the bed on my back with my eyes closed, and Lew's face immediately appeared in my mind. God, he'd looked so cute when he'd been trying not to smile at what I said about us having something in common. I couldn't wait to see him smile for real.

Wait, what?

I sat up and slapped myself on both cheeks. "Stop it! You do *not* have the hots for Captain Chess Champ."

My e-mail notification rescued me from any more self-abuse, but when I sat in front of the computer to read Flo's message, with each sentence I wanted to throw myself out the window more and more, even though it wouldn't have done me any good.

FROM: florence@blueyonder.net
TO: dead_girls_do_it_better@gmail.com
SUBJECT: RE: What the [redacted]?

Dear Miss Gayle:

Apparently, an addendum to your termination agreement was inadvertently left out of your paperwork, and the new objectives were just uploaded today. In addition to your prime directive of finding the man who killed you, you must also learn to handle normal human emotions, since you did not experience them while you were alive. This explains your feelings for the young man you mentioned. Don't be surprised if you also feel a strong desire to befriend another girl your own age. These things are not negotiable. So, in the vernacular of yourself and your peers, you need to "deal."

Don't forget to change your e-mail address.

Regards, Florence

Chapter Seven

I decided to wait until after dinner before replying to Flo's bombshell, hoping I would cool off by then so I wouldn't say something to get myself sentenced to working in the Heavenly DMV. I tried to hide my bad mood from everybody while we ate, but I guess it showed.

"Karen tells me you made some new friends at school today," Brad said as he shook hot sauce onto his fajita. "Think you're gonna like it there?"

I shrugged. "It's okay. Some of the kids are all right and some are jerks. Same as any school I guess."

Brad set down his glass of tea and frowned. "Did somebody give you a hard time about being new?"

His defensiveness about me was touching, just like Karen's offer to be my friend. Another emotion I wasn't used to and didn't know how to handle.

"Not really," I said. "Some guy named Matt didn't like it when I wasn't wowed by his football jersey, so he made a few smartass . . . I mean, smartaleck comments about how I was a foster kid. No big deal."

"How did he know you're a foster kid?" Karen was frowning as much as Brad.

"One of his minions in the office told him," I said. "It's okay. My chemistry partner shut him up pretty quick." I hurried to take a bite of my fajita so they wouldn't see the goofy smile I knew was about to spread across my whole face at the memory of how Lew had taken up for me. What a total dork I was turning into.

41

"Oh, really?" Brad said. "Who's your chemistry partner?"

"His name's Lew Stanton." I couldn't suppress a dreamy sigh after I said his name. "He's the captain of the chess team, and he's really smart." When I saw the amazed look that passed between Karen and Brad, I knew my face must look just as stupid as I sounded. Before either of them could say anything, Nathan chimed in and added another level to my personal Hell.

"Oh, man, he's *awesome*. Remember, Mom? Last month you drove me and the guys on the math team to watch one of Bay Harbor's chess tournaments. He was the blond guy who won the whole thing."

"Oh, yes." Karen still looked amazed. "And you . . . like this boy, Gwen?"

This time I knew for sure my face was as red as the peppers in my fajita, and it felt like it was being remote controlled by some whacked-out puppeteer. I looked around the table at all of them and knew it wouldn't do me any good to fight it or deny it.

"Yeah, I guess so," I said. "He couldn't stand me at first because he thought I wanted to copy his homework or something, but I think he knows different now." I took another bite of my cardboard-flavored fajita.

"Well, he sounds like a very nice boy," Karen said. "Maybe you could invite him over for supper one night."

"Oh, man!" Nathan said. "That would be so cool. Maybe he could show me *en passant*."

"Yeah, maybe," I said, my phantom heart racing at the thought of Lew coming over. "I might even get you to teach me how to play, Nateman."

Karen and Brad exchanged another amazed look, and I stuffed the rest of my fajita in my mouth to shut myself up.

Back in my room, I made a new e-mail account before replying to Flo's message.

FROM: stuck_in_nerd_hell@gmail.com
TO: florence@blueyonder.net
SUBJECT: Redact this!

This seriously bites, Flo. I'd try to sue or
something, but I'm sure it wouldn't do me
any good and all the lawyers are probably in
hell anyway. I also think your department
should have to pay a penalty for a screw-up
like this. I hope your computers get a virus
that replaces all your records with knock-
knock jokes and bad puns.

Jada

I sent the message then decided to check FaceSpace again. Maybe I'd get lucky and find the perv who killed me before I geeked out completely and started a chess club pep squad or something equally pathetic.

Five more friend requests—four from guys whose profile pictures were bare torsos or flexed biceps, and one from a girl wearing a bikini made out of beads. I accepted them all and noticed something while checking out their walls: they all belonged to some of the same groups for "meeting other people looking to have some fun."

Why hadn't I thought of that before? I typed *sugar daddy* in the search box, and seven groups came up. After I joined them all, I was able to look at the member list for each one. None of them used real pictures—at least not face shots—but I could look at their info pages and see if any of them listed the same obviously bogus stuff that BOSSMAN had put in his profile on the Sugar Daddy chat forum where I'd met him. Like how he enjoyed sailing his yachts and hand buffing his Ferrari collection. Yeah, he probably did some hand buffing all right, but not on any cars.

I found a couple of possibilities and sent them all friend requests. Once they started sending me private messages like I knew they would, I felt sure I'd recognize the lines BOSSMAN had used to hook up with me on the Sugar Daddy forum.

Before I logged off, I got another idea and typed Lew's name into the search box. The first four that came up weren't him, but the fifth one was *Lewis Mackenzie Stanton,* and the profile picture was a marble chess piece. Sidney, Leonard and Justin were all on his list of friends.

Since I obviously couldn't send him a friend request from Cherry Licious, I made another account in Gwen's name and sent the request along with a note that took me a ridiculous amount of time to compose and ended up saying nothing but *Hey from your chemistry partner.* I also sent requests to Sidney and the rest of the guys so it wouldn't look like I was singling Lew out.

Within seconds, I got notifications that the nerd battalion had accepted my friend requests, but nothing from Lew. I left FaceSpace open in case I got another notification, making sure I was offline for chat so Sidney and the guys wouldn't start sending me IMs.

Since the transdead weren't immune to accumulated grime, I still had to shower and wash my hair like everyone else, so I got my pajamas and went into the bathroom. While I was standing under the pulsating stream from the massaging showerhead, I realized I missed little things like how good it felt for a hot shower to pound away the tension in sore muscles. I could feel the water hitting me, but I couldn't tell if it was hot or cold. Apparently, the neurons and synapses of the transdead didn't continue to transmit the way they did in the living.

Wait, what?

How the crap did I know anything about neurons or synapses? And not only that, I realized I suddenly understood how the whole nervous system operated. Great, my transformation into nerd girl obviously involved more than just crushing on chess players. I was turning into some kind of freaking brainiac myself. The super zombie strength had been cool, but this had to be the lamest superpower ever.

* * *

When I got on the school bus the next morning, the guy from the day before stuck his foot out in the aisle in front of me. "Better watch your back, bitch."

I smiled at him. "How'd you get that lump on your head, Tree Boy? Unless you want some foot pain to go along with that headache, you better move that smelly cross trainer outta my way."

One of his hands wandered up to the back of his head. He muttered something about how I'd be getting mine, but he took his foot out of the aisle and didn't meet any of the curious looks from the people around him.

"Yeah, I thought so," I said before walking away and sitting in the first empty seat I came to. I'd always been able to deliver verbal punches to anybody who messed with me, but I liked knowing I could back it up with some brawn now if I needed to. I might've been a stuck-up, callous bitch in my former life, but I'd always hated bullies like this guy and the way Matt Winston treated Sid and his friends. Maybe I could add my own addendum to my assignment and let Jada the Pervert Slayer teach them not to pick on my friends.

I was still snickering to myself when I noticed the girl across the aisle—a mousy little thing wearing clothes that had to have been through at least two previous owners—looking at me curiously. I opened my mouth to ask her what the hell she was looking at, then I changed my mind and smiled at her instead. She looked startled for a second before smiling back at me.

I tilted my head in Tree Boy's direction. "Hope that guy's not a friend of yours."

"Dougie? No way." She frowned at the back of his head, then she leaned toward me and whispered, "You should've stomped on his foot."

I laughed and stood up. "Hey, is it okay if I sit with you?"

"Sure." She slid over to make room. "My name's Annalee. What's yours?"

"Gwen Stewart. I just transferred in yesterday."

"Welcome to Bay Harbor, state champions in football, softball, and worst cafeteria food."

I laughed again. "Yeah, it definitely tastes like cardboard to me. So why do you hate Tree Boy? What'd you say his name is—Dougie?"

She nodded. "Dougie Shaw, and he's been a jerk since kindergarten. He used to break all the girls' favorite crayons and laugh at us for crying. What'd he do to you?"

I shrugged. "He heard I was a foster kid and tried to give me a hard time about it."

"Why do you call him Tree Boy?"

"Oh . . ." I scrambled to think of a believable story. "When he wouldn't leave me alone, I sorta tripped him and

46

made him crack his head on a tree."

"God, I wish I could've seen that." Annalee laughed loud enough to draw Dougie's attention and make him glare at both of us. "I know a lot of people he's been picking on for years who'll be happy to start calling him by his new nickname."

"Glad I could help." I gave Dougie a little wave using just my middle finger, and Annalee giggled behind the book in her hands. I tapped it and said, "What're you reading?"

She held up the paperback. "*The Grapes of Wrath.*"

I winced. "English assignment?"

"No, I'm working my way through a list of classics I got from the circulation manager at the library. He's been trying to get me to come to his book discussion group, but I haven't gotten up the nerve yet."

"You're reading classics because you *want* to?"

She looked embarrassed. "Yeah, I'm kinda weird like that. Most of them are a lot better than I expected, like this one. The only one I haven't liked so far is *On The Road.*"

"What's that?" I said. "Willie Nelson's autobiography?"

She looked at me funny until she realized I was kidding, then she laughed. "I probably would've liked that better."

I opened my mouth to make some smartass comment about how I'd rather have my eyelids stapled shut than have to read a book, but that's not what came out.

"Hey, you think you could get me a copy of your list and mark the ones you like? Maybe I'll give 'em a look."

Wait, what?

"You like to read?" She looked even more surprised to hear it than I was.

"Oh, yeah," I said. "Mostly just popular stuff like Stephen King and Harry Potter, but maybe I'll try something different."

The lie came out so smoothly that I had to admire my deceptive skills even though I couldn't believe how far I'd sunk into nerdhood. And the weirdest thing was that I knew I wasn't doing it because I thought it might impress Lew or anything like that. No, I was pretending to be a bookworm because I really, *really* wanted Annalee to like me. Flo's prediction about finding a friend had come true, and I could just imagine her smug look.

And wouldn't you just know that the girl I wanted so much for Gwen's BFF would be somebody so completely different from anyone I would've picked when I was Jada? But it could've been worse. At least Annalee wasn't one of those perky cheerleader types who never stopped smiling and went around hugging everybody all the time.

She still looked like she thought I was pranking her about wanting the book list, but she said, "Okay, I'll get a copy made at the library and give it to you in the morning. Unless you want to go there with me after school today."

"Sure. Sounds great." The words popped out of my mouth before I had time to clamp my hand over the traitorous orifice. "What time are you going?"

"Right after school. It's close enough to walk from my bus stop."

"Okay, I'll get off at your stop and go with you."

"Great." She gave me another smile, and I resisted a sudden urge to hug her like one of the girls I'd been mocking a few seconds earlier.

Oh, yeah. Me and my new bestie chilling at the library. Maybe we could cruise by the reference section before we left to check out all the hot guys.

My sarcastic thoughts lost all their effect when I realized how much I was hoping Lew might be there and just how much my idea of a hot guy had changed since my untimely death.

Chapter Eight

When we got to school, I waited to see if Dougie tried to start something with me, but he just got off the bus and stalked away toward a group of guys standing around a mud-covered Jeep. As soon as Annalee and I stepped off, I saw Sidney and the guys—minus Lew, dang it—waving frantically at me from their spot by the cafeteria doorway.

I pointed them out to Annalee. "Hey, do you know Sid and his *World of Warcraft* buds?"

"I know Sidney from chess club," she said. "I've got some classes with a couple of the others, but I don't really know them."

"Wait, you're in the chess club too?" *Another Lew connection* flashed in my head like an Internet pop-up window. "How cool is that?"

"You think that's cool?" she said. "Really?"

"Sure. I suck at playing myself, but I love watching a good match. C'mon and I'll introduce you to the guys."

Yep, super lying ability was definitely one of my new zombie powers. I waited a few seconds then did my best to sound casual as I asked her the most important question.

"So I guess you know Lew Stanton too, huh?"

"Oh . . . yeah." Her ivory skin immediately turned a lovely shade of mauve. "He's the team captain and our best player."

Oh, God. She had a crush on him too.

I tried to keep walking normally, even though I was getting slammed with more alien emotions. Jealousy and a sudden fear that Lew might like Annalee better—pretty likely considering he couldn't stand me—along with a knot of worry that she might not want to be friends with me if she knew we liked the same guy. Jeez, why couldn't they just send me to fry instead of making me endure all this crap?

"Yeah, I heard he was pretty good," I said. "He's my chemistry partner, but he hates my guts."

She looked surprised. "I can't imagine a guy not liking you."

As if to back up her statement, Sidney and his friends greeted us with a four-part chorus of *Hi, Gwen* and began asking if I needed help with anything for the day. None of them even glanced at Annalee.

"Hey, guys," I said. "This is my friend Annalee. She's on the chess team with you—right, Sid?"

"Oh, yeah. Right." He nodded. "I thought your name was Leeann."

Annalee's ratty Converses suddenly seemed to fascinate her. "A lot of people get it wrong. I just don't correct them."

Sidney looked at me again. "Thanks for adding me on FaceSpace. I sent you a message on chat last night."

"Me too," Leonard said and got a dark look from Sidney.

"I had to get off and do my homework," I said. "Are you on FaceSpace, Annalee?"

"Yeah, but I don't get on much." She still didn't look at anyone. "And the library blocks chat on their computers."

"You don't have one at home?" Justin asked.

51

The poor guy probably didn't mean anything by it and was just surprised that anybody our age didn't have a computer of their own. But when I saw how his question made Annalee blush with embarrassment, I turned on him before I could stop myself.

"Not everybody lives a pampered little life at the end of a cul-de-sac, you know! You really need to listen to your buddies and learn to mind your own damn business, Justin." I poked him in the chest and made him stumble backward.

"Jeez, I'm sorry," he said, straightening his glasses. "I was just asking because I've got an old laptop she can have if she wants it."

Everybody—including Annalee—was staring at me in surprise, and I wished there was a hole somewhere nearby that I could crawl into.

"Oh . . . my bad, Justin. Guess I'm still kinda touchy about stuff like that. Comes from living on the street for the last year, you know?"

That little tidbit rendered everybody speechless, and I was happy to hear the bell so I could escape the awkward silence. As we all walked in, I said to Annalee, "Hey, when do you eat lunch?"

"Fourth lunch wave, but I usually go to the library and read."

Again with the library. It was almost as if somebody up there with Flo was determined to get me into one for some reason. Maybe I'd be trapped there like a poltergeist once I finally entered.

"Great, I eat then too," I said. "Wanna come sit with me at Sid's table so I won't be the only girl?"

"I don't know . . ."

I elbowed Sid and gave him a look that said he'd

better back me up.

"Oh, yeah," he said, rubbing his arm. "Come sit with us, Leeann."

Justin elbowed him from the other side. "Her name is *Annalee*."

I smiled and put an arm across Justin's shoulders. "Sorry about what I said earlier. You're all right, Justin."

He gave Sidney a triumphant look. "Thanks, Gwen. If you want to, you can call me by my screen name— Jus'Tarin."

I did my best to keep a straight face. "Maybe we'd better preserve the sanctity of that one. How 'bout if I call you Justintime?"

"I like that." He grinned and pushed his glasses up again.

"See you later, Gwen." Annalee started down the middle hall. "I need to go to my locker."

"Okay, I'll wait for you in the cafeteria foyer at lunchtime," I called after her. She waved but didn't commit to our lunch date.

Sidney tugged on my arm. "Come on, Gwen. We'll be late for Algebra."

I looked at him with my arms folded. "Okay, *Seymour*. Wait, you mean that's not your name? Oh, well. Maybe I'll remember it next time."

He smiled sheepishly. "Sorry. But she said lots of people call her that."

"Well, not anymore. At least not around me."

Yep, now I could add righteous indignation to my emotional collection. I walked down the hall toward my locker, imagining myself wearing some crazy version of a Girl Scout uniform with emotional badges pinned all over it. Golly gee whiz, maybe I could get my loyalty and empathy badges before the day was over!

* * *

When lunchtime arrived, I spotted Annalee trying to cut across the concourse outside the foyer and managed to intercept her before she reached the library steps.

"Hey, they're serving pizza today," I said. "I hear it's the least disgusting item on their menu. Come on in with me."

She shook her head and tried to slide past. "Thanks, but I want to read some more of my book. The Joad family just got to the government migrant camp in California. Lots of exciting stuff happening."

"Aw, come on," I said. "I don't want to be the only girl at the table again."

"You could come to the library with me. I've got an extra banana and some butter cookies we can share."

Great, more conflicting emotions. I really wanted some girlfriend time with Annalee, but I also knew Lew was in the cafeteria with Sid and the guys. Sad as it was to admit, I'd spent the whole morning waiting for the chance to gaze at his well-groomed countenance while he ate his lunch.

I sighed and linked my arm with Annalee's. "Okay, you talked me into it. But you gotta promise to come with me tomorrow."

She smiled. "It was the butter cookies that did it, right? I love to eat them off my fingers like they're rings."

I stopped as a memory kicked me in the gut. Me and Cassie in kindergarten with butter cookies on our fingers, pretending they were our diamond rings. Cassie had always loved coming up with make-believe games for us to play, like fancy ladies or kidnapped princesses. She told me she was gonna write books when she grew up, and I know she

54

would've done it too. If she'd gotten the chance to grow up.

"Gwen, what's wrong?" Annalee put a hand on my arm. "You look like you just saw a ghost or something."

"I did."

I swallowed the lump in my throat and wondered why it suddenly seemed like I was looking at Annalee through a heat haze, then I realized what it was. My eyes were full of tears. I hadn't cried since Cassie's funeral, and the idea of actually crying in front of somebody made me look around for a way to escape, but Annalee grabbed my arm before I could take a step.

"Come on, I know a place we can go." She pulled me around to the back of the library building and led me to a recessed doorway where we both sat down. "I come here to read when it's not so hot outside. Nobody will bother us here."

A few tears had spilled over on our way around the building. I wiped them away and thought I could keep any more from falling, until Annalee put her arm around me and really turned on the flood. I wanted so bad to tell her what had happened to Cassie and how I'd felt like my life had ended then too. But I couldn't talk to her about any of it because I wasn't Jada anymore. I was Gwen now, and she was a street kid who'd never had a best friend like Cassie.

"Tell me what's wrong," Annalee said.

I shook my head. "It was just a stupid memory from when I was a kid. Back before my mom got really bad and took off." Apparently, my zombie lying powers still worked even when I was an emotional three-car pileup. "How'd you know to bring me around here before I could run?"

Her fingers toyed with the frayed hem of her jeans.

"I've seen that panicked look staring back at me from my mirror a million times. I knew you were about to take off, I just didn't know why." She looked up at me with a little smile. "You can tell me about it if you want to, but it's okay if you don't."

"I can't right now," I said. "Maybe someday."

She nodded and squeezed my hand. "Okay. I'll tell you my story then too. We can call it the Crappy Life Contest. Winner gets a Kit Kat bar."

I laughed. "It's a deal, but I'm a Butterfinger girl myself."

"You wanna go in the library since it's like two hundred degrees out here?"

"Sure. I'm fine now," I said and meant it. I couldn't believe how just the prospect of a heart-to-heart talk with her had made everything better, even though I knew I'd have to tell her Gwen's story instead of mine. And I really wanted to know why she sometimes felt panicked enough to run. Maybe I could try to help her with it.

I could just imagine Flo up there in her cubicle, gloating over my newfound appreciation for friendship, especially since it was also getting me into a library. As Annalee and I walked through the double doors, I looked up and stuck out my tongue.

* * *

By the time I made it to chemistry class, I was floating on an Annalee-powered magic carpet, my face plastered with a goofy smile I couldn't have hidden if I'd wanted to. And I didn't. Having a best friend again was pretty awesome, and not even Lew's less-than-welcoming look when I sat down could ruin my good mood.

"Miss me at lunch, Bobby Fischer?"

"Hardly," he said.

56

His expression told me he was surprised that I knew who Bobby Fischer was—something that surprised me even more. I waited to see if he would ask where I'd been. When he didn't, I told him anyway.

"I went to the library with my friend Annalee. She's on the chess team too. You know her?"

He looked at me suspiciously. "Yeah. How do you know her?"

Oh, God. A *question*. I was making some real progress now. "We ride the same bus and found out we have a lot in common. In fact, we're going to the library today after school so she can get me a copy of her book list."

"You know how to read?"

I faked a laugh. "Cute. Your humor is surpassed only by your charming personality."

His frown deepened. "Look, you'd better not be using her for some messed-up plot to infiltrate the nerd squad or something. She's got enough to deal with already."

So much for my good mood. If there had been such a thing as an emotional overload signal, mine would've been flashing like crazy. Jealousy hit me from one side because he was so defensive of Annalee, concern slammed me from the other side over what exactly Annalee had to deal with and how he knew about it, and my feelings were hurt because he thought I was a bitch who would use innocent people. Naturally, I decided to go with my old friend—anger.

"No, *you* look, jerkface!" I poked him on one of his Oxford buttons. "I don't know what turned you into such a snob that you think it's okay to make snap judgments about people you don't even know, but you're dead wrong about

57

me. And you'd better not be spreading your snotty assumptions to my friends either. In fact, why don't you just pretend you don't know me at all and forget my name altogether!"

I opened my chemistry book to some random page and glared at the illegible words, telling myself over and over that I was pissed and not hurt so I wouldn't cry again. I bit my lip hard to keep it from quivering, then I remembered I didn't feel pain anymore and might bite through it. I was about to get up and run to the bathroom when I heard a sigh from Lew's side of the table.

"I'm sorry," he said. "You're right. I shouldn't be making assumptions about you."

Oh, jeez. Was that a freaking choir of angels I heard singing, complete with harps? I swallowed several times and did my best to resist looking at him in glorious adulation.

"Forget it," I said. "Just don't do it again, okay?"

"Okay, I'll try."

Not exactly a profession of his undying love, but I still felt giddy and didn't trust myself to say anything else. Fortunately, Mr. Forrester began to call roll, then he reminded everyone of the quiz he'd promised us the day before. While he passed out the test papers, I sneaked a look at Lew and could tell our conversation had affected him too. Maybe I could take advantage of it some more after class.

But I forgot all about scoring points with Lew as soon as I turned over my test and discovered that even though I hadn't read a single word of the chapter about atomic and molecular structure, I knew the answer to every question on the quiz. In fact, when I closed my eyes, I could see the entire periodic table of elements.

I started answering the questions as fast as I could, a smile on my face at the thought of the potential brownie points it could mean when Lew found out I had super zombie smarts.

Chapter Nine

I finished my test in no time, but I realized I'd better wait a bit before turning it in so Mr. Forrester wouldn't think I'd cheated. And I tried to look like I was struggling to remember something in case anyone was watching. Of course, Lew was too busy making sure I couldn't see his paper to notice my amazing acting skills. As soon as I saw Gary Gradepoint two rows over get up to turn in his test, I took mine up to Mr. Forrester's desk. I could tell he was surprised when I handed it to him.

"Finished already, Miss Stewart?"

I nodded. "Yep. Is it okay if I read my library book now?"

His surprise grew a little more. "Yes, absolutely. By all means."

I went back to my seat, loving the astonished look on Lew's face. I gave him a cutesy little smile as I sat down and took out the copy of *To Kill a Mockingbird* Annalee had talked me into checking out at lunch. My plan was to only pretend to read, but the story had me hooked before I knew it, and I couldn't seem to get my eyes to move fast enough across the pages. I didn't look up again until I felt somebody poking my shoulder.

"The bell rang," Lew said. "Didn't you hear it?"

I looked around and realized everyone was leaving the room. "Oh. Guess I got distracted by this crazy book. That little Scout chick is a trip."

He narrowed his eyes. "What part are you on?"

"They just found out the hole in the tree is filled with cement." I stood up and dropped the book into my backpack. "Pretty lousy thing to do if you ask me."

A slow transformation took place on his face, and I knew he hadn't believed I was really reading it until then. He was looking at me as though he were seeing me for the first time, and my knees actually got weak when he smiled at me. And to think it was all because I finally went into a library.

"It's a great book," he said. "I can't believe you've never read it before. Oh . . . sorry. Forget I said that, okay?"

"Don't sweat it." I hooked my backpack over one shoulder and walked around the table, hoping my legs would support me without wobbling. "Annalee couldn't believe it either when I told her. She's the one who talked me into checking it out."

He picked up his own backpack and walked out of the room beside me—actually walked *with* me. I wondered if we had little Cupids circling our heads but resisted the urge to look up and see.

"You just got it last period and you're already that far into it?"

I shrugged. "You didn't know speed reading was a mad skill on the streets? Can't afford to get a library fine when you got open warrants, you know."

He looked unsure whether to laugh or not, so I bumped his arm with my elbow.

"Hey, lighten up," I said. "All that's behind me now. My foster family's great, and I don't plan to ever go back to that life."

He smiled again with the same effect on my knees. "I'm glad you've got a good family. Everybody's not so lucky."

Well, that definitely screamed for some elaboration, but before I could ask him what he meant, Matt Winston grabbed a fistful of Lew's shirt and pushed him against the lockers on the left side of the hall.

"Speaking of families," Matt said through clenched teeth, "yours won't be able to protect you if you ever talk to me again like you did yesterday!"

Lew glared back at him. "You know your threats don't scare me, Matt. And my family has nothing to do with it."

His grip tightened on Lew's shirt. "Keep pushing me and you're gonna regret it, rich boy. That's a promise and not a threat."

I recovered from my stunned immobility and pushed Matt hard enough to make him stumble and let go of Lew's shirt but not hard enough to send him flying down the hall.

"Correct me if I'm wrong, Matt," I said as I moved between him and Lew, "but I believe you're the one who opened your big mouth about me yesterday just because I don't want to join your fan club. Learn to deal with rejection and there won't be a problem."

He straightened up and took a step toward me. "Yeah, but I know where I made my mistake now. I didn't give you a price." He looked at Lew then back at me. "If you're smart you'll forget about Junior here and go after his daddy or his grandpa. They're the ones with the big bucks."

I stood on my tiptoes so my face was right in front of his. "And if *you're* smart—which we both know you're not—you'll stay away from both of us unless you want to end up on the disabled list for the rest of football season."

"Ooh, I'm shaking in my shoes." He laughed and wiggled his fingers next to his face.

Mr. Forrester arrived and pulled Matt away then directed him down the hall. "Okay, let's move along. I'm sure you all have homework to get started on."

Matt sneered at us over his shoulder but kept walking. When I turned around to speak to Lew, he was already headed in the other direction.

"Hey, wait up!" I hurried to catch up with him. "I know that guy's a douchebag in general, but what was all that stuff between you and him? Sounded like some major history there."

"Ancient history," he said without looking at me. "Forget about it. And for the record, I don't need you making threats on my behalf. I handle my problems without resorting to barbarian tactics."

"Sorry." I cringed inside at the bitterness that had returned to his voice. "I'm still working on getting rid of my street survival skills. Trash talking is the first one I mastered."

He glanced sideways at me, and his expression lost some of its hardness. "I guess I can see how you'd need to excel at that. Actually, you remind me a lot of my aunt. She's good at it too because of stuff that happened to her growing up."

I added that to my list of things to get more details about. "Great. I'd love to meet her."

He stopped and looked at me with a little smile. "Maybe you can the next time she and my uncle are in town. They try to make it to at least one of my chess tournaments. I'll let you know when they're coming."

I did my best to look pumped at the idea of attending a thrill-a-minute chess tournament. "Okay, I'll bring my foster brother Nathan. You're like his chess idol."

I realized too late that I'd just told him I'd been talking

about him at home.

He narrowed his eyes. "Oh, so that's why you keep hitting on me. Is the kid paying you or blackmailing you with something?" He waited until my face was flaming and I started to stammer, then he laughed. "Hey, lighten up. That was a joke."

I elbowed him. "Yeah, you're a real comedian."

He smiled again. "I need to go talk to my chess coach about something. See you tomorrow."

I watched him walk away and could almost feel myself floating several inches off the floor. Considering all my new zombie powers, I had to check my feet to make sure I wasn't levitating for real. I managed to make it to the bus without drifting off to Lovestruck Land on a freaking cloud. Annalee was in a seat near the back.

"Hey, that bird book you talked me into isn't bad," I said as I sat beside her. "I got a chance to read some after I finished my chemistry test."

A smile lit up her face. "I knew you'd like it. It's my favorite book."

Dougie got on the bus and made an obscene crotch gesture in our direction before he sat down a few rows ahead of us.

"Looks like Tree Boy's still pissed at me," I said. "Can you hear my heart breaking in my chest?"

Annalee giggled. "Yeah, I can see how bummed you are about it."

"Does he get off before we get to your stop?"

She nodded. "Mine is one of the last stops. Why? You think he'll try to do something?"

"Who knows, but don't worry about it. I'm not taking any crap from him. I've put up with enough jerks today already."

Her fingers played with the strap on her backpack. "Yeah, I heard about what Matt did to you and Lew in the hall."

"Wow, this school's got a kickass grapevine."

"Everybody on the bus was talking about it when I got on." She kept looking at her hands. "I thought you said Lew couldn't stand you."

My stomach might not work normally anymore, but I found out it could still knot up. Was I risking my friendship with her if she found out how I felt about Lew, or would I be risking it even more if she knew I was being dishonest? My devious little mind searched frantically for something to say, and I surprised the hell out of myself by coming up with something that was pretty much the truth.

"Yeah, well . . . I guess I've got you to thank for his change of heart. Turns out he likes girls who read the classics."

"Really?" She looked up at me, and I could tell she was wondering if that might work for her advantage too.

"You like him, don't you?" I said.

"*No.*" She blushed the deepest shade I'd seen yet. "I just think he's nice."

"Yeah, right." Encouraged by the success of my honesty, I decided to keep going. "Look, I don't blame you. I like him too, but I can tell he still doesn't know what to make of me. I think he feels kinda sorry for me right now, but that won't last long. I don't want anybody's pity and sure as hell don't need anybody to protect me."

"I got that from the Tree Boy incident," she said and we both laughed. "You're probably right about Lew. He might not look like the brawny type, but he's not afraid to stand up for something important."

"Sounds like you know that from personal

65

experience." I tried to keep any hint of jealousy from my voice, but it wasn't easy. "He mentioned something about you having a lot to deal with. How does he know that?"

She sighed. "I'll tell you about that when I tell you the rest of my sad story. But remember, you have to tell me yours too."

Didn't see that happening anytime soon.

"So are we okay with both of us having a thing for Captain Chess Champ?"

She doubled over with laughter. "Oh, I'm so sure he loves you to call him that. And I don't have a *thing* for him. He's just a friend."

"I repeat—yeah, right." I wasn't exactly thrilled about the competition, but at least we'd gotten our feelings out in the open. "Okay, so give me the scoop on him. Matt said something about his family having money. Is that true?"

She nodded vigorously. "They're loaded. His grandfather owns Stanton Land and Timber, and his dad's the CEO."

"For real? So why does he go to a public school?"

"I'm not sure. He only transferred here at the end of last year. I think he went to a private school before that." She paused and looked thoughtful. "Come to think of it, Matt transferred here about the same time."

"Yeah, I can tell they have some kind of wicked bad history with each other," I said. "I don't see him spilling his guts to me about it though. Hey, maybe I can get Matt to tell me since we're such good buddies."

"No, Gwen." All trace of humor left her face. "Stay away from Matt. He's bad news."

I didn't even bother to ask what she meant by that. Apparently, everybody here had a secret, and it was gonna take some major Sherlocking on my part to find out what they were.

Shouldn't be a problem for Zombie Girl.

Chapter Ten

Julian knew it was no use trying to work when he got this way. It had been way too long. Time to arrange another rendezvous.

He left early after giving McCarthy some weak excuse about a stomach virus. Woefully unoriginal but guaranteed to work because of McCarthy's pathological fear of germs. Predictably, he'd insisted that Julian stay home for at least three days to make sure he didn't return while contagious.

Tonight he would get the girl to accept the car and arrange the details of the drop off. Of course, the actual meeting wouldn't take place until the following week when McCarthy went to Atlantic City, but Julian intended to require another naughty web cam interlude from her as payment for the Ferrari. That would tide him over until their date, and it made him eager to go home and get started.

After a quick stop at the drug store for some needed supplies, he sped home to his small apartment over his mother's garage. To keep her from hearing the car and coming to see why he was home early, he turned off the engine at the end of the street and coasted down the driveway. If she started in on him again tonight, he swore he would indulge his lifelong fantasy and finally slit her throat.

Inside his apartment, he pulled down all the shades and closed the nauseatingly ugly duck curtains. God, he hated those mallards in flight that his mother had insisted on because she thought they were so "manly." How old did he have to be before he could make his own damn decisions?

Once the apartment was soothingly dark, he undressed and booted up his laptop. As always, he smiled as he typed the password that unlocked the private world his mother couldn't infiltrate: *matricide*. The graphic images on the desktop had ceased to titillate him the way they did when they were new, but that was okay. He'd be getting some new ones very soon.

Before sending the chat message to WETNWILD16, he logged in to FaceSpace and went to the page for the new Sugar Daddy group he'd joined. He wanted to check the member list to see if any new greedy sluts had joined. There were several fresh prospects, including one calling herself Cherry Licious. Julian licked his lips and started to click on the profile picture, but he was interrupted by insistent pounding on his door. He closed his eyes and could practically see his mother's ham-like fist beating on it.

"Julian Francis Pugh, what are you doing in there? Why are you home from work so early? Let me in!"

He grimaced and hurried to the door, leaning against it with his eyes squeezed shut. "Mr. McCarthy let me come home early because I have a stomach bug, Mumsy. I just need to sleep for a while. I'll be fine."

More pounding. "Open this door right now, young man! You could be seriously ill. I'm the nurse, not you. I'll decide if you're fine or not."

"No, Mumsy. Please." He hated the pleading note in his voice, almost as much as he hated her. "I already took my temperature. It's only ninety-nine. Just a little stomach flu that's going around."

"Did you use the rectal thermometer? You know I don't trust any other method!"

"Yes, Mumsy. Don't I always do what you tell me? Just let me take a little nap, then I'll come down and you can check it for yourself." One of his hands gripped his coarse black hair and yanked hard enough to make his eyes water. God, he disgusted himself.

"Well, I don't know . . ."

"Will you make me some soup when I come down later?"

"You mean some of Mumsy's special chicken soup?" He could hear the grin in her tone and knew he had her. "You love it so much, don't you, Julie?"

"Yes, Mumsy." He pinched the inside of his thigh, relishing the pain.

"Okay, go take your nap and then come down to eat your soup. And you'll be sleeping downstairs where I can check on you tonight, so bring your pillow and jammies with you. We'll watch 'Operation Repo' together."

"Okay, Mumsy. I will." When he heard her heavy footsteps descending the stairs, he added, "Yeah, I'll bring my pillow with me. And after your fat ass is asleep in your chair, I'll smother you with it."

But he knew he wouldn't. He'd wimp out just like he'd done so many times in the past.

As he felt the familiar warm trickle run down his leg into a yellow puddle on the floor, he sobbed and twisted one of his nipples mercilessly. When his tears stopped, he went back to the computer and logged in to his favorite Sugar Daddy chat room.

WETNWILD16 was online.

Chapter Eleven

When we got off the school bus at Annalee's stop, she said, "Did you let your foster mom know you were coming to the library with me?"

"Crap, I didn't even think about it," I said. "I'm not used to having anybody who cares what I do."

I knew she thought I was talking about living on the street, but that's not what I meant. Vanessa had always been too busy scaling the corporate ladder to worry about what her whack-job daughter was doing. And I reminded her too much of my womanizing drunk of a father for her to stomach looking at me for very long.

"You don't have a cell phone?" Annalee asked as we walked.

I shook my head. "Brad and Karen said they'd get me one after my first report card if I had at least a B average." I knew better than to ask if she had one after the computer episode. "Maybe they'll let me use the phone at the library."

She nodded. "There's one they let people use to call for a ride at closing time. I'm sure they'll let you use it."

As we walked further down the sidewalk, I noticed how rundown the area looked compared to Coconut Grove. Karen and Brad lived in one of the modest sections where the houses were older, but their place still looked like a mansion compared to the low-income housing complexes separated by empty buildings or trashy-looking businesses in this neighborhood. And was that a drug deal going down on the corner across the street? I started to say something about it, then I saw the embarrassed look on Annalee's face.

"Reminds me of home," I said instead. "Hope we don't run into any of my former colleagues."

Her relief materialized in a smile. "Or any of my relatives."

"No worries there for me," I said. "All mine are either dead or doing five-to-ten."

Two guys leaning against the burglar-barred front of a barbeque joint yelled something filthy at us. I flipped them off and Annalee pulled my arm down.

"It's better if you just ignore them and keep walking."

"That's not how I roll," I said. "Don't worry. I got your back."

She shook her head. "The guys around here are a lot worse than Dougie. And neither of us are bulletproof, you know."

Speak for yourself, girlfriend.

Since I couldn't argue with her without revealing my zombie powers, I said, "Yeah, okay. I keep forgetting that I actually want to live through the day now."

We made it past the store without getting assaulted by anything worse than more obscenities, which made me feel both relieved and a little disappointed. I entertained myself with a mental viewing of what it would be like to teach the scumbags a lesson for disrespecting women. Maybe I'd come back sometime when I didn't have Annalee as a witness. Midnight shenanigans for Zombie Girl.

The library was only two blocks away, and the neat little building stuck out like a sore thumb in such a crappy area. Annalee pointed it out to me then stopped abruptly.

"What's wrong?" I followed her gaze and could tell her attention was on a red Corvette parked by the library's front door.

"That's Lew's car," she said. "What's he doing here?"

"How do you know for sure it's his?" I noticed the tag read CHKMATE and said, "Oh, never mind. Okay, let's go find out why he's creeping on us."

I managed to keep from sprinting up to the library entrance, but I still arrived way ahead of Annalee and had to wait for her to catch up. Apparently, she noticed my eagerness.

"Hey, maybe you should go in the front door and I should go in the back," she said. "You know, just to make sure he doesn't get away."

I actually considered it a second before I realized I was being mocked by a library mouse.

"Cute," I said with a cheesy smile. "But don't pretend you aren't excited to see him too. At least I'm honest about it." I braced myself for the lightning bolt that was sure to strike me for claiming that virtue.

When we went inside, Annalee was greeted by every employee in the library. I was busy looking for Lew, but I couldn't help noticing how beautiful the place was, especially the murals painted on two of the walls. One looked like a Cuban festival and the other featured famous African-Americans. There was also a display of kids' artwork in the children's fiction room.

"Don't forget to call your foster mom," Annalee said. "I don't want you to get in trouble because of me and make them not want us to be friends."

I had to laugh. "Yeah, I'm sure they don't want me

73

hanging out with somebody who takes me on unauthorized library visits."

"Well, you still should call," she said. "The phone's over there at the circulation desk." She indicated a station in the center of the fiction room. "Don't worry. I'll keep an eye out for Lew so he doesn't escape."

I stuck my tongue out at her before walking over to the desk. Just as I expected, Karen was thrilled to hear I'd made a friend and was at the library with her. I promised to call when we got to Annalee's house and purposely didn't mention what part of town we were in.

"Mr. Christopher is upstairs at the reference desk," Annalee said when I got off the phone. "He's the one who does the classic book discussion group and gave me the list. We can check the study rooms and the computer lab to see if Lew's up there."

I followed her up the stairs, admiring the framed prints on the walls. "They're really big on art in this place, huh?"

She nodded. "Mr. Christopher says it brings in a lot of patrons who might otherwise never step foot in a library. They support all the fine arts, like movies, concerts and plays."

When we got to the top of the stairs, I saw a row of chairs facing the large windows, all of them occupied by scraggly-looking people. Most of them were asleep, but one old lady who looked like she was wearing every ratty article of clothing she owned was reading a book with a lighthouse on the cover. She looked up and waved at Annalee.

"That's Hazel." Annalee waved back at the woman as I followed her into the big room in the center of the floor. "She's read just about every book in the library and

74

can remember the characters and plots from most of them."

"Is she homeless?"

Annalee nodded. "She has paranoid schizophrenia. She used to be a teacher but lost her job, her house and all her money when her medication stopped working after her husband died."

"How do you know so much about her?"

"Mr. Christopher told me, and I've talked to her some too. She's a nice lady except for thinking the government has assassins looking for her. Mr. Christopher convinced her the killers would never think to look for her in the library. That's why she spends most of her time here reading."

I gave her a suspicious look. "You sound kinda sweet on this Mr. Christopher. Is he cute?"

"Yes, but that's not why I like him." She blushed one of her medium shades. "He knows more about books than anybody I've ever known. Now, shush. There he is."

The man behind the desk smiled when he saw Annalee, and I was relieved to see it was just a fond smile and not a lecherous one. Not that I really expected the library to be staffed by perverts, but I was glad I wouldn't have to eliminate Annalee's hero.

"Hey, Mr. Christopher," Annalee said. "This is my friend Gwen. Can we get a copy of your list of classics for her?"

"Most certainly." He took a sheet of paper from one of the drawers to his left. "Glad to meet you, Gwen. Maybe you can help me talk Annalee into coming to our next discussion group. The upcoming dates are printed at the bottom of the list."

"Yeah, maybe," I said, still looking around for Lew. "Thanks for the list. Annalee, where are those study rooms and computer lab you were talking about?"

"Right through that door." Mr. Christopher pointed to the back of the room. "Annalee, did you see the new releases when you came in? There's a new Dexter book."

Her eyes lit up. "Really? I didn't know there was a new one out yet."

Mr. Christopher typed something into his computer and turned his monitor so Annalee could see it. "Here's the description. Sounds like another winner."

My patience whimpered and died a quiet death. I touched Annalee's shoulder and said, "I'm gonna go see if I can spot Lew. I'll meet you back here in a few minutes, okay?"

"Okay." She and Mr. Christopher launched into a lively discussion of the book plots versus the television show, and I wondered if she might have a crush on more than one nerdy guy. To tell the truth, I was relieved to know I didn't feel the same way about Mr. Dewey Decimal. I didn't think I could've survived the humiliation of that one.

The door at the end of the room led to a long hallway lined with windows. One side was a large room filled with tables and computer terminals. I scanned all the users and didn't see Lew among them. The other side of the hall was separated into small rooms, each with a window and a door and furnished with a desk and two chairs. In the fourth one, I saw Lew's blond head beside that of a Hispanic-looking guy, both of them bent over a textbook.

Okay, so it looked like he was tutoring this kid for some reason, but why? It couldn't be because he needed the money if his family was loaded like Annalee said. And from the looks of the tattoos on the guy's muscular arms, I didn't think he was one of Lew's chess teammates or even went to Bay Harbor at all. I was loving the chance to stare at Lew uninterrupted, but my curiosity got the best of me and made me knock on the window.

He looked up and did a double take when he saw me, shooting down the possibility that he was there hoping to see me. I gave him a little wave that he didn't return, and when the other guy saw me, I could tell by the look on his face that he'd lost all interest in studying anything but the blonde interruption. I didn't figure Lew was going to like that and tried to beat it before I made it worse, but I heard the door open behind me a second later.

"Whoa, why you run away, *chica?*" the guy said when he came out into the hall. "You knock on the window, so come on in."

I stopped and turned around. "I was just saying hi to Lew. I didn't mean to interrupt."

Lew had come out by then, and the guy gave him an impressed look. "Oh, she here to see you. It's like that, *ese?* You been holding out on me?"

"You're stalking me now, Gwen?" The corners of Lew's mouth hinted at a smile.

I was so relieved to see he wasn't mad that I didn't mind getting mocked by a nerd for the second time that day.

"Yeah, right," I said. "If you recall, I told you in class today that I was coming to the library with Annalee after school, so you're the creeper. Who's this guy, your bodyguard?"

His companion flexed his impressive biceps and flashed white teeth at me. "*Si*, I have *mi hermano's* back always." He put an arm across Lew's shoulders and cuffed him on the chin with his fist. "But you don't introduce me to this *mamácita* right now, I kick your white ass myself."

77

"Gwen, this is Javier Estrada," Lew said with a laugh. "He's one of my oldest friends. Javi, Gwen is my chemistry partner."

Jeez, he could've at least called me a friend. I tried to hide my disappointment at his bland description of our relationship, but the heat I felt coming from my cheeks told me I didn't quite succeed.

Javier looked from Lew to me and back again. "Partner like her, maybe I stay in school." He reached for one of my hands. "*Hola*, Gwen. Me and you make some chemistry, *che*?"

Only because of the way Lew had introduced him, I resisted the urge to burst Javier's conceited bubble, but I couldn't help rolling my eyes.

"Sorry, dude. I forgot to wear my fireproof jeans." With an effort, I withdrew my hand from his and looked at Lew. "What are you studying in there? Don't tell me Javier is the secret to your mad chess skills."

Both boys laughed and Lew said, "Guess I'm busted. Javi, give me a minute, okay?"

"I gotta be at work by five, *ese*."

"I know. I just need to tell Gwen something about our chemistry homework. It won't take a second."

Wait, what? We didn't have any homework. My dead heart did a few cartwheels as I wondered what Lew wanted to talk to me about in private.

Javier gave him a sly look. "Okay, I let you make some chemistry."

Unfortunately, my heart stopped its acrobatics as soon as Javier shut the study room door and Lew said, "Where's Annalee?"

"She's talking to a guy who works here," I said, trying not to scowl at him. "I don't remember getting her

78

whereabouts assigned for homework. What's with all the secrecy?"

He glanced at Javier through the window. "I just wanted to get Javi back to work. We've only got a few days before he takes his GED exam."

"Oh. Sorry I interrupted you." I couldn't help feeling a little relieved that he didn't really want to know where Annalee was. And, of course, that made me feel guilty. Jeez.

"It's okay," he said. "Did you get your book list?"

At least he wasn't trying to get rid of me as fast as possible. I held up the list and nodded. "Maybe I'll get a couple before we leave."

He took the paper and scanned it. "Want my suggestions?"

That's not all I want.

"Sure."

He took a pen from his pocket and put the list against the wall to write on it. I moved beside him as though I was looking to see which books he marked, but I really just wanted an excuse to stand close to him. He smelled so good—like a combination of soap, shampoo and ink.

"This one, this one and this one are good," he said. "I hated this one and hated this one even more. And this one"—he drew a circle around *The Great Gatsby*—"is my all-time favorite book."

"Okay, thanks for the insider tips," I said, taking the list back.

"You're welcome. Guess I'd better get back to work with Javi. Tell Annalee I said hi." He smiled before he turned to go back into the study room, and once again I wasn't sure if my knees would hold up. God, what a love-

79

struck cliché I'd turned into.

I sneaked a look into the room and saw Javier shove Lew playfully before he sat down at the study desk, making me wish I could hear what they were saying about me. And that gave me an idea. I moved away from the window and pressed my ear against the wall in case I had super zombie hearing and didn't know it yet.

"Hear anything interesting?" Annalee said from behind me.

I jumped and turned around with a laugh. "Nah. Guess I must've fallen asleep against the wall while I was waiting for you to finish making eyes at Mr. Christolicious."

She gave me a patronizing look. "You're not fooling anybody. I saw Lew go in that door a second ago."

I linked her arm with mine and showed her the list. "Yep, and he gave me some book suggestions, so let's go find 'em."

"Wait. What's he doing here?" She tried to stop and go back, but I pulled on her arm.

"He's helping some guy study for his GED, so we can't bother him again. He said to tell you hi."

"Really?" Her face lit up way too much over a little thing like that.

"Yeah, really. Now let's get these books and get out of here. I told my foster mom I'd be home by five."

When we left the library thirty minutes later, it took both of us to carry all the books since I got every one Lew had suggested. Luckily, Annalee only lived a few blocks away in a housing project that looked like it had been built back when Lincoln was president. When we walked up to the front door of the apartment, I could tell she was embarrassed for me to see where she lived.

"I wish you'd called your foster mom from the library and waited for her there," she said as she fumbled in her purse for her keys. "You're gonna be late getting home now. I told you I didn't need an escort."

"Yeah, yeah," I said. "Safety in numbers and all that crap. Take it from somebody who knows from experience."

"I hope my mom's home or you won't have a way to call now. Our house phone got cut off six months ago. Mom's been using a prepaid cell since then."

"No problem," I said. "If she's not here, there's probably a pay phone at that gas station across the street." Since I had no intention of calling anybody, I wasn't worried about a phone. No way was I having Karen or Brad drive to this neighborhood.

Annalee unlocked about a dozen locks on the door, then I followed her inside. The place was shabby but uncluttered and tidy—threadbare carpet, worn furniture, a window with a broken pane covered in duct tape. Nothing like Karen and Brad's place, but way better than the vacant warehouse where Gwen was supposed to have been living.

"Mom?" Annalee called down the hall. "Mom, are you here?" She turned to me and shrugged. "I guess she had to work a double again."

"Where does she work?"

"She's a cashier at the Publix in Flagler Park. It's a really nice store—a lot better than the Food Barn where she worked before." She dropped her book bag on the couch and walked toward the kitchen on the other side of a small bar. "I'll get a plastic bag for your books."

I started to follow her until I heard a thump coming from somewhere in the apartment. "Hey, maybe your mom's here after all."

Annalee rushed around the bar to look down the

hall, then she turned to me with eyes full of panic. "You need to go, Gwen. Now."

"Why? What's wrong?" I looked down the hall and noticed a pair of men's work boots sitting outside the door at the end. "Who's here?"

Annalee picked up the books she'd carried in for me and started toward the front door. "Come on. I'll walk to the gas station with you."

I wasn't going anywhere until I found out who she was so afraid of. "What about the bag for my books?"

"We can get one from the station. I know the man who works the counter." She opened the front door and motioned for me to follow.

"Well, well, well," said a male voice behind us. "Who's your little friend?"

Chapter Twelve

"None of your business, Rufus." Annalee grabbed my arm and tried to keep me from turning around. "Let's go, Gwen. *Please*."

I could tell she was desperate to get me out of there, but I had to know who this Rufus was and why she was so freaked out by him. I pulled my arm free and turned around to see a man wearing nothing but a pair of grimy boxers, his skinny body covered in tattoos featuring swastikas or women with huge breasts. His eyes moved up and down my body and he grinned at me with teeth that looked like the defective kernels in a cheap bag of microwave popcorn.

"Well, ain't you a hot little piece o' ass?" He scratched at his greasy ponytail. "Why the hell you running with Little Miss Nothing here?"

I mimicked his redneck accent. "Well, ain't you a disgusting sack o' shit? Why the hell ain't you in the walls with the rest of the cockroaches?"

His grin disappeared and he took a step toward me, but Annalee ran to get between us.

"Get out of here, Rufus! Mom told you not to ever come back when she kicked you out."

He sneered at her. "Yeah? Then why's she passed out in the bed right now with a satisfied smile on her ugly face? Get the hell outta my way, you little bitch!"

He raised his hand to hit her, and I literally saw red—the same as when I'd sent Dougie flying into the tree. Before I could stop myself or even think about what I was

83

doing, I had my hand around his throat and pinned him to the wall with his feet dangling ten inches from the floor like stinky wind chimes.

"Big mistake, Rufus," I said. "Nobody talks to my friends like that, and you're even stupider than you look if you think you're gonna touch her. I'm gonna give you exactly thirty seconds after I put you down to get your shit and get out of here for good. If you're not gone by then, I'm gonna break off two important body parts, the loss of which are gonna keep you from hitting anybody ever again and also from being able to pee without a catheter. You got that, douchebag?"

Even with the red filter over my vision, I could tell his face was turning a deep purple shade that meant he couldn't breathe, let alone speak. But he managed to nod and signal his agreement. I released his throat and he fell to his knees on the floor, coughing and gasping for breath.

"One Mississippi, two Mississippi, three Mississippi . . ."

He looked up at me in terror and struggled to his feet, then he stumbled down the hall and disappeared into the room at the end. When he came out a few seconds later with his clothes clutched in his arms, he grabbed his boots and made it back to the living room just as I got to twenty Mississippi. Without saying a word or even looking at me or Annalee, he skittered out the door like one of the cockroaches I'd compared him to a few minutes earlier.

I went to the door and yelled after him. "And if Annalee tells me you showed up here again, you can bet I'll be back to keep my promise!"

My vision gradually returned to normal as I watched him run down the street to a chorus of jeers and laughter from the people on the front stoops of the other apartments. If I'd had any doubt before about whether or not I could carry out my mission with BOSSMAN when the time came, I knew now I'd have no problem. In fact, I couldn't wait.

I turned to find Annalee looking at me with her eyebrows raised and her arms crossed.

"You want to explain that?" she said. "I know he's a scrawny excuse for a man, but he still outweighs you by at least fifty pounds. How did you lift him off the floor like that?"

"Oh, it was just . . ." I waited for my super lying power to kick in, but it was nowhere to be found. "You know, it was just . . . adrenaline. It happens when I get mad."

She shook her head. "Uh-uh. Try again."

"Would you believe . . . steroids?" I almost winced at the lameness of that one.

"Strike two."

I looked around the room in desperation, as though I might find an answer hidden somewhere in the flowers on the faded wallpaper. "Okay, how 'bout this? While I was living on the street, I got abducted by government goons who were using homeless people for military experiments, and they injected me with . . ." I stopped and looked disgusted. "Forget it. I got nothing."

"Why don't you try the truth?"

I sighed. "The truth makes that last story sound perfectly believable."

"Try me."

I knew I didn't *have* to give her any kind of explanation at all, but I was too afraid our friendship would be at risk if I refused to tell her the truth. And the thought of losing Annalee as a friend was every bit as unthinkable as letting Rufus get away with hitting her. I opened my mouth to explain but shut it again quickly when I heard a woman's moans coming from down the hall.

Annalee looked stricken. "Wait here. I'll be back in a minute."

I thought about making a run for it before she got back, but I knew it would only postpone the inevitable until the next day, and I didn't want to tell her my crazy story on the bus or at school where somebody might overhear. It was also better to tell her in private in case she totally freaked out over it. I tried to wait for her in the living room, but when I heard her mom yelling and demanding to know where Rufus was, I got pissed again and went down the hall.

I stopped in the doorway when I saw her mom—a haggard-looking version of Annalee with bleached blonde hair and raccoon eyes—puking into a plastic basin that Annalee held under her face. The odor of whiskey, sweat and something else I didn't want to identify filled the room, making me wish my sense of smell didn't work anymore.

Annalee looked up, her eyes pleading with me to go back to the living room without saying anything. I didn't want to make things any worse than they already were, so I went back and sat on the couch until she returned.

"Please don't judge her," she said, sitting beside me on the couch. "I know it looks bad, but it's not her fault. She does pretty good when she stays on her meds."

"What does she have?"

"Borderline Personality Disorder. It's a mental illness that keeps her emotions out of control and makes her do rash things and make terrible decisions. Like taking Rufus back for the millionth time." She stared at her hands in her lap. "When she drinks or does drugs, it makes

86

everything worse."

"I'm sorry," I said. "Is there anything I can do to help?"

She shook her head then looked up at me. "You already got rid of Rufus. And I still want that explanation from you."

"Okay, look," I said. "It's too long of a story to tell right now since I'm already late getting home, but I promise to tell you everything tomorrow after school. You can come home with me and we'll have a nice long talk in my new, unfrilly bedroom. Okay?"

"Annalee, baby . . . I *need* you!" Her mom's whiny, tearful voice came from down the hall.

"Coming, Mom!" To me she said, "Okay, tomorrow after school. Do you want to use my mom's cell phone to call home?"

"No, I'll walk back to the bus stop we passed on the way here. I'm sure I don't have to convince you now that I'll be fine."

"Okay, see you in the morning." She started to get up but stopped. "Thanks for standing up to Rufus for me. It's great to finally have a friend I don't have to hide anything from." She leaned over and hugged me until her mother's pleas made her hurry down the hall.

With my eyes full of tears, I had a hard time gathering all my library books from the floor where I'd dropped them before I went off on Rufus. When I got outside, I walked the two blocks back to the bus stop and sat down on the bench, still sniffling because of what Annalee had said.

But all my sappy emotions vanished when I saw a red Corvette coming down the street.

"Get in," Lew said through the passenger window

when he pulled up to the bus stop. "I'll drive you home. It's not safe for you out here."

He was wrong, of course. But I wouldn't have disagreed with him for all the heavenly brownie points in the world.

Chapter Thirteen

Using incredible restraint, I managed to walk over casually and get into Lew's car instead of running to it and jumping in like a moron.

"What're you still doing over this way?" I asked.

"I drove Javi to work so he wouldn't be late. Why are you out here by yourself? This isn't the Grove, you know."

I shrugged. "Pretty tame compared to my old neighborhood. Besides, I didn't think anybody would proposition a girl with an armful of books."

"I see you took my recommendations." He picked up the copy of *The Great Gatsby* from the stack on my lap. "Think you can read all these in two weeks?"

"Speed reader, remember? Street skills."

"Oh, yeah." He smiled and put the car in gear. "Tell me how to get to your house."

I gave him the address and he pulled out into traffic. "You and Javier are pretty tight, huh? Did he go to Bay Harbor before he dropped out?"

"No, he went to school in Little Havana."

"So how do you know him?"

"His mother's been our housekeeper since before I was born. Javi's just a few months older than me, and Yelina used to bring him to work with her before we started school. We pretty much grew up together. He's like a brother to me."

I took a break from hoping we'd hit all the lights

red and debated with myself about whether or not to mention the big differences between the two of them. Lew saved me the trouble of deciding.

"I know he looks like a gangbanger, but he's done with all that. He went through a rough time right after—" He broke off and glanced sideways at me. "He got mixed up with the wrong people for a while and messed up pretty bad, but he's back on track now. I'm helping him get his GED so he can go to college."

Uh-huh. More secrets added to my investigation list.

"That's great," I said. "Everybody deserves a second chance. Sometimes a third or fourth."

He nodded. "He wants to surprise his mom by getting his GED. That's why we study at the library instead of my house."

"I knew you weren't really creeping on me," I said. "But why'd you pick a library in this neighborhood?"

"It's close to Javi's job. He works at a Cuban sandwich shop two streets over—the Medianoche Mezzanine. Food to die for, by the way."

Cardboard Cuban cuisine. Yum-yum.

"Oh, yeah?" I said. "I've never had one of those whatayoucallem sandwiches before." I'd also never had to drop hints to guys before.

"Medianoche," he said. "It means midnight sandwich."

"Are you supposed to sneak out at night to eat them?"

He laughed. "No, they're a lighter fare than regular Cuban sandwiches. Easier to eat after a night of partying."

"Sounds great," I said. "Maybe you can take me to get one the next time I run into you at the library." Forget hinting. Subtlety was overrated anyway. And we were almost to Karen and Brad's house, so I was running out of time. Luckily, he didn't seem to mind my brazen hussy-ness.

"Javi takes his test this Saturday. You think you'll be going back before then?"

Nuclear war couldn't have kept me away, but I played it cool.

"Sure, I'll have a couple of these read by Friday that I can swap for more." He pulled into our driveway, and I managed not to whoop when he turned off the engine.

"Okay, it's a date then." He turned to look at me. "You think Annalee can go too?"

Really? *Really?* Talk about getting your bubble busted. My first impulse was to tell him Annalee was a vegetarian or an Orthodox Jew or she was allergic to Cuban food. I even opened my mouth to say one of them, but that's not what came out.

"Yeah, she'd probably love the chance to get away and have some fun for a change."

Wait, what? Damn friendship.

"You must've met her mom," he said.

I nodded. "How do you know about her?"

He looked at his hands on the steering wheel. "I don't really know anything but what I saw when I took Annalee home after a chess match once. Her mom was on her way out with some guy who looked like he'd just escaped from the drunk tank. Both of them were so wasted they could barely walk."

"Yeah, her mom's pretty messed up," I said. "I don't know if it's because we've got crappy families in common or what, but Annalee talks to me. I'm working on getting her over that shyness stuff too."

He turned sideways in the seat. "I'm glad she's got you for a friend. You definitely don't have a problem standing up to anybody, and she needs somebody on her side."

"You mean like you're on Javier's side?"

He smiled again. "Guess we've got more in common than just Matt. Wonder what else there might be."

"Yeah, I'm wondering the same thing." I was glad it was too dark for him to see me blush like a sixth grader.

"Sorry for misjudging you at first," he said. "I guess I'm too wary about people from getting burned in the past. You know, because of my family."

"You make it sound like you're in the mafia." I arched an eyebrow at him. "Funny, you don't look Italian."

He laughed. "Sometimes it feels like a mafia family, but I meant because of our money."

"Yeah, about that," I said. "I didn't know anything about your family until Matt said that stuff in the hall today, but it wouldn't have made any difference to me if I had. Money doesn't impress me." I realized that probably sounded strange coming from a street kid, so I added, "Never had any and don't expect to get any, so why waste my time thinking about it?"

"Smart girl," he said. "I don't care about it either."

I ran my hand over the car's dash. "Whatever you say, Mr. Corvette."

He laughed again. "Okay, other than the car I don't care about it. At least I didn't get a Ferrari like my granddad wanted me to."

Flashing back to the last time I was in a Ferrari, I couldn't suppress a shudder.

"Yeah, I really hate those. Glad you stuck with something domestic."

He picked up the copy of *The Great Gatsby* on my lap. "My family's the reason I love this book so much. Fitzgerald does a great job of exposing the shallowness and pretense of the wealthy."

Sounded like a trip down memory lane. I'd definitely be reading that one first.

"Okay, I'll give it a shot," I said. "So is money the reason Matt's got such a problem with you?"

All trace of humor left his face. "No, it doesn't have anything to do with why he hates me. But that's a long story, and you probably need to get inside."

I really wanted to know what the deal was with Matt, but he was right. "Yeah, guess I'd better go in before Karen and Brad think I ran away."

"Hold on and I'll carry your books for you." He got out and came around to open my door and take the stack of books from my lap. We walked to the front door together, and Brad opened it as soon as we reached the porch.

"Thank God you're all right, Gwen." His face was a mixture of worry, anger and relief. "Karen said you told her you'd call when you got to your friend's house." His gaze shifted to Lew. "And we thought you went to the library with a *girl*friend."

"Sorry I didn't call," I said. "Annalee's phone wasn't working. Lew saw me at the bus stop and gave me a ride home."

Nathan and Karen appeared behind him in the foyer. "For goodness sake, Brad," Karen said. "Let the boy come in and put those books down before he gets a hernia."

"Oh, sorry." Brad opened the door wider and motioned toward the foyer table. "You can put them over there."

"You're Lew Stanton, huh?" Nathan's face glowed

with hero worship. "I saw you beat that guy from Riverside last month with St. Andrew's Cross. You really suckered him."

Lew put the books on the table and turned to smile at Nathan. "Thanks. Gwen told me you play chess too. Maybe we can have a match sometime and I'll show you an easy way to bait somebody."

"Oh, man, that would be *awesome*."

I put my arm around Nathan. "Okay, kid. I did my part and brought him here. You owe me a hundred bucks."

"Huh?" Nathan looked confused.

"Inside joke." Lew laughed and nudged me with his elbow. "Introduce me to your family, Gwen."

"Oh, sorry," I said. "This is Karen and Brad Sherman, my foster parents, and your number one fan here is Nathan. Lew is my chemistry partner." Let's see how *he* liked that description.

Brad held out his hand. "Your last name is Stanton? Any relation to the Stantons who own half of Florida?" He laughed as if there was no likelihood of that, and I cracked up.

"Unfortunately, yes." Lew said, laughing a little himself. "But please don't hold that against me."

Brad looked as if he hoped one of Florida's famous sinkholes would suddenly appear under his feet. "I, uh . . . didn't mean any offense by that." He shrugged helplessly under Karen's glare. "Sorry."

"No problem," Lew said. "It was nice meeting all of you, but I'd better get home." He started toward the door then turned to look at me. "I can bring you and Annalee home Friday night too."

"Sounds great," I said, then I remembered that I needed to ask permission. "Lew offered to take us to eat after we go to the library on Friday. Is that okay?"

"Oh, yes. Certainly." Karen gave him a big smile. "Thank you so much for bringing Gwen home. Come back anytime."

As soon as the front door closed behind him, everyone began talking at once.

"Brad, how could you have said such a thing about his family?" Karen demanded.

"I didn't know who he was!" He gave me a scornful look. "Gwen, why didn't you tell us he was a Stanton at dinner the other night?"

Nathan was pulling on my arm. "You think he'll come in with you when he brings you home on Friday? Can I ask him to play chess with me then?"

Karen crossed her arms and gave me a smile. "You were right about how cute he is. I don't know why I didn't notice it before when I took the boys to the chess tournament."

Brad put an arm across my shoulders and pulled me toward the living room. "Never mind that. Do you have any idea how rich his family is? I read in the paper the other day about a billion-dollar deal their company just made with a Brazilian firm."

I stopped and pulled away from him. "I didn't know anything about his family until today, and I don't give a crap about their money. Please don't bring it up when he's here. I don't want him to think that's why I like him."

"Don't worry, Gwen." Karen glared at Brad again. "He won't say anything about money *or* business deals when Lew's here. In fact, he'll be lucky if I let him talk at all."

Brad sighed. "Maybe I should submit a list of topics for approval."

"Not a bad idea," Karen said, linking her arm with his. "Get it to me by tomorrow night."

I laughed and turned to Nathan. "I'm sure he won't mind playing chess with you if he's got time to come in when he brings me home Friday night." Anything to keep him here longer was okay with me. "Oh, I need to ask you something else, Karen."

"Sure, what?"

"Can my friend Annalee come home with me tomorrow and sleep over?"

"On a school night? Couldn't you wait until Friday?"

For all my friendship loyalty to Annalee, I had no intention of sharing Lew with her after our "date" Friday night if I could help it. Lucky for me my super lying powers had returned.

"We've got a project due on Friday that we need to work on tomorrow night."

"Oh, then I guess it's okay," Karen said. "Now let's go eat before my chicken marsala is beyond rescue."

I couldn't enjoy the food, but I still ate with a dopey smile on my face the whole time while I thought about Friday night. When I got to my room, I logged in to the Transdead Trustee blog and got my journal caught up about everything that had happened over the past few days. I finished with a couple of reflective paragraphs.

> I guess all this friends and family stuff doesn't suck as much as I thought it would. (Stop gloating, Flo!) In fact, I probably wouldn't have minded it when I was alive if I hadn't been cursed with Vanessa

Vanity and David-the-Drunk as parents. But if you expect me to end up thinking they weren't so bad after seeing Annalee's mom, you can forget it. The only difference between them and her is they had money.

And speaking of money, I don't know if that's why you made me fall for Lew or not, but I think it's gonna backfire on you. We might feel the same way about money, but I can't exactly talk to him about it, now can I?

Of course, I didn't plan to let that stop me from getting to know him better. I was pretty sure I could find some other things we could talk about, but there was no sense giving Flo and her buddies more reason to gloat. I could just picture them hovering around one of the monitors in Afterlife Admissions, reading the blog like it was an episode of *The Dead and the Restless*. No way was I giving them anything juicy.

I logged off the blog and checked the FaceSpace account for Cherry Licious. Just as I figured, all the friend requests I'd sent had been accepted, and I had a few private messages inviting me to exchange photos or meet in a private chat room. One guy sent me his cell phone number and invited me to "sext" him anytime. Gross.

None of them sounded like BOSSMAN though. He'd been quick to tell me what an important man he was and how much money he had and how willing he was to send expensive gifts—especially jewelry—in exchange for naked pictures and web cam sessions.

I accepted all the new friend requests, then I logged off the account and logged in to the one I'd made for Gwen. Sidney, Justin and Leonard had all posted welcome messages on my wall along with links to songs and funny videos, but nothing from Lew yet. Maybe he hadn't had a chance to get on FaceSpace since he'd been home.

I killed time by searching the Internet for an avatar to use as my profile picture, and I cracked myself up by choosing an animated girl zombie with blonde hair and huge black eyes. Nothing like a good inside joke with yourself. Still laughing, I got out my copy of *To Kill a Mockingbird* and finished it in twenty minutes.

Still no sign of Lew on FaceSpace, so I lay on my bed staring at the ceiling while I thought about him. Karen was right—he *was* cute despite being a nerd, and he was also funny and a lot more confident than I would've expected him to be. Probably because he'd grown up with money and was used to people sucking up to him, even though he obviously didn't want anybody treating him that way.

I still wanted to find out why he and Matt had such bad blood between them, and he'd also clearly been leaving something out when he was talking about what had made Javier go rogue for a while. I wanted to find out more, but I had to be careful not to push him to talk or make him think I was prying. God, it had been so much easier when I was Jada and hadn't cared about anybody enough to want to know anything about them.

Easier, but not better. I knew that now.

With a sigh, I rolled over to check my computer screen again and almost fell off the bed when I saw the red number one telling me I had a response to a friend request.

I clicked on it as fast as I could and actually squealed when I saw it was from Lew. A few seconds later, he posted a note on my wall.

> *Interesting profile picture.*
> *Doesn't really do you justice*
> *though. See you tomorrow.*

I sat there gazing at it with a stupid grin on my face as though it were a freaking love sonnet instead of basically saying that he thought I was better looking than a zombie.

Chapter Fourteen

I spent the rest of the night trying to figure out how much of the truth to tell Annalee, reading the books I got from the library, and thinking about Lew. Okay, mostly thinking about Lew. Good thing I didn't need to sleep anymore or I would've been totally zonked the next morning.

When I passed Dougie on the school bus, he gave me a dirty look and called me a slut.

"And yet I turned you down," I said, stopping to smile at him. "How pathetic does that make you?"

The guy sitting next to him snickered, and Dougie's face went an ugly shade of red. Annalee laughed when I told her what I'd said to him, then she gave me a curious look.

"Hey, how did he really get the knot on his head? Did you do something to him like you did to Rufus?"

I hiked one shoulder up and down. "I pushed him and he ended up against a tree. That's how I found out I'm a lot stronger than I used to be." I could tell she was about to ask more so I stopped her. "Listen, we don't need to talk about any of that stuff where somebody might overhear us. I'll tell you after school today like I promised."

"Okay," she said. "I guess I can wait until then."

"Karen said it was okay for you to sleep over tonight. You think you can?"

"Sure. My mom's working a double to make up for missing yesterday. I'll call her when we get to your house."

"Was she pissed when she found out Rufus was

100

gone?"

"She cried over the jerk for about an hour." Annalee sighed and looked out the window. "But I think she was glad he was gone after she sobered up. She's really a good mom when she's not drinking."

I wasn't sure *good* was the best word choice, but I kept it to myself. Who was I to judge anybody?

"Hey, I do have some good news we can talk about now," I said. "Guess who we're going out to eat with Friday night?"

She frowned at me. "What are you talking about?"

"I ran into Lew after I left your house, and he gave me a ride home. He wants to take us to this Cuban sandwich shop where his friend Javier works when we're done at the library on Friday."

"Okay, back up." She held up one hand. "Who's Javier, why are we going to the library on Friday, and how did you run into Lew last night?"

I explained it all to her, then I said, "Isn't that great?"

"You're something else, Gwen." She shook her head, clearly in awe of my social skills. "And I can't believe you included me when I know you'd rather be alone with Lew."

"Oh, well . . ." I tried to look like it was no big deal. "What are friends for?"

A twinge of guilt poked me for not telling her it was Lew's idea to invite her, but it disappeared when I saw the way she smiled at me. Okay, yeah, I was happy to take the credit. So kill me—again.

Friendship had sure been a helluva lot simpler when it was just me and Cassie. Boys definitely complicated things. Especially when you both liked the same one.

All morning at school, I discovered that my sudden genius status in chemistry didn't extend to my other classes as well. No big deal, but I had to wonder why Flo's department hadn't at least made me smart in math to impress Lew. Guess they thought that was just too much for anyone to believe.

Annalee reluctantly agreed to eat with me in the cafeteria, so we met in the foyer at lunchtime. Sidney waved us over to their table when he saw us walk in.

"Hi, Gwen. Hi, *Annalee*. We saved a place for you."

I could tell he'd stressed Annalee's name to point out that he'd gotten it right. I gave him a punch to the shoulder and said, "Thanks, Sid. You're all right."

He winced and rubbed his arm. "Wow, you're strong for a girl."

I traded looks with Annalee, and we both tried not to laugh.

Justin stood up and slid his lunch tray over to make room beside him. "You can sit here, Annalee. I want to tell you about that laptop to see if you think you might want it."

She smiled shyly at him as she sat down. "Thanks, Justin."

I'd noted that Lew was missing as soon as I came in, but I knew he was at school because I'd seen his Corvette in the parking lot that morning. Trying to be casual about it, I took out the apple I'd brought for lunch and turned to Sidney.

"Where's Lew today?"

"He's helping Ms. Fountain with the computers in her keyboarding class," Sidney replied. "Somebody keeps putting passwords on them and locking her out. She's a nice lady, so Lew always fixes them for her."

I saw Annalee listening to Sidney while she pretended to be engrossed in Justin's animated description of the laptop's specs. I gave her a smile to let her know I was on to her and got an eye roll in return.

"Yeah, you told me he was a computer whiz," I said to Sidney. "Maybe I'll see if he can help me with a little problem I've got."

"Oh, he can for sure," Sidney replied. "He hacked into the school's enrollment database once and added a couple of new students named Tony Stark and Peter Parker. Everybody cracked up when they got called to the office for skipping."

I was glad to hear Lew didn't mind yanking authority's chain sometimes despite being such a model student. Not that I intended to lead him astray or anything, but it was good to know he might be a little understanding if I got into trouble from any zombie shenanigans.

Loud voices behind us made me turn around just in time to see a girl at Matt's table stand up and pour a carton of milk on one of his jock buddies then run out of the cafeteria in tears. The rest of the guys at the table collapsed in rude laughter. Most of the girls giggled, but a couple of them looked disgusted and left the table.

"What do you think that's about?" I asked Sidney.

He turned to look. "I heard two cheerleaders talking in second period about something that happened at a party over the weekend. I think the girl that dumped the milk on Scott's head was who they were talking about."

"What happened to her?"

He shrugged. "All I heard was that she asked for it by getting so drunk."

"Sounds like she could use some less bitchy friends."

103

I didn't know why, but it really pissed me off the way this unknown girl was getting treated. I decided to find out what had happened to her.

"Hey," I said to everybody at the table, "does anybody know that girl's name who just ran out?"

"It's Caitlin Warner," Justin said. "She's in my World History class."

"You know her?"

"Just her name. But she did tell me thank you one day when she dropped her pen and I picked it up for her."

I bit my lip to keep from laughing. "Sounds like she might be sweet on you, Justintime."

He smiled then sobered when he looked at Annalee. "There's nothing between us though—for real."

"Oh, okay." She smiled then looked at me. "Why do you want to know about her, Gwen?"

"I'll tell you tonight at my house. It kinda goes along with that other stuff I promised to tell you."

From the look she gave me, I could tell she had a pretty good guess about what I meant and felt the same way. Who knows, maybe Annalee would end up being Zombie Girl's sidekick—Book Babe.

* * *

When Lew smiled at me as I walked up to our table in chemistry class, I managed to keep from breaking into a skip like a total dork.

"Hey, partner," he said. "Glad to see you didn't adopt the look in your profile picture as your new style."

"Inside joke," I said as I sat down. "I could explain it to you, but then I'd have to eat your brain."

He laughed. "From what I've seen of zombies, I'd like to think I could outrun you."

"Yeah, but what about when you stop to look

104

behind you in horror until I'm almost there and then trip over nothing when you finally start to run again?"

"You're right, I'm a goner. May as well give up now."

Oh, man. That definitely begged for some further interpretation that I would have to examine under a microscope later on. I studied his face closely to see if I could detect any hidden meaning, but all I saw was amusement.

"You know it, Captain Chess Champ."

Oh, crap. Did I really just call him that out loud?

He laughed again. "Wait, with a name like that, maybe I'll turn out to be your nemesis."

Okay, that could have more than one meaning too. At least he didn't seem to mind the nickname.

"Yeah, I'm sure I'll be in big trouble if we ever play a chess match to the death," I said.

•   Matt walked past our table and sneered at both of us. "Still settling for Junior when you could be tapping Daddy's bank account?"

I returned his sneer. "Still wasting oxygen meant for people with a brain?"

Lew laughed and Matt slapped the back of his head. "What'd I tell you, rich boy?"

I stood up, ready to throw Matt through the window, but Lew pulled me back down.

"Ignore him, Gwen. He's just trying to prove he's a tough guy to everybody, including himself."

Mr. Forrester walked over before Matt could do anything else. "Mr. Winston, I thought I made myself clear yesterday when I told you I wasn't going to tolerate any more aggressive behavior from you. Do I need to go have a talk with Coach Morton about it?"

"No, sir." Matt's arrogance disappeared. "Please don't say anything to Coach. He'll bench me for the Coral Gables game Friday night."

"Then I suggest you keep that in mind the next time you let your testosterone dictate your actions." He waited for Matt to take his seat before looking at me and Lew. "And I would also remind you two of the warning signs at the zoo about taunting the animals."

"Yes, sir," we said at the same time.

Oh, yeah. I definitely had to find out the story behind Lew and Matt's feud. And that reminded me of the other mystery I was working on.

"Hey, do you know a girl named Caitlin Warner?" I asked Lew.

He shook his head. "Not really. I know who she is. Why?"

I told him what happened in the cafeteria at lunch and what Sidney had told me. "Any idea what it's about?"

"No telling with that crowd. Why do you care?"

"I'm not sure I do. But even if she was stupid enough to get so drunk that she didn't know what she was doing, I don't like the idea of those jockstraps taking advantage of her and laughing about it."

He looked at me intently for a moment. "I can't believe I was so wrong about you at first. You're really something."

"Yeah, there's a lot more to us zombies than meets the eye," I said. "Don't forget that, Triple C."

He laughed loud enough to get a warning look from Mr. Forrester. Guess I was leading him astray after all.

When Mr. Forrester passed out the test papers from the day before and handed me mine, he said, "Congratulations, Miss Stewart. Yours was the only perfect

106

score in the class."

"Wow, I'm impressed," Lew said. "Let me guess—chemistry is another street skill."

"Actually, yeah," I said, "but I don't think the meth labs use chemical analysis or the scientific method." I could tell he didn't know how to take that, so I added, "I was strictly a cheap wine girl myself. Thunderbird, vintage 2010." I didn't think Flo would mind if I tweaked Gwen's rep a little.

When the bell rang, Lew walked me to my locker. Matt made sure to bump him with his shoulder when he passed us, but he didn't say anything or stop.

"Say the word and I'll take him out," I said, only partially joking.

Lew sighed. "Not worth it. Just ignore him like you would a gnat."

"I squash gnats," I said. "Are you ever gonna tell me why the two of you hate each other so much?"

"Probably not. Can't afford to lose my mystique, you know. See you later." He winked and turned to walk down the hall.

I stood there watching him go, grinning like an idiot because he'd winked at me, and more determined than ever to find out his secret.

* * *

Annalee was already on the bus when I got on.

"Ready for our slumber party?" I said. "Do we need to go by your house and get you some clothes for tomorrow? You can always just wear some of mine if you want. We're about the same size."

She looked from her chest to mine and laughed. "The same height maybe."

I rolled my eyes. "Look, I've got a couple of shirts

107

and some jeans Karen bought me that don't fit right. She can't take them back because they've been worn. You can have 'em."

I could tell she was embarrassed by the charity offer, but I could also tell she was happy at the prospect of some new clothes. I was pretty sure she'd been wearing the same pair of jeans all week.

"Okay," she said. "If you're sure your foster mom won't mind."

"Karen's great. If I'd had a mom like her, maybe I wouldn't be so screwed up right now."

"Trust me, I know what you mean."

She slipped her hand into mine and squeezed. I *did* trust her, and I decided I was gonna tell her everything once we were alone.

Unfortunately, when we got off the bus and saw Dougie and two other guys standing beside a car parked down the street, I knew it was gonna be awhile longer before we'd get to have our talk. And I also knew I wouldn't need to convince her of my super zombie strength, because she was about to see it for herself.

"Let's go the other way," she said. "The bus stops again on the next street. Maybe we can catch up to it and get back on."

"No, I got this." When she started to argue, I took her by the shoulders and looked into her eyes. "You wanted to know everything, right? Well, you're about to witness some of it."

She looked from me to the boys walking toward us. "You sure you can handle all three of them?"

"Positive," I said, although I was just guessing. "Make sure you stay far enough away that you don't get caught in the crossfire. Okay?"

She nodded and we started walking again.

"'Sup, slut?" Dougie said when they were about fifteen feet away from us. "Teaching your little white trash friend how to make some extra cash?" He and his two friends looked at Annalee and laughed. "Good luck finding anybody desperate enough to hit that."

Oh, no he didn't just say that about my best friend.

The red filter reappeared over my vision. I stopped walking and glanced slowly from him to his two friends, then I took a step closer and looked Dougie in the eyes.

"You shoulda brought more backup, asshole."

Chapter Fifteen

I had always laughed at movies where the good guy whips five or six thugs at a time, but I knew without a doubt that I could've easily handled three or four more besides Dougie and his two buddies. And I didn't even need them to dance around stupidly while they waited their turn to get their butts kicked.

Dougie grabbed my left arm and twisted it hard enough to dislocate it. I laughed in his face and punched him in the gut with my right hand, laughing harder when it lifted him off the ground several inches. All the wind came rushing out of his mouth in one big *oof,* and he fell to his knees with his arms wrapped around his belly, his eyes bulging like an astonished trout.

The other two guys were startled enough by what I did to Dougie to make them freeze for a few seconds, then I guess their clueless male egos took over because they each grabbed one of my arms and tried to pull me toward the car.

"Let's go, bitch!" the taller one said. "We got a little party planned for you. Pete, go help Dougie up."

"Nah, Pete," I said. "Don't bother."

I jerked my arms free and grabbed both of them by the back of the neck, then I banged their heads together the way countless goons had met their fates in cheesy action flicks. When I pulled them apart, their rolling eyes convinced me they were no longer conscious, so I threw them on top of Dougie who hadn't yet regained the ability to speak. I waited a couple of seconds for the red to fade from my vision, then I bent over the pile of bodies on the sidewalk.

"Gonna have to pass on that party invite," I said. "And if you get any brilliant ideas about trying something like this again or bothering my friend here in *any* way, the next party you go to is gonna be a kegger in Hell. I took it easy on you this time, but this is your last chance. Better remember that, asshole."

Annalee had watched the whole thing from about ten feet away on the edge of somebody's lawn, so I waved her over. She looked around like she was checking to see if there were any witnesses to the brawl, then she ran over.

"Let's get out of here before somebody shows up and we have to explain what happened," I said.

"Hold on a second." She bent over the pile so Dougie could see her face. "I've hated you since kindergarten, Dougie Shaw. You're nothing but an ugly bully with toxic breath, and watching you get your fat ass kicked by a hundred-pound girl was the funniest thing I've ever seen. Open your mouth about this to anybody, and I'll tell the whole school how she creamed you. Oh, and here's my white trash contribution." She did a little pirouette on the hand sticking out from under Pete's shoulder.

Dougie managed a groan, although he hadn't gotten enough wind back to make it very loud. The two morons on top of him must've been hampering his respiratory recovery.

I took Annalee's hand and ran down the street as fast as our laughter would allow us to run. When we turned the corner and reached Karen and Brad's yard, we fell on the grass, still laughing.

"Guess I don't have to worry about scaring you off

111

with my mutant strength," I said when I could speak again.

Annalee rolled over and rested her head on her bent arm. "That was the coolest thing I've ever seen. You were like a female Chuck Norris."

"Nah, Chuck Norris doesn't bother with less than six at a time. Smaller groups just beat themselves up out of embarrassment at being so pathetic." We laughed some more, then I said, "Seriously, I'm glad that didn't freak you out, 'cause there's a lot more that's even freakier. Sure you want to hear it all?"

She nodded. "I'm sure. Besides, it's not like I can pretend I didn't see that and go around wondering whether you're from Venus or you're Superman's long lost sister."

"Nope to both, but you're getting a little warmer." We heard a siren approaching and got up. "Somebody must've seen the pile of assholes and called the cops. We better get inside."

We ran to the door but slowed to a walk inside so Karen wouldn't wonder what was going on. She was on the phone when we went through the kitchen and just waved at us as we went by. I grabbed two Cokes and a can of Pringles for appearances before we went upstairs to my room.

"You think they'll tell the cops who did it?" Annalee said after we shut the door.

I set the Cokes and chips on my nightstand before flopping across the bed. "Not if they don't want to be the biggest joke around. And even if they do, the cops are gonna have their doubts when they see me. I'm sure I can convince them that Dougie's lying to get me in trouble because I turned him down. Do you know the other two guys?"

She took off her backpack and sat cross-legged on

the bed. "I think the tall one was Dougie's older brother. Never seen the other one before."

"I'm guessing they'll quit while they're ahead and make up a story to tell the cops," I said. "But even if they've got some stupid idea about trying anything else, they're not gonna want any connection to me or you. Either way, they shouldn't tell the cops anything about us."

Annalee sighed. "I hope so. But maybe we need to get our stories straight in case we get asked about it."

"Okay," I said, "we can say Dougie tried something with me a couple of days ago and got a knee to the nuts, so he brought his brother and a friend to get even with me today. Somebody drove by and yelled at them to leave us alone, then we ran. That's all we know."

"They'll want a description of the car and the person who yelled. Our descriptions should match."

I gave her a playful shove. "Look at you with your devious little brain. Okay, we'll say it was a guy in a black SUV who looked like Chuck Norris."

A knock on the door interrupted our laughter, then Karen stuck in her head. "Sorry I was on the phone when you got here. Mind if I come in and meet your friend?"

"Come on in." I sat up and introduced them.

Karen smiled at Annalee. "I'm so glad you and Gwen hit it off so well. Do you . . . um, have a lot in common?"

"Yes, ma'am." Annalee kept her gaze on her hands in her lap.

Karen sat beside her on the bed. "Gwen tells me you love to read. What's your favorite book?"

Annalee looked up, her face brightening. "Oh, there are so many I love, but if I had to pick one I guess it would be *To Kill a Mockingbird*."

"I love that book," Karen said. "I've read it at least four times."

"Yeah, it was pretty good," I said. "I finished it last night."

Annalee looked at me in surprise. "You just got it yesterday. How'd you read it that fast?"

"Oh, I . . . " I looked from her to Karen and back. "I've always been able to read fast. Guess it's one of those idiot savant things you hear about sometimes. You know, like Rainman." I poked Annalee meaningfully in the arm. "Hey, we should probably get started on that project now. It could take us all night."

"Okay, I can take a hint," Karen said. "I'll call you when dinner's ready. Nice to meet you, Annalee. We'll have a book chat sometime when Gwen is more willing to share you."

Annalee smiled. "I'd like that, Mrs. Sherman."

I followed Karen to the door and whispered to her before I closed it. "Thanks for knowing what to say to her."

"Glad to help. You girls have fun gossiping. Oh, I mean working on your project." She winked at me before walking down the hall.

"Huh, she knows we don't really have a project," I said after I shut the door. "How cool is that?"

"Yeah, she seems really nice," Annalee said. "Did you finish the book already for real?"

I nodded and sat on the bed again. "I'll explain that to you when I'm done with the big stuff." I handed her one of the Cokes and the can of Pringles. "Maybe you'd better eat something before I start. We don't want you to faint from lightheadedness or anything like that."

She put the chips aside but popped the top on the Coke. "I'm not hungry. Start whenever you're ready."

114

I opened my mouth to begin, but another knock on the door interrupted me. "Who is it?"

"It's me!" replied Nathan's excited voice. "I gotta tell you something!"

I sighed. "Come on in."

"Guess what I just heard!" He ran in but stopped when he saw Annalee. "Oh, hi. I'm Nathan." He turned back to me, his eyes wide. "My friend Bobby said the police are out in front of his house over on Plaza Drive. Three guys from Bay Harbor just got beat up by some Cuban gang. They told the cops there was a whole carload of them cruising around looking for people to mug."

I looked at Annalee and we did our best to keep a straight face, but it was a lost cause. We fell back on the bed and laughed so hard that she almost spilled her Coke.

"What's so funny?" Nathan looked confused and a little miffed. "It just happened a few minutes ago, so it's lucky you didn't run into them on your way home from the bus stop."

"Yeah, lucky for us," I said, still laughing. "Thanks for letting us know, Nateman. We'll be on the lookout for those gangbangers for sure."

He left muttering something about girls being from outer space.

"Guess we don't have to worry about them opening their mouths," I said. "At least to the cops."

"Yeah, Dougie'll probably lie and say he stood up to the whole gang." Annalee was still giggling. "You think he'll say anything to you tomorrow?"

"Who knows, but it doesn't matter. It's not like I have to explain anything to him like I do to you. You ready to hear it now?"

She took a sip of Coke as if for strength. "Go."

115

I pulled my feet under me and took a deep breath—solely out of habit since I didn't breathe anymore.

"Okay, nobody else knows any of this. My real name is Jada Gayle, and I was murdered two weeks ago because I was stupid enough to get mixed up with an online predator. Instead of sending me to Hell where I probably belong, they told me there was a hold placed on my Afterlife Account. To clear it, I have to stay here and pretend to be a homeless girl named Gwen until I find and eliminate the scumbag who killed me. I'm what they call *transdead*, which means not quite dead or alive. That's why I have super zombie strength. Here—feel."

I took her hand and put it over my heart.

"See, no heartbeat."

Her expression had been confused at first and had slowly grown into shocked surprise by the time she felt my chest. "But . . . that's not possible. It's some kind of trick."

I sighed. "I figured you were gonna need more proof." I reached over to pick up a pen from my computer desk, then I turned to face her again and jabbed the pen into my dead heart. "See, no biggie."

I barely managed to grab the Coke before she fell over in a faint.

Chapter Sixteen

"Oh, crap! I finally get a best friend and then scare her to death."

I pulled the pen out of my chest and threw it aside, then I turned Annalee onto her back and patted her cheeks, probably a little too hard.

"Annalee, please wake up! I'm okay—look at me!"

Her eyes fluttered before they opened and focused on my face. "Gwen, what hap—oh my God!" She sat up and put her hand over the hole in my shirt. "Did you really just stab yourself with a pen?"

"Yeah, that was really stupid of me. I'm sorry, I should've known it would freak you out." I held her hand in both of mine. "I'm fine though, okay? I didn't even feel it."

Her gaze remained on the hole in my shirt. "There's no blood. Can I . . . see what it did to you?"

I pulled the neckline of my shirt down far enough for her to see where the pen had punctured my chest below the collarbone. The hole was already starting to close up and disappear. She touched it tentatively, as if she needed proof that it was real and she hadn't imagined the whole thing, then she looked up at me with tears in her eyes.

"You must've felt so alone until now. I'm glad you trust me enough to tell me, and I promise I'll do whatever I can to help you."

With everything that had just been dumped on her, I couldn't believe her biggest concern was how I felt and how she could make it easier for me. And I also couldn't believe I'd been given the chance to have a friend like her after all the stupid things I'd done when I was alive.

I pulled her to me in a tearful hug. "I guess you're wondering why I can still blubber like a baby if I'm supposed to be dead, huh?"

"Well, I guess it *is* kinda strange," she said when we let go.

I sat cross-legged on the bed in front of her. "Okay, here's the whole story, starting from when I found myself in Death Detention."

I told her all about Afterlife Admissions—finding out that I had to be a Transdead Trustee and what I had to do to clear my account, the guidelines Flo had given me, and the stupid addendum to my assignment that I didn't find out about until later.

"I guess that's why they made me have a crush on Lew and why I have to deal with stuff like being part of a family and having a real friend. Pretty lame, huh?"

Her forehead creased. "You didn't have a family or friends in your other life?"

"Yeah, but they're pretty much what got me into trouble in the first place."

I could tell she didn't understand what I meant, but I was so used to keeping my feelings about Cassie locked up inside me that I didn't know if I could talk about it, even with her.

"Look," I said, "why don't I tell you the basics about my life, then you can ask me questions about anything I don't explain well enough."

She squeezed my hand. "Whatever's easiest for you. I know this has to be hard for you to talk about."

God, she was so understanding. I swallowed the

lump in my throat and struggled not to cry again.

"Okay, I'll start with my parents, Vanessa and David Gayle. Two of the most vain, spoiled, selfish people in the world. Both of them came from rich families, but all they cared about was making more money. Well, until David decided to take up getting drunk as a hobby. Then they spent half their time fighting and trying to run the other one off. As you can guess, neither of them had any time for me, their little tax deduction."

Annalee shook her head. "So all that stuff about living on the street and having a prostitute for a mother wasn't true?"

"No, that's just the fake identity they gave me," I said.

"So . . . should I call you Jada now?"

I kinda wanted her to, but I figured we'd better stick to the story. "No, you might forget and call me that in front of somebody. Just keep calling me Gwen."

She nodded. "Okay. But I think Jada is a really pretty name."

"Thanks. Anyway, I grew up with a flock of nannies and housekeepers taking care of me until I got to middle school and met Cassie." Tears filled my eyes as soon as I said her name, and I had to stop for a second. "She's the only real friend I ever had besides you. Her mom was the greatest—a lot like Karen. She kinda took me in because she knew Vanessa and David didn't have time for me."

"I'm glad you had somebody who cared." Annalee squeezed my hand again.

"Yeah, I was actually happy for a little while," I said. "Then Cassie got leukemia."

"Oh, no. How old was she when she died?"

I couldn't stop my bitter laugh. "Oh, she beat the cancer. That's not what killed her."

"What do you mean?"

I looked away and stared out the window. This was the real test of whether or not I could talk about the thing that had changed my life forever. I'd never talked about it to anyone before, not even the dozens of doctors and therapists Vanessa had sent me to. Ever since Cassie's death, I'd locked myself away in a dark place where I didn't feel anything at all, and I realized now just how many memories I'd blocked out because of the gut-wrenching pain I felt every time I thought about them.

"It took almost two years of chemo and radiation and surgeries, but Cassie finally went into remission. She got the good news from her oncologist the day before my fifteenth birthday. It was the best present I could have gotten. God, I wish I'd convinced her that's all I wanted. She'd still be alive if I'd done a better job of making her believe me."

I sobbed into my hands as the memories of that horrible night came rushing back to me. And the most vivid memory of all was how much I'd wanted to die afterward. How I'd shut down and cut myself off from everybody after my suicide attempt had failed. Without Cassie, there'd been nobody I could talk to, so I just went away. My body was still there, but the rest of me was curled up in a dark place where it didn't hurt to live.

"I'm sorry," I said. "I can't do this."

I had every intention of stopping right there, but then I felt Annalee's arms go around me and remembered that I had somebody again. Somebody who understood the loneliness of not having a family you could depend on for help. Somebody who knew what it felt like to get your heart broken by one of the two people in the world who were supposed to love you more than anyone else.

"It's okay," she whispered. "You don't have to talk about it if it's too hard for you."

I turned so I could look in her eyes, because I knew the understanding in them would make it easier for me.

"Cassie wanted to go shopping for my birthday present. She said she had something special picked out and wanted me to go to the mall with her to get it, and afterward she wanted us to get chocolate chunk cookies at Sharon's Bakery like we used to do all the time before she got sick. Her mom dropped us off at the mall, and Cassie's dad was supposed to pick us up when it closed at nine."

Annalee pushed the tear-soaked hair out of my eyes. "What happened?"

"Cassie's dad got called to the hospital to deliver a baby right before it was time to come get us and her mom was gone somewhere too, so we had to call my house. I figured Vanessa would send our housekeeper to pick us up, but for some ungodly reason, she sent David. I should've known better than to get in the car with him!"

Realization dawned on her face one feature at a time. "He was drunk?"

"Yeah." My tears dried as anger quickly took over. "Just like he was every night. But I was so stupid and pathetic that I was actually happy because he remembered it was my birthday and said he wanted to take us to get ice cream on the way home. So I ignored all the warnings in my head and got in the car with him. Ten minutes later, he and Cassie and the driver of the car we broadsided were all dead. I made it out with a broken arm and a concussion. Lucky me, huh?"

"Oh my God." She hugged me again. "I'm so sorry,

121

Gwen."

"Yeah, me too." I pulled away, my old detachment returning with the details of the story. "I don't remember a lot of what happened after that. A bunch of doctors and counselors who never stopped talking and Vanessa getting more and more embarrassed by her nut job daughter until I finally got disgusted myself and decided to take one of those bloody baths you see in the movies all the time. Just my luck Vanessa picked that night to come home early and found me before I had a chance to bleed out."

Annalee's eyes were huge. "You tried to kill yourself?"

"Sure, why not?" I said. "I wasn't really living anyway. Why not make it official and let Vanessa turn my room into that home gym she'd been wanting? I think it was pretty damn thoughtful of me."

"What happened after that?"

"Vanessa had me committed to a nice upscale facility for crazy rich kids. They put me on a balanced diet of Prozac and hospital haute cuisine and forced me to talk about my feelings in group therapy every day. Lucky for me it was easy to play them all like a bunch of gullible violins."

"How did you fool them?"

"Oh, I went through the whole process for them. See, they're stupid enough to give you pamphlets and literature about the goals of therapy. First I pretended to be in denial, then I was angry, then I fell into depression, and then—hallelujah and praise Freud—I began to see how much my dear, devoted mother loved me and needed me. That enabled me to make all kinds of positive revelations about myself." I paused to laugh. "Too bad I was faking everything just so they'd let me out of there."

"What happened when you got out? You didn't try to kill yourself again?"

I sighed. "No, they made sure I stayed on the happy pills that kept me from caring about anything enough to try again. By the time I finally quit taking them, I was so used to feeling nothing that it was all I knew. That's what got me into trouble with the sicko who killed me."

"You said before he was an online predator. Did he trick you somehow?"

My laugh dripped with bitterness. "Yeah, but not until I'd been tricking him for weeks—or at least I thought I was. Maybe he was planning to kill me all along and I was the sucker."

I hadn't really thought much about the events leading up to my death until then, but it started to make sense that I had been the victim from the start. And that made my anger grow like a flame that suddenly gets a dose of oxygen.

"You know, now that I think about it, I'm sure he *did* plan it all along. I thought he just got mad when he finally realized I'd been playing him, but I bet he knew what I was doing and was stringing me along until I took the big bait that would get me alone somewhere so he could rape and kill me."

"He raped you too?" A look of horror overtook her face. "Oh, God . . ."

I shook my head. "No, I got the last laugh and made him mad enough to kill me before he could get his jollies. Man, I bet he was pissed when he realized I was dead."

She was starting to look way too pale, so I took one of her hands. "Listen, don't sweat it. I didn't feel anything after he hit me in the head with the gun."

Tears spilled over onto her cheeks. "I don't know

how you can talk about all of it so casually. And how'd you ever get mixed up with somebody like that in the first place? What did you mean about playing him?"

I sighed and lay across the bed on my stomach because now I didn't want to see her face while I told her just how stupid I'd been.

"Remember what I said about the pills? When I got out of the hospital, it was like I couldn't feel *anything* anymore. Happy, scared, angry, sad—nothing. I went through the motions at school and had lots of pretend friends, mainly because it gave me an excuse not to be at home and have to see Vanessa. The truth is I was bored out of my mind and desperate to find anything that would make me feel *something*. One night when I was online in a chat room with some girls at my school, I got a private message from a guy inviting me to a Sugar Daddy room. I was curious, so I went to see what it was like, and it was full of older men looking for some hot young thing to play around with online. All of them claimed to be super rich and were willing to send gifts and money in exchange for messages, pictures and videos. Pretty pathetic, huh?"

"Disgusting," she said. "Why would you have anything to do with that?"

I traced the pattern on the comforter with my finger. "Because when I realized how easy it was to find pictures and videos on the Internet to send them and how much fun it was to yank their chains with badly written schoolgirl sex scenes I copied, I felt this incredible *rush* that I was making total fools out of them. I didn't know why, I just knew I was finally feeling something again, and I was hooked like it was some kind of drug. At one time I had four of the pathetic losers sending me money and jewelry and things like sold-out concert tickets. I didn't want any of it. It was just the excitement of doing it that gave me the thrill."

I sat up again and turned to look at her. As hard as it was to see the confusion on her face, I had to make her understand.

"I swear I hated all the nasty stuff. That's why I never wrote them anything myself or sent any pictures that were really me. It was just that rush I felt every time I got one of them to send me a present and knew I'd cheated them. It felt so good to make them pay for something they weren't really getting. They thought they were such big shots with their CEO salaries and their cars and their fancy offices, and I hated them all!"

She stared at me a second, then she nodded. "Because they were men like your father."

Her words hit me like the back draft from an explosion. I didn't know why I hadn't been able to see it before, but she was right. My hatred for my own father had made me want to punish men like him over and over, and it had gotten me killed.

Chapter Seventeen

Nathan knocked on the door again to tell us supper was ready, so Annalee and I had to postpone the rest of our talk until later. Luckily for me, Karen kept Annalee talking about books then Nathan practically grilled her once he found out she was on the chess team with Lew, so no one noticed I wasn't talking while we ate. I was glad because it gave me the chance to think about what Annalee had said about my father. I couldn't believe I'd never realized it myself, but there was no denying it now that she'd pointed it out.

While we were loading the dishwasher after we finished eating, I nudged Annalee and said, "Hey, you want to take a walk before we get back to work on the project? Maybe we can burn off the million calories Karen made us consume with her awesome cooking."

"I probably need to," she said, handing me two glasses. "But you hardly ate anything."

"Actually, she ate more than usual," Karen said. "Most of the time she doesn't eat enough to keep a bird alive."

Annalee looked as if she were going to say something else about it, then she gave me an oh-I-get-it look.

"I don't think a walk is a good idea," Brad said from the doorway. "Nathan told me about the incident with the gang members this afternoon."

Annalee and I managed to stifle any giggles, and I

126

said, "Yeah, but they probably won't come around here again now that they know the cops are on the lookout for them."

Brad shook his head. "Maybe so, but I'd rather you stayed here where I know you're safe. I don't want to take a chance on anything happening to either of you."

"Okay," I said. "Guess we'd better get back to work anyway."

Up in my room, Annalee lay across the bed and rested her chin on her hands. "Your foster parents are so nice, and Nathan's a little cutie. I wish I had a family like them."

I put a couple of pillows behind me and leaned back against the headboard. "Yeah, I got lucky this time. Maybe Flo and her buddies felt sorry for me."

"Do you want to talk about your father some more?"

I thought about it a few seconds then shook my head. "No, I need to sort it all out in my mind, but I know you're right about what you said. I can see it now. And as much as I hate to admit it, I guess I can also see why they're making me pay a penalty for it. I knew how dangerous it was and didn't care. It's really no different from doing drugs or driving drunk, so I'm no better than David."

"That's not true, you're nothing like him!" Her outrage surprised me. "Your breakdown wasn't your fault. You were just dealing with it the best you knew how."

"Well, no matter why I got mixed up with the bastard who killed me, he's still gonna pay for what he did. I've just gotta find him."

"Do you have any idea where he lives?"

I shook my head. "Not really. The Sugar Daddy

chat room was for people in Florida, so I guess he's somewhere in the state, but that's all I know."

"Then how are you gonna find him?"

"I'll show you."

I went to my computer desk and logged into the FaceSpace account for Cherry Licious. There were fifteen new friend requests, most with private messages included.

"None of these sound like him," I said after scanning them with Annalee reading over my shoulder.

"How can you tell?"

"I'm not sure. I just know I'll recognize the way he talked."

"Do you know what he looks like?"

"No, he had a bandana covering his face, plus it was dark. All I know is that he was short and had dark hair. And he was kinda . . . twitchy."

"What name did he go by?"

"BOSSMAN." I couldn't help rolling my eyes as I said it. "But he's probably got sense enough not to use the same name since it could tie him to me."

"Have you done a search for news stories about . . . you know, what happened to you? How do you know they didn't catch him?"

I shrugged. "I don't, but I figured they wouldn't give it to me as an assignment if he'd been caught."

"Yeah, I guess you're right." She sat on the edge of the bed. "But maybe the police have some leads that could help you find him."

I swiveled the chair around to look at her. "They wouldn't put them on the Internet, would they? Don't they usually keep stuff like that a secret so they won't tip off the killer?"

She nodded. "They usually keep a few details

secret, but the public and the press would be putting a lot of pressure on them to solve the case right after it happens. They'd want to show some kind of progress in the investigation."

"How do you know all that stuff?"

"I know it's kinda weird." She looked a little embarrassed. "I love reading true crime books and watching shows like 'Forensic Files.'"

I laughed. "Guess that explains why we were destined to be friends, huh?"

"Maybe." She reached for one of my hands again. "Or maybe you were meant to save me from Rufus. Whatever the reason, I'm just glad we found each other."

"Me too." I squeezed her hand then swiped at my eyes. "Jeez, I'm turning into a freaking faucet."

I turned back to the computer and opened a new window so I could Google my name, but I paused with my fingers hovering over the keyboard, considering what the results might be. What if there were crime scene photos of my dead body? Did I really want to see that?

"I know what you're thinking," Annalee said, "and I don't think there'll be anything graphic posted, especially this early in the investigation."

I nodded and typed my name. The first link that came up in the results caused both of us to gasp.

SEARCH CALLED OFF FOR
MISSING TALLAHASSEE
TEEN. MOTHER REFUSES
TO ACCEPT RUNAWAY
THEORY.

"They don't even know I'm dead?" I said in

disbelief. "What the hell did he do with my body?"

"Click the link and see what it says in the story."

It took us to an article from the *Tallahassee Democrat*. We both read in silence how Jada Celeste Gayle, age 18, was last seen two weeks ago by her friend Courtney Madison, age 17, when she was dropped off at a remote location in a rural area of Leon County east of Tallahassee, purportedly to meet a boy she'd met online. This led police to believe that Jada had run away with her boyfriend. Mrs. Gayle had insisted that her daughter would not run away and had been pressuring the police to conduct a search of the entire county. When no trace of the runaway was found after a week, they'd called off the search and officially listed Jada Gayle as missing. Since Amber Alerts were only for abducted children under the age of seventeen, Vanessa Gayle was quoted as saying that she was hiring her own private investigator to find her daughter.

"I don't understand," I said when we finished reading. "Why haven't they found my body yet?"

"Where were you when it happened?" Annalee asked. "The story said a remote location."

"It was a dirt road leading down to a lake, close to where I picked up the Ferrari he baited me with. It was in the boonies, but I could tell people used the road to launch boats and stuff for fishing. Somebody should've been back there by now."

"Maybe he buried you, or . . ." She paused to wince. "Weighted down your body and threw you in the lake."

"Yeah, maybe." A much more gruesome possibility occurred to me, but I decided to keep it to myself. "Vanessa must be going crazy."

"I know." Annalee put a hand on my shoulder. "How awful for her not to know where you are. She must

130

be so worried."

My bitter laugh came out in a huff. "Yeah, I'm sure she cries over my picture every day. Oh, wait—I don't think she has any pictures of me. Maybe she cries over some of my old hospital bills."

"But you said—"

"I meant she must be going crazy because they're calling me a runaway. How does that make her look? Hell, it could cost her a promotion and that big corner office she's had her eye on for so long."

"But the article said she hired an investigator to find you."

"Yeah, I'm sure she wants him to find some proof that I was either killed or abducted. Actually, she's probably hoping I'm dead so they can close the case. She hates loose ends."

Annalee sat on the bed with an amazed look on her face. "Is she really that heartless?"

"Yeah, she is." I turned back to the computer. "Let's see what the other stories say."

An earlier article from the Tallahassee paper reported a lot more details about what really happened that night. Courtney had told police that the only thing I'd said about the boy I was supposed to be meeting was that he attended Florida State. She told them she dropped me off at an abandoned BP station on rural Canopy Road not far from Lake Miccosukee, and she remembered seeing a black sports car there but hadn't seen anyone inside it or nearby. She also remembered seeing a horse logo on the car's front grill, leading police to think it had been a black Ford Mustang. The only other information she'd provided was that I'd had my laptop with me. A search of our home computer had revealed nothing, and a check of our wireless network was also a bust because a proxy server had been used to mask Internet activity, reinforcing the theory that I'd been planning to run away and had covered my tracks.

"Why *did* you do that?" Annalee asked when we got to that part.

"He told me to. He said it would protect both of us from getting caught if his wife found out. I was stupid enough to swallow it along with the rest of his bullshit. Trust me, he didn't have a wife. From the looks of him, he probably never had a girlfriend that didn't need to be inflated first."

"What about the car? I thought you said it was a Ferrari."

"It was. They have a horse on the front too, but I guess the cops figured it was a Mustang since it was supposed to be a college kid's car."

The rest of the article described how interviews with my classmates had revealed nothing about my plans or a relationship with anyone at Florida State. They all told the police that I was popular but didn't have any close friends and didn't date anyone they knew.

I closed the browser window and turned the chair around. "At least I don't have to worry about anybody seeing my picture in a news story about my murder. And with all the runaways and missing teens they've got already, one more shouldn't be big news."

"Unless your mother makes it big," Annalee said.

I shook my head. "That won't happen unless her private detective finds proof that I'm dead, and I don't think he will if they haven't found it by now. Who knows, maybe Flo's department had something to do with this so my cover won't get blown."

"Yeah, maybe so." Annalee looked past me at the

computer screen. "Hey, the FaceSpace button on your taskbar says you've got four notifications."

They were all new friend requests from Sugar Daddy group members. I read the private messages and deleted all but one.

"This one's a possibility," I said. "See how he offers to send jewelry for a few pictures and videos? BOSSMAN offered to send me diamond earrings right off the bat."

"You think it's him?" Annalee's voice was an excited whisper.

"Maybe. I'll send him a message and see what he says."

"You're not gonna send him any pictures, are you?"

"No," I said as I typed, "but I might have to send some later on to keep him on the hook. They won't be pictures of me though."

"What are you gonna say to him?" I could hear the disgust in her voice, and it made me want to stop talking about this stuff with her.

"I'm just gonna ask him about himself. You know, tell him I've been burned in the past by guys who didn't make good on their promises and say I need proof that he's not a phony." I sent the message then closed the window. "Okay, enough of that crap. Do you want to check your FaceSpace or your e-mail?"

"No, that's okay," she said. "I don't get online much."

I grinned at her. "That'll change pretty quick if Justin's got anything to say about it. He's got a major crush on you."

"Yeah, right."

"Hey, didn't you see how quick he made sure you

knew there was nothing going on between him and that Caitlin girl?"

She rolled her eyes. "That reminds me, you said you'd tell me why you were asking all those questions about her at lunch."

I told her what Sidney had overheard about Caitlin getting drunk at the party. "I don't know what happened to her, but if those jocks drugged her or took advantage of her while she was wasted, they shouldn't get away with it."

"You're right," Annalee said, "but she's probably not gonna tell anybody about it if she hasn't already, and I don't think anybody would back her up if she did. They'd be too afraid of getting kicked out of the popularity club."

"Yeah, I know all about how that works," I said. "I used to be president of that club, remember? But from the way they acted at lunch today, it's pretty clear she's on the fringe already, and a couple of the other girls didn't look too happy either. If I can get any of them to tell me what happened, maybe I can get some justice for Caitlin on my own."

A smile spread slowly across Annalee's face. "You mean the way you handled Dougie and his pals?"

"Yeah," I said. "Zombie justice dealt out Chuck Norris style. The way I see it, those guys are predators just as much as the ones online. Taking care of them is part of my assignment."

"I like it." She raised her hand for me to slap. "And I hope Matt Winston is the first one you take out. In fact, you should kick his butt even if he didn't have anything to do with Caitlin. He deserves it for what he did before."

"What do you mean?" I asked, excited about finally getting some information. "What'd he do before?"

"Well, I don't know it for a fact," she said, "but

right after he transferred to Bay Harbor, there was a rumor going around that he left his other school because a girl accused him of rape."

"Oh, really?" I said. "If that turns out to be true, I'll definitely be paying Mr. Matt Winston a visit he won't ever forget."

"How are you gonna find out if it's true or not?"

"I get the feeling Lew knows all about Matt's past," I said. "But if he won't tell me anything, I'll have to see if I can find out from Matt himself."

She frowned. "How are you gonna do that?"

"He hit on me the first time he saw me," I said. "I can't see him passing up a chance to take Gwen out even if he thinks she's trash. And I'm sure his true colors will come out as soon as we're alone." I leaned back in my chair and crossed my arms. "Alone with no witnesses."

Chapter Eighteen

Dougie wasn't on the school bus when we got on the next morning.

"Maybe he's at the police station looking at mug shots of gangbangers," I said as Annalee and I sat down.

She laughed and tried to stifle a yawn. "Sorry. Guess we stayed up too late talking last night."

I knew better. I'd seen her tossing and turning all night and heard her muttering in her sleep. She was a lot more bothered by everything she'd seen and heard from me than she was letting on. I just hoped it wouldn't be too much for her.

For my part, I'd spent most of the night online reading every word of every article I could find about my case. It actually seemed as if Vanessa was truly upset by my disappearance, and I couldn't help wondering if she might've cared a little bit about me after all. If she did, she'd sure done a helluva job keeping it a secret. But could I have been wrong about her? And did I want to be wrong?

I'd also waited until Annalee went to sleep before logging in to Gwen's FaceSpace to see if there was anything from Lew. Good thing, because I would've died a second death if she'd seen me giggling like a dork when I read his post on my wall.

> *Spent the evening plotting your downfall like a good nemesis. Triple C saves the world from the Zombie Apocalypse. Story at 11.*

Was he just being funny, or did that mean he'd really been thinking about me all night? And, God, what a ridiculously big thrill it had been to see him use the nickname I'd given him.

Annalee interrupted my private Lewfest when she said, "Be sure to tell your foster mom thanks again for letting me have these clothes."

"Okay, but I think the dozen times you thanked her already is enough. Those jeans do look great on you though. I saw a couple of guys checking out your butt when we got on."

"Yeah, right." She blushed, but I could tell that made her happy. I really needed to figure out a way to help her find some confidence.

When we got off the bus at school, we headed toward Sidney and his friends in their usual spot, but the sound of angry voices across the parking lot made me stop and turn to look. The group from the cafeteria the day before was standing around Matt's Silverado, and the guy who'd gotten the milk poured on his head was holding Caitlin's arm while she struggled to get free.

I was about to go help her when the guy said something that made her rear back with her free hand and hit him square in the mouth. He barely even flinched, but he let go of her arm before saying something else with a hateful laugh. Caitlin held her hand in obvious pain and said something back to him before running away in tears. Nobody in the group followed her.

I turned back to Annalee and said, "Here's my chance to see if she'll talk to me. Tell the guys I'll see 'em at lunch."

Caitlin had fled to a green Volkswagen Beetle parked a few rows away from Matt's truck, and she was sitting in it with her face hidden in her arms against the steering wheel. The passenger door was unlocked, and she looked up at me in surprise when I got in.

"Who are you, and why are you in my car?"

"My name's Gwen. It looked like you could use a friend."

Recognition registered on her face. "Aren't you the girl Matt said used to be a hooker?"

I couldn't help laughing. "Do you always believe everything Matt and his friends say?"

She wiped her eyes angrily. "No. I'll never believe anything that comes out of their lying mouths again."

"See, we're on the same team." I reached over and squeezed her shoulder. "Wanna tell me what they did to you?"

She shrugged off my hand. "Why do you care?"

I stared out the windshield and forced myself to remember how pathetically helpless I'd felt when I'd been at BOSSMAN's mercy, then I channeled all that anger into my answer. It was still basically a lie, but this way it had a ring of truth to it.

"Because I know what it's like to be taken advantage of and forced to do things against your will. Matt was right about me living on the street, but the things I did weren't my choice." I turned to look at her and really meant what I said next. "Nobody deserves to be used like that. And anybody who does it sure the hell shouldn't get away with it. If you tell me what happened to you, I can help you make the assholes pay."

She stared at me a few seconds without saying anything, then her eyes filled with tears again. "Nobody will believe me. Or back me up."

"I'll believe you," I said. "And since I wasn't talking about going to the cops, you don't need anybody to

138

back you up. In fact, nobody needs to know you said anything at all. I can make them pay in private." I gave her a wicked smile. "Unless you want to be there to watch."

"What can you do to them?"

"Trust me," I said. "I've got some special skills I had to learn in order to survive. A 'very particular set of skills' to quote Liam Neeson."

She still looked confused. "You mean like karate?"

A light bulb went on in my devious little head. "Yeah, kinda. It's something I learned from an Asian kid I met on the streets—a mixture of karate and a few other martial arts. It's called zomjitsu."

She seemed to think about it a moment, then she said, "I didn't want to go to Scott's stupid party in the first place . . ."

* * *

I thought I was gonna die all over again waiting for lunchtime when I could tell Annalee what I'd found out. Even though it meant I'd have to wait until sixth period to see Lew, I snagged Annalee in the cafeteria foyer and pulled her behind the library so we could talk in private.

"I take it from the way your eyes are blazing that you got Caitlin to talk," she said as she took out the turkey sandwich I'd made her that morning for lunch. "What'd she say?"

I told her everything. The previous weekend, Caitlin's best friend Kinslee had talked her into going to a kegger that Scott Murphree—the guy she'd dumped the milk on—threw at his house while his parents were on a cruise. Kinslee said Scott had invited them personally, and since freshmen didn't usually get invited to his parties, not going would have been social suicide.

Caitlin said she'd felt uncomfortable as soon as they

arrived, mainly because there were about twice as many guys than there were girls, and all the guys were football players. She'd also noticed that all the other girls were either freshman or JV cheerleaders. As soon as they walked in the door, Scott had shoved two big glasses of beer in their hands and announced that anybody caught with a full glass had to take off an article of clothing.

Kinslee didn't seem to mind any of it and told Caitlin to stop being such a baby when she said she wanted to leave. Caitlin said she'd never had beer before and didn't like the taste. She tried to sip it instead of chugging like all the other girls, but she started feeling weird before half the glass was gone. All the guys kept telling her to drink the rest of her beer and get another one or she'd have to take something off.

Then she noticed that the other girls were disappearing with two or three guys at a time, and she really started to freak out. When Scott came over and ordered her to "drink your fucking beer, bitch," she threw it in his face and tried to run for the door, but Scott and several other guys caught her and held her down while they poured beer in her mouth and made her swallow it. The next thing she remembered was puking her guts out in her front yard just before dawn.

Annalee had stopped eating a few sentences into the story. Now she wrapped up the rest of her sandwich and put it back in the bag. "How did she get home?"

"She vaguely remembers somebody putting her in the back seat of a car, but she can't remember anything about him except that he said he was taking her home and kept saying he was sorry."

"Did they . . . rape her?"

"She doesn't know," I said, "but she feels pretty sure they made her do some things she wouldn't normally

140

do."

"Did she tell her parents?"

I rolled my eyes. "No, she said she was too ashamed for going in the first place. And when she talked to Kinslee about it the next day, Miss BFF claimed that Caitlin got way drunker than everybody else and made a fool of herself by stripping and begging Scott to sleep with her. She also warned Caitlin that the other girls at the party would say the same thing if she tried to cause trouble for Scott or any of the other guys."

Annalee frowned. "Why would they cover for them?"

"I'm not sure, but I have my suspicions." I picked up a rock and threw it against the side of the building, leaving a chink in the brick. "Caitlin told me one of the varsity cheerleaders named Fallon said something this morning about how freshmen have to pay their dues like everybody else."

"What did Scott say that made her hit him?"

"He told her she left the party before she was done paying, so she could get on her knees and finish whenever she was ready."

Annalee was starting to look ill. "God, why does she still have anything to do with them?"

"Oh, you know," I said, "it's that whole stupidity thing that makes her care more about being popular than what they did to her."

"Makes it kinda hard to feel sorry for her," she said.

I sighed. "I'm sure I would've agreed with you when my name was Jada, but my opinion of what stupid girls deserve has changed since I became one of them. Caitlin might be dumb and shallow, but she didn't deserve to be drugged and used by a bunch of jocks who think rules

141

don't apply to them just because they run up and down a football field."

"You think they put a roofie in her beer?"

"Yeah, they probably drugged all the girls there, which is why none of them know what really happened to anybody, including themselves. And since they're just as stupid as Caitlin, they'll say whatever Scott and the other jocks tell them to say because they don't want to make waves. Actually, from what that Fallon girl said, it sounds like it might even be some kind of initiation all the cheerleaders have to go through."

"I think I'm gonna be sick." Annalee turned and heaved a couple of times, but nothing came up.

Maybe she wasn't cut out to be Zombie Girl's sidekick after all.

I patted her on the back. "Hey, we don't have to talk about this anymore if it's bothering you this much."

She shook her head and took a couple of deep breaths. When she looked at me again, her eyes had a determined glint to them. "No, I'm okay. Sorry for being such a wimp. I want to hear what you're gonna do to Scott and his disgusting friends."

I smiled. "Caitlin doesn't remember much about the night of the party, but she remembered enough to give me directions to Scott's house." I picked up another rock and crushed it in my fist. "I'm gonna pay him a visit tonight and see if he wants to party with me."

"Awesome," Annalee said. "But maybe you should check with your advisor first to see if it's okay. I mean, what'll happen if you break a rule or something? Will you get sent somewhere else?"

"I don't think so, but I'll check with Flo when I get home just to be sure. Don't worry, okay?"

She nodded. "What are you gonna do to him?"

142

I told her the brainstorm I'd had about pretending to know martial arts. "All I have to do is give him a chop here and a kick there like I know what I'm doing. He'll think it's the power of the Force or *feng shui* or whatever it is those karate guys use that's helping me kick his ass. And you can bet I'll make sure he knows *why* I'm doing it too, even though I promised Caitlin I'd keep her name out of it."

"Good idea," she said, "but I wish you could keep yours out of it too. You know, like wear a disguise or something so he can't identify you and get you in trouble."

"Maybe I can," I said. "Do you know where I can find a thrift store around here?"

"Are you kidding?" She gave me a wry look. "I've got a frequent shopper card from the Goodwill store around the corner from my house."

"Great. We can go there after school and find an outfit for Zombie Girl."

* * *

My preoccupation with Caitlin's problem for most of the day made me almost forget how much I wanted to see Lew, but when he greeted me with that smile of his as I walked into chemistry class sixth period, it all came back to me in a smoking hot rush.

"We missed you at lunch," he said as I sat beside him. "You and Annalee hitting the library again?"

He missed me! Well, he said *we,* but that meant him too, didn't it?

"Nah, we were just talking."

"Everything okay?"

"Just girl talk," I said. "You know, which lip gloss is the best, how to keep your nail polish from chipping, who's our latest crush."

He gave me a look I couldn't quite read. "So who

are the lucky guys?"

Just you for both of us, Mr. Clueless. Wait, he did say *lucky.* But did he mean me or Annalee? God, I was so pathetic. If I hadn't already been dead, I would've been tempted to scream *Kill me now!*

"Justin Bieber and Morgan Freeman," I said instead. "I'll let you guess who likes whom."

He laughed. "Give it up. I know you got it bad for the Biebs."

"Busted," I said. "Hey, we're still on for tomorrow, right? My mouth's been watering for one of those Cuban sandwiches ever since you told me about them." Yeah, I couldn't wait to bite into all that cardboard deliciousness.

"Sure," he said. "I'll meet you and Annalee at the library. How many of the books did you finish?"

"All of them," I said without thinking. When he gave me a doubtful look I said, "Okay, only half."

"Which ones?"

I named off the first five that came to mind and ended with *The Great Gatsby.* "Thanks for the tips. They were all pretty good, especially Gatsby."

Mr. Forrester called the class to attention just then, so Lew leaned over and whispered, "We can talk about it tomorrow night."

I nodded then spent the rest of the class hoping that Annalee would get sick and couldn't go with us. Nothing serious—just a mild stomach virus or something that would keep her home and let me have Lew all to myself for the night.

Guess I wouldn't be getting that friendship badge anytime soon.

Chapter Nineteen

As soon as I got home, I e-mailed Flo to make sure it was okay to put Scott on my list of predators. While I was waiting to hear back from her, I created a new FaceSpace account so I could message Scott and set up our meeting. Within minutes of sending him the request to hook up with Hotgirl Jones—an admirer from Coral Gables High who just *loved* the way he looked in his football pants—Scott replied and invited me over. And since his parents were still out of town, he said we'd have the house all to ourselves. Woohoo!

It was after eleven before I got an answer from Flo, but the news was good.

> FROM: florence@blueyonder.net
> TO: stuck_in_nerd_hell@gmail.com
> SUBJECT: RE: Late Night Fun
>
> Dear Miss Gayle:
>
> Your request to punish the young man
> you described has been approved as a
> codicil to your termination agreement.
> However, while you may inflict injuries
> on him or others like him, you must stop
> short of taking their lives if they have
> taken none themselves. One more
> caveat: be careful to protect your
> anonymity so as not to jeopardize your

mission.

Additionally, our Network Administrator
has instructed me to inform you that your
new e-mail address is still not acceptable.

Regards,
Florence

I logged off and quickly dressed in the clothes Annalee and I had gotten from the Goodwill that afternoon. No ski masks to be found in Miami, but we did find a red and black Mardi Gras mask with an elastic band. Even better, we'd found a black T-shirt emblazoned with a big red Z. I knew Zorro might sue if he found out that Zombie Girl had stolen his logo, but I decided to risk it. Black leggings completed the ensemble since I decided to go barefoot for comfort and fleetness of foot.

When I checked my reflection in the mirror after I was suited up, I got another idea. Using my FaceSpace profile picture as a model, I smudged some mascara around my eyes, then I used lipstick to add some "blood" dripping from my mouth. A little more red and black streaked through my hair and nobody should recognize Gwen even if the mask happened to come off. As a finishing touch, I applied some glittery black polish to my nails and toes. I might be dead, but I was still a girl. And totally fabulous.

I was about to slip out of the room and tiptoe through the house when I realized I didn't need to use the front door. Since I didn't have to worry about broken bones or sprains, I could jump from the window even though I was on the second floor. I dropped the fifteen or so feet to the ground without so much as a twinge of pain. I'd need a way to get back in when I came home, so I looked around and decided the banyan tree on the side of the house looked like my best bet.

I cut across the back yard and easily scaled the privacy fence. Super strength apparently improved my agility, a good thing since I'd need it to climb the tree when I came back.

Scott's house was three blocks over in a more upscale part of the Grove. I probably could've made it there in just a few minutes if I cut through some yards, but I didn't want to risk setting off any security alarms. Fortunately, the streets were enclosed in a canopy of trees that offered plenty of shadows for cover in case any night owls were out walking Fido.

Scott's Spanish villa style house turned out to be quite the showpiece. Not exactly a mansion like the ones that bordered Biscayne Bay, but a lot ritzier than Karen and Brad's house. I dashed across the brick courtyard that led to the keyhole doorway and saw a note taped to the front door. In handwriting that would've earned a smiley face sticker for a first grader, Scott had left me instructions to take the side portico to the pool area in the back.

When I went through the gate leading to the deck, I saw him lounging on a chaise by the pool wearing only a pair of red gym shorts, a wooden tub on the ground beside him filled with ice and beer, and music blasting from somewhere nearby. Good, that would make it less likely for the neighbors to hear Scott's cries for help.

He had his eyes closed, so he didn't know I'd come through the gate. I walked over and took one of the beer bottles from the tub, then I twisted off the cap and tilted the bottle slowly until the beer splashed onto Scott's muscular chest.

"Shit!" He jumped up, nearly knocking the chair

147

into the pool.

"Hope you didn't bother to put anything in the beer this time." I tossed the empty bottle into the water. "I won't be drinking any, but it wouldn't do you any good if I did."

"What the—who the hell are you?" Confusion battled with anger for control of his face.

"I know it sounds incredibly cliché," I said, "but I'm your worst nightmare, Scott. I'm here to teach you a lesson about taking advantage of stupid girls."

"I don't know what you're talking about," he said. "And I don't take lessons from nobody, especially some psycho chick who thinks she's freaking Catwoman."

"What's the matter, Scott? No fun hooking up with a girl who's not drugged and at your mercy?" I grabbed the chaise and threw it aside so there was nothing between us. "Don't you wanna party with me?"

He laughed unpleasantly and looked me up and down. "Guess I could shut my eyes."

I beckoned him with my fingers. "Come get some, asshole."

He was in front of me in three steps and tried to grab my arms, but I met him with a punch to the throat that sent him reeling backward, coughing and gasping. He managed to stay on his feet, but I didn't give him a chance to attack again. In an awesome imitation of all the roundhouse kicks I'd seen in action flicks, my foot connected with his hip and knocked him completely off the deck onto the lawn where he lay sprawled on his back.

Before he could recover, I dropped to the ground on top of him. With his arms pinned under my knees, I gripped his throat with one hand and held the other over his face in a claw like Mr. Miyagi in *The Karate Kid.*

"Time for your lesson, Scott. The next time you and

148

your football buddies decide to put the new cheerleaders through an initiation at one of your parties, better stick to dunking them in the pool. I don't care how stupid or slutty or willing to grovel they are, they don't deserve to be drugged and raped."

He obviously didn't realize the gravity of his situation, because he tried to argue despite my hand around his throat.

"I told you I don't know what the hell you're talking about," he said. "Me and my boys don't need to drug *anybody*. We got girls begging us for it all the time."

"Liar."

I released his throat and drove my knuckles into the bridge of his nose, hard enough to break it but not hard enough to send bone fragments into his brain. He uttered a distinctly unmasculine scream and tried to free his arms, but I held him down as easily as if he were the little girl he sounded like.

"Okay, I'm sorry—shit!" Blood ran into his mouth from his shattered nose and mixed with his tears.

"Much better," I said. "And you'd be smart to spread the word to your teammates too, because if I hear about anything like this happening again, every guy on the team is gonna pay with a broken bone. And it's gonna be whichever bone they need the most to play football. You're the quarterback, huh? Right-handed or left?"

"No . . . please!" His eyes were wide with fear. "I swear it won't happen again!"

I shrugged. "Guess I'll just have to break both of them."

"The left! The left!"

I lifted my knee so I could deliver a karate chop to his right forearm. "Sorry. Don't trust you."

I stood up and watched him rolling around on the ground, holding his broken arm and sobbing. Was I a monster because I didn't feel even a speck of sympathy for him? Maybe. But he sure as hell hadn't felt any sympathy for the girls he'd drugged, so I guess that made us even.

"Okay, Scott, let's review our lesson. Girls are not objects created to entertain the male of the species, and even when they're drugged or drunk or just too stupid to make intelligent decisions and tell you no, that doesn't give you the right to take advantage of them. Got that?"

"Yeah, I got it," he whimpered.

"Excellent. And don't forget to share your newfound knowledge with the other guys, 'cause I'm holding you personally accountable for anything they do. Oh, and in case you're wondering how I found out about your little roofie parties, you can thank Fallon and her bitchy cheerleader pals for gossiping in the bathroom without checking to make sure nobody's in the stalls."

I went back to the deck and picked up the tub of ice and beer, which probably weighed close to seventy-five pounds. Scott was still on the ground, although he tried to scramble to his feet when he saw me coming back.

"I said I'd do whatever you want. Please don't break anything else!"

"Dude, how cruel do you think I am?" I gave him an offended look and pushed him back to the ground with my foot. "I'm not gonna break any more bones. I just think you need one more little reminder about why this happened in the first place."

I set the tub on the ground beside him and smiled.

"Take off your shorts."

* * *

When I left Scott's house ten minutes later, I was still so

pumped that I knew I couldn't go back to Brad and Karen's yet. I took a detour down Bayshore Drive, hoping I could find a spot between the houses where I could get to the water. I needed a quiet place to de-charge or I was liable to wake everyone in the house when I went home.

I had to keep going south until I got to where Bayshore intersected with McFarlane, but I found a spot where I could cut through Peacock Park and get to a small pier. Sitting cross-legged on the end of the dock while I looked out at the moon's reflection on Biscayne Bay, I could feel the electricity in my body slowly draining into the worn boards beneath me.

It felt so good to get vengeance for Caitlin and the other girls who'd been used by Scott and his douchebag friends. If I could've found something to make me feel this amplified while I was alive, maybe I wouldn't have messed around and gotten myself killed. Of course, if I hadn't gotten myself killed, I wouldn't be here now playing Superhero. That was some irony that even Alanis Morissette should be able to recognize.

Ironic or not, one thing I knew for sure was that it felt incredible to do something that could actually make a difference in this crappy world. And I also liked being teamed up with the good guys for a change. My life before had been such a total waste. Maybe it would've been different if Cassie hadn't died—I liked to think so at least—and this made me hope I was right. That there was some good in me after all.

But, yeah, I could totally get used to this Zombie Girl gig. In fact, I was starting to hope I wouldn't find BOSSMAN anytime soon and have to leave, which was why I hadn't even bothered to see if Cherry Licious had any new messages on FaceSpace when I got home from school that afternoon. I'd love the chance to take care of a few more junior scumbags like Scott and Dougie before I moved on to the big guys.

I lay back on the pier and looked up at the stars. Who was I kidding? There was another reason I wasn't ready to leave yet, and it had to do with a certain blond chess champion. Maybe by this time tomorrow night, I'd know whether he felt anything besides friendship for me or if Annalee was the reason he'd asked us on our "date."

Something to my left drew my attention and I sat up. About a quarter mile away, I could see a light at the end of another pier that stretched out behind one of the humongous houses on Bayshore Drive. It reminded me of the green light at the end of Daisy Buchanan's dock and how Jay Gatsby had loved her for so long even though he knew she belonged to another man.

A shooting star streaked across the sky just then, almost like an omen, and I decided to make a wish. It was incredibly selfish of me, but I wished with all my dead heart that Lew would like me better than he liked Annalee. I sat there a little while longer, thinking about things like the perfect crease in his khakis and his crazy math watch, and it didn't even bother me anymore that I thought they were sexy.

Before I left, I paused and looked up at the sky again. "Hey, Flo, I don't know if wishes are your department or not, but maybe you can put in a good word for me since I just struck a blow for the guys in white."

Chapter Twenty

Julian loosened the fishing line just enough to allow the girl one last gasp before he finished her off. He wanted her alive a little longer for a final bit of fun.

"Let's recap, shall we? This is what happens to snooty little tramps when you get so greedy that it makes you lose the tiny amount of intelligence you were born with. Now would you like to beg for your sorry life one more time? Just make sure you choose your words carefully, because one little slip means no more fun and games for you. Ever."

"Please let me go." The girl's voice sounded as if her throat were coated with sandpaper. "I promise I'll be nice to the losers at school from now on. I'll even sleep with them and send you pictures if you—"

"Not even close, you stupid little slut." Julian's disdainful laughter echoed through the clearing as he tightened the garrote around her throat and held it until she stopped thrashing.

An hour later, after he'd taken his souvenir pictures and disposed of her body, he drove back to Jacksonville in a black fury despite all the delicious things he'd made her do before he killed her. The comment she'd made when she first arrived about telling her friend they'd met in the Sugar Daddy chat room had him more than a little concerned.

Not that he was worried about them finding her body, just as they'd never found any of the others. The efficient disassembly and disposal process he'd perfected made sure of that. His IP address was masked so the cops couldn't trace him, and he always changed his e-mail address and screen name after a kill. Still, he couldn't shake the feeling that he'd rushed this meeting too much because the one before had been such a disappointment.

Yes, he should have ended this correspondence as soon as he'd found out that WETNWILD16 was really WETNWILD14 and didn't even have a driver's license, which meant he couldn't use the Ferrari to lure her to a meeting. But her uncanny resemblance to a certain blonde cheerleader from middle school who'd mocked him mercilessly because his mother walked him to and from school every day had made it impossible for him to let this look-alike go on living.

Since the Ferrari couldn't be used as bait this time, he'd had to talk her into meeting him at a motel in Ocala with the promise of tickets to a sold-out Lady Gaga concert. After checking to make sure the friend who'd dropped her off didn't hang around, he watched her on the hidden camera he'd planted in the room to make sure she wasn't talking to someone on a wire.

Once he felt certain the meeting wasn't a trap, he'd drugged her drink and had some preliminary fun with her in the room while he waited for it to get dark enough for them to leave. He loved the way the drug turned them into slutty little puppets who did whatever he told them to do. Once it was dark, he tied her up and drove to a remote campsite in the Ocala National Forest. Then the real fun began.

But now, because the stupid tramp had opened her mouth to one of her friends, he'd have to stay out of the Sugar Daddy chat rooms for a while and lay low until they gave up on finding her. No telling how long that would take, and he hated the thought of having to settle for those filthy hookers in the meantime. Even when he indulged himself and killed one of them instead of just knocking them around, he didn't get the same satisfaction that came from turning one of the snooty little suburban tramps into a sniveling, bloody pulp that would never laugh at anybody again.

He slammed his hands against the Ferrari's steering wheel and knocked his head against the window until his ears rang from the impact and his eyeballs vibrated painfully in their sockets. He didn't even care if he broke the window. He'd blame it on one of McCarthy's garage monkeys and get them fired. He hated those muscle-bound mouth breathers anyway. Always flirting with the maids and probably screwing them in McCarthy's cars. Barely literate immigrants, all of them.

By the time he pulled through the gates of the McCarthy estate, he'd consoled himself with the realization that even if he had to stay out of the private chat rooms, WETNWILD16 hadn't been part of the Sugar Daddy group on FaceSpace, so he could still pursue some new connections there.

And he cheered up even more when he got home and saw that he had a private message from a hot little thing calling herself Cherry Licious.

Chapter Twenty-one

When I got on the school bus the next morning, Annalee pulled me down beside her as soon as I reached the seat.

"Did you go to Scott's house? Tell me what happened! Did he know who you were? Did anybody see you? What did you do to him? Tell me!"

I laughed. "Dial it back a notch, girlfriend. Give me a chance, okay?" I relayed the story of Scott's lesson as quietly as I could, but Annalee's periodic squeals of laughter still drew some curious looks.

"Did he really cry?" she said between giggles. "I thought he was supposed to be such a tough guy."

I scoffed. "Guess he's only tough if he's wearing pads and has an offensive line in front of him. You should've heard him beg when I packed his junk in ice before I left."

She covered her mouth with her hand. "You saw his. . . you saw him naked?"

"Trust me, it was no big deal," I said. "And the ice made it even less of a deal."

She giggled even more. "You think it did any permanent damage?"

"Who knows and who cares? But I made sure he knew I'd be back to put him out of commission for good if I heard about any more roofie parties. I think he got the message."

"Awesome." She looked at me with open

156

admiration. "Zombie Girl is my hero."

"Thanks. I kinda like her myself."

"Did you bring your library books with you so you can come home with me after school today?"

I patted my backpack. "Yep. I finished them all. Hey, can we go by your house and primp a little before we head to the library?"

She looked skeptical. "I guess so, but why?"

"Did you forget about our date with Lew?" I couldn't help hoping she might not be able to go.

"No, but you don't need to primp, and it wouldn't do me any good even if I had a reason to do it." Her fingernails suddenly became oddly fascinating.

All my selfish hoping from a moment before disappeared, and I reached over to take her hand. "We'll have to see about that. Did I ever tell you about my mad cosmetology skills?"

"Are they part of your zombie powers?" She still looked doubtful.

"No, they came from countless hours of playing with a giant Barbie head when I was little."

When we got off the bus at school, I could tell something had just happened in the parking lot from the way people were huddled together whispering and staring in the direction of Scott's crowd, although he was nowhere to be seen. When Caitlin saw me, she ran over and grabbed my arm.

"I have to talk to you, Gwen." She glanced at Annalee and added, "Alone."

I winked at Annalee. "I'll catch up with you and the guys in a few minutes."

Caitlin pulled me over to her car. "Get in so nobody can hear us." Once we were inside with the doors closed,

157

she said, "Oh my God, you did it! You said you could make Scott pay and you did!"

I tried to keep my face expressionless. "Why, what'd you hear?"

"Scott called Kyle in the middle of the night, freaking out because he said some psycho in a mask broke into his house and went off on him about what happened at the party. Kyle said Scott's throwing arm is broken."

"Wow," I said, still giving away nothing. "What else did he say?"

"Scott said for all the football players to be at his house after practice today or else. Matt told Kyle he doesn't take orders from Scott and they could all kiss his ass if they didn't like it. That's when Kyle decked him. Mr. Kopelecki took both of them to the office right before your bus pulled up."

I couldn't hide my surprise at that. "I thought Matt was tight with all of them."

"Me too, but yesterday when Scott was being such an asshole to me, Matt's the only one who told him to shut up."

"But I thought . . ." I broke off before saying anything about the rape rumor since Annalee had said she didn't know if it was true. "Never mind. So what makes you think I had anything to do with Scott's broken arm? Didn't you say this psycho was wearing a mask?"

She smiled. "Yeah, but I know you must've sent him. Scott told Kyle the guy was huge and knew karate or kung fu or something. Was it your Asian friend?"

I doubled over with laughter. I thought about telling her what was so funny, then I realized it was probably better if nobody knew the vigilante was a girl.

"Yeah, it was my friend . . . Kato," I said. "I'm

158

laughing because Scott said he was huge. Kato's my size. Actually, we're exactly the same size."

She giggled. "I bet Scott cried like a baby when he broke his precious throwing arm. I hope he loses that full ride to Florida State he's always bragging about." She reached over and put a hand on my arm. "Thanks for making it happen, Gwen. Is there some way I can repay you?"

I started to tell her to just forget it, then I changed my mind. "Yeah, the next time you hear some girl getting called a slut or getting talked about for something she did, take up for her—at least until you know the whole truth. Us girls need to stick together like we did when we were little and we thought all the boys had cooties, remember?"

She nodded. "You're right. You know, one of my best friends from middle school told me yesterday that she didn't believe what people were saying about me. I haven't hung out with her since I made cheerleader. I think I'll see if she'll forgive me for being so stupid."

"Hey, we all make stupid mistakes," I said. "The important thing is not to make the same ones again."

* * *

By lunchtime, the news of Scott's broken arm had spread over the entire school, although the account of what happened to him ranged from an attack by a couple of Coral Gables' linebackers to an extraterrestrial encounter. I didn't care how many stories circulated as long as none of them featured a blonde girl with a smart mouth and sparkly nails.

Annalee had to make up a test during lunch and said she'd see me on the bus after school. When I joined the guys in the cafeteria, I almost kissed Sidney when he moved over and made a place for me between him and

159

Lew.

"Hey, guys," I said as I sat down. "Did you hear about the jock who got his ass kicked by Chuck Norris last night?"

Sidney's eyes widened. "I heard it was his homeroom teacher's husband."

Lew laughed and took a bite of his sandwich. "I heard it was Wolverine."

I tried not to hyperventilate because Lew's thigh was touching mine. "Well, it's bad news for football fans no matter who it was. Hope you guys didn't have money riding on the rest of the season."

"No worries." Lew opened a bag of Fritos and offered it to me.

I took one and savored the cardboard crunchiness. "Good, but I hope this isn't the first in a series of hate crimes against jocks, Triple C. They might be targeting you next."

He almost spit his SoBe LifeWater across the table. "Maybe you're right," he said when he recovered. "Should I be on the lookout for somebody who might eat my brain?"

"You never know." I shrugged and took another Frito. "Somebody could be thinking about nomming on that super cerebellum right now."

"Could we please talk about something else?" Sidney had a lovely green tint to his face. "People are trying to eat lunch here you know."

I put an arm around his shoulders. "Sorry, Sid. We'll try not to ruin your fine dining experience."

* * *

I was already sitting at my table when Matt walked into the room sixth period and gave me a dirty look. Because of what Caitlin had said about him and my curiosity about why he and Lew hated each other, I decided to quiz him a little before Lew got there.

"Sucks about your buddy Scott, huh?"

He kept walking and took his seat behind me. "He's not my buddy."

I turned around but kept an eye on the door for Lew. "I thought all you jocks were tight. Hanging at the same parties and all." Was that a slight wince at my mention of the party?

"Shows you don't know shit." He kept his gaze on his hands. "Just shut up."

"Hey, I think it's great that you stood up for Caitlin like you did."

His head jerked up and he looked around to see if anybody had overheard. "I don't know what you're talking about. I didn't take her home from—"

I'd been talking about when he told Scott to shut up in the parking lot, but the way my surprised look had stopped him in mid-sentence made me realize that he must be the mystery guy who'd taken Caitlin home from the party. Before I could process that shocker, Lew walked into the room.

"Fine, just forget I said anything," I whispered to Matt before turning around.

Lew gave me a curious look as he sat down, but since the bell rang and Mr. Forrester began calling roll, I managed to put off any questions. When Matt practically ran out of the room as soon as the period ended, Lew looked at him and said, "What were you talking to him about before class?"

"Just ragging him about the football crisis," I said. "He must be in a hurry to go cry about it with the rest of the

161

team."

"No, he's probably a little glad it happened," he said as we walked to our lockers. "Maybe he'll get to play quarterback now."

I turned to look at him. "How do you know that?"

He seemed to think about it a second, then he said, "He played quarterback at the school we both went to before. He's pretty good, but Scott already had the position. They've been playing Matt at running back and defensive end."

I leaned against the lockers with a hand over my heart. "You're a football fan?"

He rolled his eyes and kept walking. "Not anymore, but I used to be."

Oh, this was getting good. I hurried to catch up with him.

"So you and Matt went to the same school and both transferred here? What's up with that?"

He shook his head. "Sorry, that part's classified. You don't have sufficient security clearance."

"Oh, really?" I said. "And what would I have to do to get it?"

He stopped at his locker and began working the dial, but I could see a little smile teasing the corners of his mouth. "I'll think about it and get back to you. See you tonight."

I walked away wondering if I could survive that long. Then I remembered it wasn't really an issue for me anymore.

* * *

Annalee's mom was at work when we got to her apartment, so we were free to primp our little hearts out with her flat iron and assortment of drugstore makeup. Annalee said her

162

mom had been trying to get her to use them for a long time and knew she wouldn't mind if we borrowed them.

When I was done working my magic, Annalee still looked like Annalee, but her mousy hair framed her face softly instead of being pulled back in a careless ponytail, and her hazel eyes and full lips were enhanced just enough to be noticeable. She didn't say anything at first as she stared at her reflection, then she turned to look at me with a light in her eyes that was all the thanks I needed.

"I can't believe the difference," she said. "I think I might even be able to do it myself since you showed me how. Thank you so much, Gwen."

She practiced using the flat iron by straightening my hair, then she watched me put on just enough makeup to take Gwen from high school girl to Hollywood starlet. I usually didn't bother with makeup, but tonight I was using every weapon in my feminine arsenal to get Lew's attention. Especially since I had just armed my competition with some ammo of her own.

On our way to the library, we got plenty of unwanted confirmation for our efforts from the thugs along the route, but this time Annalee didn't try to stop me from talking smack to them. One guy wearing a wifebeater and a greasy do-rag tried to follow us after I told him off, but a well-placed knee and a shove that sent him sprawling made him suddenly realize there was somewhere else he needed to be.

We spotted Lew's Corvette as soon as we got to the library, parked in the same spot by the door where it had been the last time, making me wonder if he paid the security guard to keep an eye on it for him. Probably not a bad idea considering the neighborhood.

While I returned my books, Annalee checked the

new releases, then we went upstairs so she could talk to Mr. Christopher and I could look for Lew. I spotted him with Javier in the same study room they'd been in before, but I decided not to interrupt them. The sooner they got done studying, the sooner we could leave for our date.

When I got back to the reference desk, Annalee and Mr. Christopher were talking to the homeless woman who'd waved at Annalee the last time we were there. She looked at me suspiciously and started to leave.

"It's okay, Hazel," Annalee said. "This is my friend Gwen. We go to school together."

Hazel squinted at me. "Do you work for the MCP?"

"I don't work for anybody," I said. "But what's the MCP?"

She sighed with obvious exasperation. "The Mind Control Police. Everybody knows that."

Mr. Christopher patted her hand. "Gwen is new in town, Hazel. The MCP doesn't have a unit where she comes from."

She didn't look convinced by any means. "Where is she from, outer space?"

I was tempted to tell her I came from the Great Beyond, but since Annalee liked the poor woman, I said, "I come from a little town on the Louisiana bayou where the gators scare off anybody who bothers us." When she looked like she was considering a change of address, I added, "I left after Hurricane Katrina wiped out the whole town."

Mr. Christopher put a hand on the woman's shoulder. "Did you see the new arrivals, Hazel? There's one by Barbara Kingsolver I think you'll really like."

Her whole attitude changed, as if she had morphed into another person before our eyes. She smiled at Mr.

Christopher and took his arm. "Oh, I love the way she writes, and I always learn something new from her books." She paused to giggle. "And her sex scenes are smoking hot."

Mr. Christopher threw us an uncomfortable look as they walked away.

"I hope he's safe with her," I said. "You think I need to follow them in case he needs Zombie Girl's protection?"

Annalee laughed. "She's harmless as long as she doesn't think you're in the MCP. Get her talking about books and she forgets her paranoia for a little while. Did you find Lew?"

"Stalking me again, huh?" His voice made Annalee and me both turn around a little too quickly.

"Conceited much, Triple C?" I tried to sound scornful. "We're just hungry. And broke."

He laughed, then his eyebrows went up in surprise. "Wow, Annalee. If you do your hair like that for the next chess tournament, you're gonna wreak havoc on your opponent's concentration."

She blushed—no surprise there—but when she looked up at Lew through the long eyelashes I had so recently enhanced for her, I almost gasped.

Annalee didn't just have a crush on Lew. She loved him.

Chapter Twenty-two

Javier said he had somewhere to be and left the library in a hurry. Good thing, because there was no way the four of us could've fit into Lew's Corvette. Annalee and I barely squeezed into the passenger side together on the ride to the Medianoche Mezzanine. Since she was shorter than me, she was the logical choice to sit on the console next to Lew— *right* next to Lew. Yeah, I'm talking squeezed up against him. But I guess it was actually for the best, seeing as how he spent the entire drive talking to her about chess. They definitely shouldn't have had a problem hearing each other.

I kept hoping the intricacies of chess strategy would miraculously become clear to me, but no such luck. Maybe Flo and her crew considered it an exercise for me in learning to deal with jealousy and inferiority because I definitely felt like a clueless third wheel. So much for granting my wish as a reward for my good deeds.

By the time we arrived at the restaurant, I was practically sulking. But the funny thing was, I wasn't mad at Annalee at all. In fact, mixed in with my jealousy and hurt feelings, I actually felt proud of her for the way she was coming out of her shell because of Lew's attention.

After we got our sandwiches and snagged one of the tables outside the restaurant, Lew and Annalee finally noticed that I wasn't saying much.

"Sorry, Gwen," he said as he sat on one side of the table. Beside Annalee, of course. "All this chess talk must be boring you to death."

166

Annalee flushed. "I'm sorry too. We'll shut up now and talk about whatever you want to talk about."

Great, now they pitied me. A little sprinkle of humiliation added to my emotional gumbo.

"Don't sweat it," I said. "I'm more interested in talking to this sandwich right now anyway." I pretended to savor a bite. "God, it's *so* good."

Lew smiled. "I knew you'd like it. Not too spicy?"

"No, just right," I said. *Maybe a touch too much wood pulp and a little heavy on the corrugation.*

Annalee took a bite of her own sandwich and rolled her eyes with ecstasy. "That's the most delicious thing I've ever put in my mouth. I can't believe I've lived in Miami all my life and never had one of these."

"Javi used to beg his mom to make them for us when we were kids," Lew said.

"You think he'll pass his test tomorrow?" Annalee asked.

Lew shrugged. "He should be okay if he can get through the math part. We've been working on that the most."

"He sure took off in a hurry from the library," I said. "Hot date?"

"More than one probably." He laughed as he wiped his mouth with a napkin. "I gave him a midnight curfew so he wouldn't fall asleep during the exam, but he'll be doing good if he makes it home before three."

I'd actually felt a little slighted when Javier left us at the library without so much as a glance in my direction, especially after the way Lew had made such a big deal over Annalee's appearance. I probably should've taken it as an omen to my night of invisibility.

For the next hour, I tried not to let them see me pout

167

while they made token attempts every now and then to include me in their conversation, which only made me feel more pathetic. When Lew finally said we needed to leave, I couldn't wait to get away.

"Why don't you take me home first?" I suggested as we walked to the car.

"Annalee's house is closer," he said. "We'll drop her off and then head to the Grove."

She did a fair job of hiding her disappointment. "Oh, do you live in Coconut Grove too?"

He nodded as he opened the passenger door for us. "My dad wanted to stay on the water when we moved from Fisher Island last year."

From the look on Annalee's face, I could tell Fisher Island must be a pretty big deal around there. I was more interested in why they had moved and would've asked him about it if I hadn't been stuck in my sinkhole of self pity. At least he hadn't jumped at the chance to get rid of me so he could be alone with Annalee the way I'd expected. That small consolation allowed me to peek over the edge of my hole as we drove to Annalee's apartment, but I slid back into the muck when he parked and got out with her.

"Be right back, Gwen," he said, taking Annalee's backpack from her when I let her out.

I turned to get back in the car, but I made the mistake of glancing at Annalee first. The look of happiness mixed with guilt on her face reminded me of how much this had to mean to her.

"Hey, tonight was fun," I said. "Talk to you tomorrow."

Her relieved smile made me glad I'd hidden my feelings, especially when she hugged me.

"Thanks for everything, Gwen."

168

I watched them walk to the front of the apartment, Lew's hand casually on her back as they disappeared into the shadows of the porch. At least there was no porch light so I couldn't torture myself further by watching him kiss her goodnight. I thought about getting out of the car and running away before he came back, but I didn't want to have to explain it to him later.

At least this made me want to get back to my search for BOSSMAN so I could leave as soon as possible. In fact, I intended to spend all night online looking for him as soon as I got home. Maybe this date was a message from Flo that I needed to focus on my assignment and stop playing stupid romance games.

When Lew got back in the car, I discovered that my lack of anger at Annalee didn't extend to him as well, even though he hadn't done anything wrong. It wasn't as if he'd led me on or done anything to suggest we were anything more than friends. But that didn't keep me from wanting to zomjitsu chop him upside his neatly-groomed head.

"I wanted to make sure she got inside safely," he said as he started the car. "She said her mom should be home from work soon."

I stared straight ahead. "Great."

He didn't seem to notice my snippiness. "Mind if we make a little detour before I take you home?"

"Detour to where?" I said, still not looking at him.

"You'll see when we get there. Don't worry, it's not far from your house."

I turned to see if his face gave any hint as to what he had in mind, but he only looked back at me expectantly.

"Fine. Whatever." My gaze returned to the street in front of us. "But I can't be out too late."

He kept asking me trivial questions about school as

we drove, but all he got were one-word replies. By the time we reached Coconut Grove, he had to have noticed that I was pissed about something. When he didn't ask me what was wrong, I figured it meant he didn't care. I tried to convince myself that I didn't either. No such luck.

"Okay, where are we going?" I said when he turned east on Grand Avenue.

"To my house." He gave me a smile as if it were the most normal thing in the world.

The momentary hope that flooded my zombie heart disappeared just as quickly when something horrible occurred to me: what if he was taking me there because he thought I was easy? Gwen was supposed to have been a hooker, after all. Maybe he'd only been nice to me because he wanted to—

"You promised me a book discussion, remember?" he said, yanking me back to reality.

"Oh, right." I was relieved but still confused. "We could've talked about it earlier though. I'm sure Annalee's read Gatsby too."

"I know, but you were a good sport all night about all the chess talk, so I wanted to save this for you and me." He looked at me and smiled again. "And there's somewhere special I want to show you too."

"Oh," was all I could manage while I flailed helplessly in the emotional tide that washed over me— excitement that he wanted to be alone with me, guilt over the way I'd doubted him earlier, and nervous speculation about how the night would end.

He turned down a driveway leading to the gated entrance of an estate on Bayshore Drive that made Scott's place look like low-income housing. My home with Vanessa and David had been nothing to sneeze at, but we'd been living in squalor compared to the Stanton estate. The stories about Lew's family hadn't been exaggerated. He was straight-up loaded.

He opened the gate with a remote mounted above the car's rearview mirror, then he drove down a circular driveway with a lighted fountain in the middle. We parked on the far side next to a brick walkway lined with palm trees.

"Let's go," he said with a wink that made me ridiculously happy.

Despite my wobbly legs, I managed to get out of the car and go around to where he was waiting for me at the top of the walkway, which I could now see led down to a private beach.

"This way." He inclined his head toward the opening. "Careful on the steps at the end. The sand makes them slippery sometimes."

I didn't trust my voice any more than I did my legs, so I nodded and followed him silently down the path. When we reached the steps, he led the way to a wooden boardwalk that curved around the beach toward a boathouse. He stopped just past it where the boardwalk branched off into a pier stretching out onto Biscayne Bay.

"I know it looks narrow," he said, "but there's plenty of room for two people to walk on it. I can hold your hand if it'll make you feel safer."

Safer was definitely not what it would make me feel, but I nodded. "Okay, thanks."

Because I spent the next few minutes marveling over the electric current passing from his hand to mine, I didn't notice until we were halfway down the pier that there was a covered deck at the end. When we reached it, he stopped and let go of my hand to flip a switch mounted on

171

one of the roof supports. A light came on at the corner of the deck and revealed a wooden swing swaying gently in the breeze blowing in off the bay.

"This is where I come when I want to be by myself and get away from my family's craziness," he said. "Sometimes I stay out here all night."

I was once again speechless. Not only was I afraid I might squeal like a fangirl because he'd brought me to his sanctuary, the main reason I couldn't speak was because I recognized Peacock Park off to my right about a quarter mile away. The light Lew had just turned on was the one I'd seen the night before. The one that had reminded me of Gatsby and Daisy.

Maybe Flo had granted my wish after all.

Chapter Twenty-three

We sat beside each other in the swing with our shoulders touching. I considered telling him that swings made me even more nervous than narrow piers so he would hold my hand again, but I didn't think he'd fall for it.

"So tell me what you thought of Gatsby." He turned toward me slightly, his elbow resting on the back of the swing. "And I want you to be honest."

I wasn't sure I remembered how to do that anymore. Fortunately, I really liked the book.

"Okay, I honestly wanted to slap all the characters except Nick," I said. "I ended up feeling sorry for Gatsby, but he was really just as stupid as everybody else. I suppose Fitzgerald wrote them like that on purpose to prove his point about rich people being clueless."

Lew nodded. "Exactly, and I agree. I love the way he exposes the shallowness of wealth, their prevailing moral deficit and how quickly they can be knocked off their self-made pedestals."

Okay, wow. That was some deep stuff, but I actually understood exactly what he meant and agreed with all of it because of personal experience. Of course, I couldn't tell him that.

"Yeah, what you said. And I did feel a little sorry for Gatsby when Daisy broke his heart after everything he did to get her back, but since she was basically a whore, he kinda deserved it. I guess the thing I liked the most was

Nick and the way he saw through all of it and had sense enough to get the hell away from them."

A smile spread slowly across his face. "Do you really mean that?"

"Sure. Why would I lie to you?" *About this anyway.*

"Nick is the main reason I love that book," he said. "Sometimes I feel like I'm cast as him in the whacked-out version of the plot that masquerades as my life."

Yeah, this was way more than just a book discussion. I knew that if I was ever gonna get him to open up, now was my chance. As casually as I could manage, I put my hand on his forearm.

"Tell me about your family, Triple C. What is it about them that drives you crazy?"

He stared out at the water. "Trust me, you don't want to hear about it."

"I wouldn't have asked if I didn't. And you must need to talk about it or you wouldn't have brought me out here."

I could tell he was fighting with himself over it, so I scrabbled around in my head for something to convince him he could trust me.

"What if we make a deal?" I said. "I'll answer a question for you, then I get to ask you one. Ask me anything you want to know."

He looked at me intently a second then sighed. "Okay. What made you decide to get off the streets?"

Oh, crap. Maybe I should've thought this through a little more. I tried to stall by staring up at the night sky, as if I was pondering how to phrase such a deeply emotional revelation. Within seconds, I was rewarded with a flash of deceptive brilliance so perfect that I had to wonder if Flo was my wingman.

I turned to look at him with all the fake earnestness I could manage. "My life's never been perfect, but it didn't suck quite as bad until my mom decided to run off with a piece-of-shit meth head and I got sent to a state group home where I met my friend Jada. She came from a rich family like yours, but she kept running away because her dad was a drunk and her mother was a selfish bitch. For some reason, we hit it off from the start and were like sisters in no time. Things were actually pretty good until she got murdered by a pervert who worked at the home as a chaperone."

"Oh my God," he said. "Was he arrested for it?"

I put a hand over my eyes, shamelessly playing on his sympathy.

"They never found her body. I knew he did it, but nobody listened to me. They said she just ran away again. I decided I'd better take off before he made me disappear too, and I ended up turning tricks on the street so I wouldn't starve."

I looked up at him and almost managed to squeeze out a tear.

"I know it's gotta be hard for you to understand how I could do something like that. I don't blame you if you don't want to have anything to do with me anymore."

He reached out and tucked a strand of hair behind my ear. "You did what you had to do to survive. It just makes me admire you more."

I gave him a brave smile. Nope, not a shred of decency left.

"Anyway," I said, "after a year of that, I woke up one morning in the filthy warehouse I'd been living in and found a rat gnawing on my finger, and I realized I didn't have any more of a life than if he'd killed me. So I turned myself into the cops and decided that if I got sent back to the home, I'd fight instead of running. I knew it's what Jada would want me to do."

He took my hand. "I'm glad you got a good family this time."

"Yeah, me too," I said. "And I feel like I owe it to them to do good in school and stay out of trouble. That's why I tried to pick a better crowd to hang out with from the start. But when I hear about stuff like what happened to that Caitlin girl, I have a hard time keeping my mouth shut and playing nice. I guess it reminds me too much of how I lost Jada."

"I understand how you feel," he said. "I know what it's like to lose the person you're closest to in the world."

Okay, this was it. My fingers tightened around his. "Who did you lose?"

He looked at our hands and hesitated, but only for a second.

"My twin brother committed suicide last year— eleven months, twenty-four days, twenty-three hours and fifty-nine minutes ago. I come out here every night at the exact time I found him hanging from the tree in our back yard where we built a tree house with Javi when we were ten."

He looked up at me, and I recognized the same anguish I'd felt when I lost Cassie reflected in his eyes. I forgot all about my petty jealousy, my lame attempts at flirting, and the deceitfulness I'd just used to play on his sympathies. His pain was *real*, and it was the only thing that mattered to me at that moment. My arms went around him before I had time to think about it or worry about what he would think it meant.

"I'm so sorry, Lew. I know how bad it hurts, and I'd

176

do anything if I could make it stop for both of us."

I could tell the embrace had surprised him, but he must've heard the sincerity and grief in my voice, because he returned the hug and said, "Thank you, Gwen. It feels good to have somebody who understands."

I pulled away to look at his face. "Why did he do it, Lew? Can you talk about it?"

He shook his head. "Not yet. But maybe soon."

"It's okay." I put my hand on his cheek. "I'll listen whenever you're ready."

I honestly hadn't meant the gesture to be anything but comforting, but I sensed the change in him immediately. Even in the darkness on the deck, I could see the pain in his eyes replaced with softness as they looked into mine, and I felt his breathing double in speed.

"I can't believe how wrong I was about you when we first met," he said. "It's always been hard for me to trust anybody, and it got worse after Drew died. I didn't think I'd ever find anyone I could talk to like this." He took my hand from his face and held it in both of his. "It's almost like we were destined to meet."

"Maybe we were," I said. "They say everything happens for a reason."

Maybe I had to die so I could come into your life.

"Whatever the reason," he said, "I'm glad you're here."

His hands encircled my waist, but he made no move to pull me closer. I could tell it wasn't because he was nervous or anything like that, it was because he was leaving the choice up to me. I didn't make him wait long for my decision.

My arms went around his neck, and I could tell he knew it wasn't for comfort this time. When he pulled me to him, I felt his heart beating hard enough to cover the stillness of the dead one in my chest. I forgot to close my eyes because I couldn't stop watching the way his lids descended slowly over the blue of his eyes as he bent to kiss me.

I'd never had any feelings for the guys I'd dated when I was Jada, but I still had kissed more than my share of them. Nobody had impressed me much, but a couple had been respectable. Lew put them all to shame.

And although the rest of the world disappeared while I was lost in the wonder of his lips against mine, I didn't miss the strength I felt in the arms holding me so tightly that I would've had trouble breathing if I'd still needed to do it. The long-sleeved Oxfords he always wore buttoned up to the neck were more than just a personal fashion statement. They were hiding muscles he clearly didn't want anybody to know he had.

When the kiss ended, I pulled away to look at his face. "You sure kiss great for a nerd, Triple C. Care to explain that?"

He threw back his head and laughed for a good ten seconds, then he turned to face the water with his arm behind me on the swing. "I didn't realize intelligence was an impediment to knowing how to kiss, but I guess I should be flattered by the praise."

"You've been holding out on me in more ways than one." I put a hand on one of his biceps. "Am I supposed to believe you got these guns from lifting all those heavy chess pieces?"

"Hey, those pewter sets can be pretty hefty."

"You're not gonna tell me the truth, are you?"

He shook his head. "Can't talk about that right now either, but your inquiry is duly noted." He turned toward

178

me again and touched my chin. "Besides, if I'm using my mouth for talking, I can't use it for the other activity I had in mind."

Forget it. I'd grill him later.

"Shut up, Triple C. You talk too much."

Chapter Twenty-four

Despite my kiss-happy state when we left, riding in the car with Lew when he drove me home reminded me of how mad at him I'd been earlier, and I had to say something about his conflicting behavior.

"So . . . am I the only girl you kissed tonight?"

He looked surprised. "Of course. Why would you ask me that?"

"Don't try to be cute. You only had eyes for Annalee until we took her home. Please tell me that wasn't some whacked-out plan to make me jealous, because if you hurt her—"

I had to brace myself against the dash with my hands when he braked the car to an abrupt stop. He looked at me without a trace of amusement.

"If you really think I'd ever do that, we have a big problem."

"Then why did you basically ignore me all night and hang on her every word?"

"Why'd you do her hair and makeup for her?"

"What does that have to do with anything? And how do you know I did it?" When he gave me a patronizing look, I said, "Okay, fine. I just wanted to make her see how pretty she is and give her a little confidence."

"Same here."

I shook my head. "What you did is different. Now she thinks you want to be more than just her friend, and when she finds out about you and me—"

"She already knows," he said. "When I walked her to the door, I told her why I wanted to be alone with you. She said you were the best friend she ever had, and anything that made you happy made her happy too."

Two embarrassing tears leaked from my eyes before I could stop them. I really didn't deserve a friend like Annalee. I turned away to hide the tears from Lew, but I wasn't fast enough. He turned my face toward him with a finger on the side of my chin.

"When I saw the way you let her have the spotlight all night, it just confirmed what I'd already decided—that you're nothing like any girl I've ever known. And I knew I wanted to find out everything there is to know about you."

He brushed the tears from my cheeks with his thumbs, then he leaned over to kiss me. I almost told him to turn the car around and go back to his house so we could spend all night in the swing.

"You're not gonna be able to distract me that way forever you know," I said when he returned to his side of the car. "After the novelty wears off, I'm gonna get the truth out of you,"—I leaned over to do air quotes in front of his face—"nerd boy."

He laughed and put the car in gear. "We'll see about that. I didn't become an international man of mystery by accident."

He walked me to the door when we got to Karen and Brad's house. Holding both my hands in his, he looked down at me with a smile. "How about a date by ourselves tomorrow night?"

"What'd you have in mind?"

He shrugged. "A few hours not talking in the swing would be fine with me, but we can go to a movie or something if you want to."

"I'm not too big on Hollywood," I said. "Why don't we just hang out here so I won't have to pay Nathan back the twenty bucks I borrowed from him?" He laughed a little too loud and I said, "Shh, he'll be out here in a second if he hears you."

"Oops, sorry." He put his arms around my waist. "Okay, I'll come over and show him a few chess tricks if you promise to go to the swing with me later."

"Deal," I said. "Come at six for supper. Karen will be almost as happy as Nathan."

"What about you? Will you be happy to see me?"

"Sure," I said. "I've been thinking about learning chess for a while."

His eyes lit up. "For real? Because I could teach you easy."

I laughed louder than he had. "You're way too gullible, Triple C."

* * *

After he left, I floated up the stairs and stopped briefly to let Karen and Brad know I was home when I passed their bedroom. I couldn't wait to get to my room and replay the night in my mind, frame by frame. Pausing and rewinding certain parts over and over and over again.

When I got out of the shower and had relived the best parts for an hour or so, I had to admit I was still confused about a lot of it. There was no question I was happy about Lew's feelings for me, even though I had no idea how I was supposed to act around him in public now. Cassie and I had barely begun to talk about boys when she got sick, and I'd never talked about things like that with anybody else.

And his surprising confidence in the romance department was another piece of the puzzle surrounding

182

him. I'd finally come to terms with having the hots for a nerd, then I find out he's not as nerdy as I thought he was and obviously didn't want anybody to know it. I suspected it had something to do with his brother's death, but I couldn't figure out how or why.

And what about Annalee? She had probably been in love with Lew for a long time, so I could just imagine how crushed she must have been when she realized he'd only been paying attention to her all night because he was just so freaking sweet. Yet she'd been happy for me. Too bad neither of us had a cell phone so I could call her or at least text. Maybe I could go to her house in the morning and talk to her in person.

I went to the computer and logged in to Gwen's FaceSpace account, trying not to be embarrassed at how much I was hoping to see something from Lew and then giggling like a sixth grader when I read his status.

> *It's been a long, long time since I've looked forward to anything as much as I'm looking forward to tomorrow night.*

I "liked" it, then I spent the next five minutes composing my own status and impressed myself with my cleverness.

> *Miami sure has a lot to offer the taste buds. Never thought I'd find anything yummier than brains, but I did tonight. Looking forward to seconds.*

Lewis Mackenzie Stanton likes this popped up within seconds, making me grin like an idiot. I was just about to send him a private message when Dexter's theme music alerted me to a new e-mail message from Flo. She said I needed to add another entry to the *Paying it Upward* blog. And she reminded me to change my e-mail address.

A few hours earlier, I'd been planning to spend the night online searching for BOSSMAN, but now I had even less interest in finding him than before. Maybe I could get by with posting the details of what I'd done to Scott and why he'd deserved it. That should qualify as part of my assignment. And I was also making good progress on the emotional addendum part, so that ought to count for something.

I wrote the blog entry about Scott and changed my e-mail address before sending Flo a message to let her know I'd done what she told me.

> FROM: zombiegirl@gmail.com
> TO: florence@blueyonder.net
> SUBJECT: Obedience
>
> Check the blog for the latest
> installment of my adventures in
> Zombieland. I didn't say anything
> about it on there, but I wanted you
> to know I'm also getting quite a
> workout dealing with those
> emotions you and your buddies
> seem to think are so important.
> Thanks a lot for screwing with my
> head.
>
> Jada

I wasn't sure if Flo—or somebody higher up—was monitoring everything I did, but no way was I gonna write about my feelings for Lew like some middle school kid mooning over her first crush in the pages of her diary.

After replaying the night in my head again—private mooning was another thing altogether—I spent the next hour trying to decide what to say to Annalee when I talked to her. What if she was mad at me and what she'd said to Lew had just been an act?

The more I thought about it, the more worried I got that my friendship with Annalee was at risk. I decided I couldn't wait until the next day to see her and made up my mind to go right then, no matter how late it was. I remembered seeing a broken pane in the living room window that I could use to get into the apartment, so I should be able to talk to Annalee without her mom knowing anything about it.

I donned my Zombie Girl outfit minus the mask and makeup, hoping the dark clothes would let me make the trip as inconspicuously as possible. Annalee's neighborhood wasn't far from Coconut Grove, typical of Miami's hodgepodge layout that put mansions back-to-back with high crime areas. I could easily make it there on foot in a half hour or less. I stuffed my hair inside a black ski hat I found in the closet, hoping that anybody who saw me would take me for a skinny guy and leave me alone. Not that I couldn't handle anybody who bothered me. I just didn't want any delays.

Thanks to a lift I got from a creepy old man in a Cadillac Escalade who leered at me so much that I ended up getting out after a mile, I made it to Annalee's in under twenty minutes. Since it was Friday night, there were still quite a few people outside the other apartments, but I managed to make it up to Annalee's door without drawing anybody's attention. The scraggly bushes in front of the apartment were half dead, but they gave me enough cover to push my fist through the duct-taped pane and unlock the window to climb inside.

The apartment was completely dark except for a light I saw coming from under a door to my right. I knew the room at the end of the hall belonged to Annalee's mom, and I remembered that the other door in the hall had been a bathroom, so the one with the light must be Annalee's.

I started to turn the knob as quietly as possible and stopped when I heard muffled voices. At first I thought they were coming from down the hall, then I realized they were inside Annalee's room. Maybe her mom had seen that she was upset when she got home and was in there talking to her, trying to soothe her daughter's broken heart. I put my ear against the door and heard sobs, but they weren't the kind caused by heartache.

They were the kind caused by abject terror.

The door was locked, but one shove with my shoulder banged it open. In the dim light made even dimmer by the red filter over my vision, I could barely make out Annalee on the bed with Rufus on top of her, his scrawny ass grinding obscenely between her legs and one of his hands covering her mouth. She saw me and her terrified eyes pleaded for help as her muffled scream filled the room.

I grabbed Rufus by his greasy ponytail and threw him against the far wall where he slid to the floor in a crumpled heap. I was both furious and terrified at the same time, but I had to see how bad Annalee was hurt before I finished with him. Her shirt was bunched up around her neck and her jeans were off, but her underwear was only partly pulled down from her hips, making me hope I'd stopped him in time. She was sobbing uncontrollably, and I wrapped my arms around her.

"Shh . . . it's okay, you're safe now. Did he—"

"Hey, I got something for you, bitch!" Rufus yelled behind me. "You fucked with the wrong dude this time!"

I straightened up and turned to see him pointing a small pistol at me, his pants still puddled comically around his ankles.

"What little old lady did you mug to get that thing?" I said. "Or is it a cigarette lighter?"

"It's big enough to blow your ass away," he said. "Big enough to put you on your knees in front of me like your little friend was before you got here!"

My vision went blood red.

I tackled him and got both hands around his throat, vaguely registering the sound of the gun going off as we fell to the floor. The astonished look on his face when the shot had no effect on me almost made me laugh while I choked the life out of him, especially with the way his eyes were bugging out in his reddening face. But just before I tightened my grip to finish him off, I felt Annalee pulling on my shoulder.

"Don't kill him, Gwen! We need to make it look like suicide."

Her words penetrated my fury and made the red filter recede enough to let me think rationally a moment and realize she was making sense. The gun was pressed into my stomach between Rufus and me, and as soon as I released his throat, he pulled the trigger again, probably thinking he must've missed the first time. I sneered at him and grabbed his wrist, then I forced his arm up so the gun was pointed at his temple.

187

"Annalee, don't look," I said. "I'm about to make this maggot blow his brains out."

"No, not here." Her voice sounded eerily calm. "I don't want his disgusting blood in my room. There's a vacant lot across the street behind the gas station. Let's take him there."

I took the gun from Rufus then turned to look at her in amazed admiration. "You were right, girlfriend. We were destined for each other."

Rufus began babbling incoherently, so I clocked him upside the head with the gun to shut him up. I couldn't stand his sniveling, plus he'd be easier to transport that way. Annalee got a trash bag from the kitchen and we stuffed him into it, then I hoisted the bag over my shoulder.

"You need to stay here," I told her. "It's not gonna be pretty, and we shouldn't take a chance on connecting you to any of this."

"No way," she said. "After what he did to me and the things he's done to my mom for so long, I can't wait to watch him die."

I couldn't really blame her.

"Speaking of your mom, where is she?"

"Passed out in her room." She looked at the floor. "She's been drinking and doing drugs with him all day while I thought she was at work."

"You sure you can handle this?" I asked, although I felt certain she could. She was pretty freaking awesome.

"Positive."

"Okay, let's get it over with."

She went outside to make sure the coast was clear, then we sprinted across the street and ducked into the shadows behind the closed Chevron station. The vacant lot was littered with trash and abandoned items, so I picked a dark spot in the middle between the rusted shell of a washing machine and a pile of old tires. Rufus groaned inside the bag when I dropped him on the ground.

"Make him pull the trigger himself so there won't be any gunpowder residue on your hands," Annalee said while I was opening the bag. "And make sure you wipe your fingerprints off the gun before you give it to him."

"Wow, you really pay attention to those forensic shows." I laughed, then something occurred to me. "Be sure to stand behind me so he can't shoot you after I give him the gun. You're not bulletproof like me." I kicked Rufus in the side. "Pull up your pants then get on your feet."

He tried to crawl away, but I stopped him with a kick to the middle of his back.

"I'm gonna give you a choice here, asshole. You can do what I tell you and die quickly, or I can rip off little pieces of you one by one and let you bleed out. And guess which part I'm gonna tear off first."

He started blubbering but stopped when I rolled him over with my foot and kicked him in the gut.

"Which is it gonna be, maggot? Quick or slow?"

"No, please! I'll do it—gimme the gun!"

I made sure Annalee got safely behind me while I wiped off the gun with my shirt before I tossed it to him. Predictably, he pointed it at me.

"You stupid bitch! I'm gonna blow you away!"

"Go ahead and shoot, dumbass. Here, I'll give you a target." I pulled down the neck of my shirt and patted a spot over my heart. "Aim for here."

He looked unsure for a second, but he pulled the trigger and hit a spot between my collarbone and my bra. The tiny bullet made a bigger hole than I expected but began closing up immediately. I watched until it was gone, then I looked up at Rufus with a smile.

"Nice shot, shithead. Now put the gun in your mouth and point it where your brain would be if you had one."

"No, please . . ." He dropped the gun and crawled over to clutch at my feet. "I swear I'll leave and never come back if you let me go! *Please* . . ."

"Shut up!" I shook him off my foot like something I'd stepped in. "I don't believe anything you say."

He rolled over and got to his knees, sobbing into his steepled hands. "No, I swear it! I'll never come around her or her old lady again. Please don't kill me!"

"Why should I have any pity for you, you pathetic waste of oxygen?" The red filter was returning rapidly to my vision. "You sure as hell didn't have any for Annalee when she was crying and begging you not to rape her. You thought you were some kinda badass, didn't you? I bet it even got you off to hear how terrified she was. Well, look who's on their knees now!"

"I'm sorry, plea—"

I kicked him in the head and sent him sprawling onto his back, then I went to stand over him with my foot on his throat. It took all my self control to keep from decapitating him.

"I'm sick of your bawling! You're a worthless piece of shit who made the mistake of hurting my best friend, and I'm gonna make sure you never hurt any other girls." I kicked his legs apart and moved my foot to his crotch. "Pick up that gun and blow your brains out, or I'm gonna stomp your balls into the pavement and start ripping off pieces of you to go in that garbage bag."

He might've been a moron dangling from the

bottom rung of the intellectual ladder, but he understood enough to know when he was totally screwed. His hand searched the ground beside him until it touched the gun, then he grabbed it and put it in his mouth, tears and snot running down his arm.

I pressed down with my foot. "Pull the trigger, asshole."

For all her earlier tough talk, Annalee ended up hiding her face against my back and didn't see his head implode.

"Wow," I said. "That cute little gun had more kick to it than I thought."

Chapter Twenty-five

When we were safely back in Annalee's room, she fell apart. I held her until she stopped shaking and her sobs had become sniffles.

"It's okay if you don't want to talk about what happened," I said. "But I'll listen if you want to tell me. It's up to you."

She told me how Rufus and her mother had arrived shortly after she got home, before she'd had a chance to wash off her makeup or change clothes. Rufus had never given her a second glance before except to mock her or tell her how ugly she was, but she said she could tell immediately that he noticed the change in her looks. After he went to the bedroom with her mother, Annalee had locked her own bedroom door, but it was a flimsy lock that anyone could easily pick. Rufus came into her room sometime later and started talking about how good she looked and saying filthy things to her. When she threatened to scream if he didn't get out, he showed her the gun he said he'd gotten to take care of her "psycho friend" and told her he'd shoot her if she didn't do what he told her.

"He made me kneel in front of him, then he made me . . ." She started to sob again and buried her face in her pillow.

I put my arms around her and cried with her. "You don't have to talk about that. He can't hurt you anymore."

When she could speak coherently again, she said, "It was bad, but not as bad as it would've been if you hadn't got here when you did. How did you know I was in trouble?"

"I didn't. I came to talk to you about what happened with Lew tonight. I was afraid you were mad at me."

She looked totally confused. "Mad at you for what?"

Considering what we'd just been through together, it all seemed pretty stupid now and made me wish I'd pretended I was there because I'd had some kind of premonition like she had thought.

"I was afraid your feelings were hurt because Lew paid all that attention to you tonight and then told you he wanted to be alone with me."

"You really thought that?" When I nodded, she said, "I knew he was just being nice to me. And anybody could see how he feels about you from the way he kept looking at you all night."

"What are you—?"

"Gwen, he's crazy about you. Besides, I told you he and I were only friends."

I knew better, but I didn't think I should let on that I knew she loved him. It would only embarrass her.

"Are you sure you're okay with it?" I said. "Because our friendship means more to me than any guy."

She hugged me. "Thank you, but I know that's a lie. And like I told Lew, I just want you to be happy. Even more now after everything you've done for me."

We checked on her mom and knew she hadn't choked on her own vomit when we heard her snoring. It was hard to do, but I kept my opinion about the woman to myself for Annalee's sake. We spotted Rufus's shoes and wallet on the floor, so I put them in the garbage bag to drop in a Dumpster on the way home. Annalee walked outside with me when I left, and we both looked across the street.

"I guess they'll find him sometime tomorrow," I said. "You think they'll come around asking questions?"

She shrugged. "Maybe as a formality to see if anybody heard anything. But it's not like gunshots or dead junkies are anything unusual around here. And since he doesn't have any ID on him, at least they won't be asking about him by name in case my mom is functional tomorrow."

"You think she'll just figure he took off again?"

"Yeah, he did it all the time. Maybe she'll finally get straight without his influence."

I thought that was about as likely as Flo doing standup at God's next birthday party, but I kept that to myself too.

"If anything happens, make sure you call me," I said. "I left Karen and Brad's number on your nightstand."

"Okay, I will." She hugged me one last time. "Thanks again for saving my life."

I returned her hug. "Maybe I could've saved my own life if I'd had you for a friend."

I took off and was glad to make it home without encountering anybody else. Both Zombie Girl and her alter ego had definitely had enough excitement for one night. All I wanted was a scalding hot shower to wash off every trace of Rufus then to lie on my bed and spend the next couple of hours thinking about nothing but Lew. Not very Superhero-ish, but I was still a rookie after all.

And the truth was I didn't want to think about what I'd done to Rufus, because I was afraid to admit how much I had secretly been hoping he would refuse to pull the trigger so I'd get the chance to rip him apart. The thought horrified me now, but while I'd been consumed with the red fury, the prospect had been scarily exciting. I was afraid I was starting to enjoy my job too much. The truth was I liked playing Zombie Girl and getting justice for girls like Annalee and Caitlin.

And that made me even less eager to find BOSSMAN and have to stop.

* * *

At breakfast the next morning, when I told the family I'd invited Lew over for supper, domestic pandemonium reigned.

"Good Lord, what am I going to serve!" Karen abandoned her omelet and began pulling out cookbooks.

"You don't need to impress him," I said. "He took me to a Cuban sandwich shop in West Flagler. Anything you want to fix will be fine."

"Did he say he'd play chess with me?" Nathan asked breathlessly.

"Yes, Nateman." I threw a piece of onion from my omelet at him. "Try not to hyperventilate when he gets here, okay?"

"Did you know his family moved to the Grove from Fisher Island?" Brad asked. "The president of our homeowner's association told me they paid their dues in advance for the next five years and threw in three grand as a donation." He shook his head and sighed. "Can't imagine why anybody would move here from that place."

"Well, for God's sake don't ask him about it," Karen said before I had the chance. "In fact, don't mention money to him at all."

"Karen's right," I said. "He doesn't like to talk about that stuff."

Brad frowned at both of us over his coffee cup. "Maybe you should give me that list of approved topics so I

195

won't embarrass you and Gwen with my crass ignorance."

"Just talk to him like he lives down the street," I said. "He's not a snob. And he's not slumming either in case you're wondering why he wants to hang out with me."

"That never entered my mind," Brad said. "He obviously appreciates young ladies who are beautiful and smart."

I smiled. "Thanks, Brad. And you're allowed to say stuff like that as much as you want."

* * *

Karen decided on lasagna for supper since it was one of her specialties. She wouldn't let me help her cook—as if I would've been much help—but she did let me give the already spotless living room and den another cleaning.

At quarter to six, Nathan yelled up the stairs from his stakeout post at the front window to tell me he saw Lew's Corvette coming down the street. For all my casual attitude with the family, my stomach felt as if it were hosting the butterfly Olympics as I checked my hair and makeup in the mirror one last time before going downstairs to let him in.

When I opened the door, Lew greeted me with a bouquet of flowers and a smile that still did a number on my knees.

"I hope those are for Karen," I said.

"Yep." He winked at me. "Got something else for you, but you can't have it until later."

The butterflies in my stomach concluded their qualifying events and commenced with the semi-finals.

"I see you're still wearing the camouflage." I pulled him inside. "You know I'm on to you, Triple C."

"I have no idea what you're talking about," he said. "Oxfords are classic."

196

The lasagna was a hit with everyone, and I thought I gave a convincing performance for my part. The conversation was polite and pleasant with nothing embarrassing for anyone. Lew was so comfortable talking to Karen and Brad that he quickly put them both at ease, and I could tell they really liked him. Nathan, of course, spent the whole meal gazing at Lew in unabashed hero worship. Karen had forbidden him from asking Lew to play chess, so when Lew suggested a game as soon as we finished dessert, Nathan polished off his cheesecake in two bites.

Lew explained the game to me while they played, and although I learned the names of the pieces and their moves, the strategy remained a complete mystery to me. After two games, Lew must've felt sorry for me because he set up the board in a famous problem composed by Vladimir Nabokov and challenged Nathan to solve it on his own after we left.

I hadn't cleared the rest of the night with Karen and Brad yet, and I wasn't sure how to ask their permission to go with Lew. I obviously couldn't tell them I was joining him for his nightly memorial to his dead brother, and I also couldn't say I wanted to go suck face with him in the swing at the end of his pier. In keeping with his talent for surprising me, Lew solved the problem for both of us.

"Thanks for inviting me to supper, Mrs. Sherman," he said. "That was the best lasagna I've ever had, including when I was in Italy."

Karen blushed. "Thank you, Lew. And thank you for the beautiful wildflowers."

Brad held out his hand. "Come back anytime, son. It was a pleasure having you."

"Thank you, sir. Actually, I was hoping you'd let

197

me borrow Gwen a little while longer. The Draconid meteor shower peaks tonight, and the end of our pier is a great place to see shooting stars."

I had to bite my lip to keep from laughing at his word choice.

Karen patted me on the shoulder. "I had no idea you were so interested in astronomy, Gwen. Glad to see you're broadening your horizons."

Unlike Karen, Brad apparently didn't pick up on anything. "Sounds like a fine educational activity. You can even stay out an hour past your curfew, Gwen."

"Thanks, Brad." I gave him a hug that surprised us both. "I'll let you know when I get in tonight."

As soon as we were in Lew's car, we both cracked up.

"You charmed the whole family, Triple C. Nice job."

"I like them. They're good people." He smiled as he started the car. "Why are you looking at me like that?"

"Pretty suave for a nerd. Another flaw in your façade?"

He shrugged. "I've had to attend business functions with my family since elementary school. I can make idle chatter about every boring topic you could possibly come up with. In several languages."

"Pretty lame for a superpower." I slapped him on the arm with the back of my hand. "Your nemesis training really sucks."

"Ah, but I make up for it with my mastery of the double entendre," he said. "I expect to see quite a few shooting stars in the swing tonight."

"Is that what you have for me that you were talking about earlier?"

198

"No, I'll be the one seeing stars," he said. "But I'll do my best to show you some."

I wasn't sure, but I thought I heard the starting pistol for the butterfly decathlon go off in my stomach. When we reached the circular driveway in front of Lew's house, he pulled in behind a black Jaguar that hadn't been there the night before.

"Nice ride," I said. "Yours too?"

"No, it's my grandfather's."

"Is that a problem?"

He shook his head and turned off the car. "No, just a surprise. He's got a business meeting with my dad and my uncle on Wednesday, but I didn't think he was coming until tomorrow. Want to meet him now or Tuesday at my chess tournament?"

My eyebrow went up. "What chess tournament?"

"Didn't you hear me talking to Annalee about it last night?"

"No, I kinda tuned you both out after awhile. Sorry."

He laughed. "Oh, I forgot that was while you were busy pouting."

"Cute." I socked him in the arm, careful not to break it. "Is your grandfather as funny as you?"

"Yep, and twice as charming." He opened the car door to get out. "I'll be keeping an eye on him for sure."

We started toward the front door, but the sound of an approaching car made us stop and turn around. I could feel Lew tense beside me as soon as he saw the white limousine coming down the driveway.

"Shit. Let's get out of here," he said.

He ignored my questions and pulled me toward the entrance to the beach walkway, but the limo came to a stop

199

before we reached it.

"Master Lewis!" a distinguished male voice called behind us. "Your mother wishes to speak with you."

Lew stopped and sighed heavily. "You're about to see firsthand why my family drives me crazy. I apologize in advance."

We walked back to the limousine where a chauffeur opened the door for a beautiful, stylishly dressed woman who didn't look at all happy to see us. And the closer we got to the woman, the more I noticed that her beauty seemed a bit worn around the edges. I'm sure Lew's grip on my hand would've been excruciating if I had still felt pain.

"You were taught better manners, Lewis," she said. "Introduce your mother to your friend."

"Gwen, meet Belinda Stanton." Lew looked at her with blatant contempt. "First runner up to Miss Florida in 1981, and last place finisher in perpetuity for Mother of the Year."

Wow. I braced myself for his mother's reaction, but she appeared only slightly annoyed at what he'd said. On the other hand, her disdain for my clothes and my hairstyle was abundantly clear.

"You must be one of Lewis's classmates from that horrible public school he insists on attending," she said. "And what do your parents do, Gwen?"

"Mostly meth, but occasionally they do a little crack for old time's sake."

I swear to Flo I had intended to be polite, but once Lew had made it clear from his introduction how he felt about her, how was I supposed to resist giving her a smartass reply after she'd practically set me up? When Lew literally bent over with laughter, I knew he didn't mind.

Belinda's beauty queen features were arranged in an unflattering frown. "I see what this is, Lewis. Bring home a piece of trash to antagonize your mother. I'm sure you think you're quite clever, but you're only doing the same thing your Uncle Bud did to your grandfather. Not very original for someone who thinks they're such a genius."

Lew straightened up and put his arm around my waist. "She just gave you a big compliment, Gwen. My Aunt Jaycee is the one I can't wait for you to meet. They'll be here Tuesday for the tournament. You're gonna love her."

"Sweet." I smiled at Belinda. "Thanks, Mrs. Stanton."

She walked away in a derisive cloud of Chanel No. 5. "Don't even think about bringing her into my house, Lewis."

"Wouldn't dream of it now that you're home, Belinda." Lew's arm tightened a little more around me. As soon as his mother disappeared through the entrance, he picked me up by the waist and spun around. "Oh, God. Thank you for that!"

I looked down at him and scowled. "Put me down before you strain your big chess muscles, Triple C."

Chapter Twenty-six

A n hour later, I was leaning against Lew's chest in the swing with his arms around me and our hands clasped together at my waist.

"I warned you that the novelty would wear off eventually," I said. "Since you seemed to enjoy that little scene with your mother so much, it's time to repay me for it."

"I thought that's what I've been doing since we got out here." He laughed and nibbled my ear.

"You know that's not what I mean. What's the deal between you and your mother?"

I could feel him tense again. "I guess I do owe you an explanation after putting you through that."

I turned around to look into his eyes. "Listen, I want you to talk to me, but only if you're okay with it. Don't do it if it's gonna bother you too much."

"No, I want to tell you," he said. "I just don't want to dump all my problems on you."

"I can take it. I'm a lot stronger than I look." *You have no idea.*

"I don't doubt that at all," he said. "Okay, but turn back around. It'll be easier to talk about it if you're not looking at me."

I had no problem with that. I could easily have stayed inside his arms in perpetuity, to borrow his phrase. When we were settled again, I heard him take a deep breath.

"My brother killed himself because the day he finally got up the nerve to tell us he was gay, Belinda's response was to tell him she wished he was dead. And the worst part was that it wasn't being gay that she had the problem with, it was because he wanted to go public with it. She told him she'd send him away to military school so they could beat some sense into him before she'd let him embarrass her like that."

"God, what a bitch," I said. "Just like Vanessa."

"Who?"

"Oh . . . my friend Jada's mother. She was all about appearances too."

"Yeah, that's Belinda. All she cares about is her social status. I don't know why my dad ever married her."

"How did he take the news from your brother?"

"It wasn't like it was a big surprise to any of us. Dad had always been okay with Drew being different from me, but Belinda never stopped hounding him about playing sports and being popular and dating debutantes—her idea of the perfect son." He paused to sigh. "What I used to be before Drew died."

A light suddenly went on in my head. "You used to play football, didn't you?"

"Yeah, I was the star running back for Fisher Island Academy. And my best friend Matt was the quarterback."

I'd thought I was beginning to get the picture, but that really threw me for a loop.

"You and Matt were friends? Why do you hate each other now?"

"I never said I hated him, but he's been mad at me ever since I quit playing football and left the academy. He blames me for ruining his chance to play college football, and that's all he's ever wanted to do."

"How is that your fault?"

"My family had been paying his tuition for him so we could play football together, and Belinda cut him off when I transferred. My dad offered to keep paying it for him when he found out what Belinda did, but Matt's parents wouldn't take it since I wasn't going there anymore. They couldn't afford to pay it themselves, so Matt had to transfer too."

"How did you ever talk your mother into letting you go to Bay Harbor?"

He scoffed. "She didn't have a choice. If she didn't want her society friends to find out why Drew committed suicide, she had to let me transfer. Nobody outside the family knows the truth except for Matt. And I know he won't tell anybody."

"How can you be sure if—" I broke off and gasped. "Oh my God. He's gay too?"

"Of course not." He laughed without any humor. "He's a big football star, and can't you see what a chick magnet he is? He couldn't possibly be gay just because he loved my brother."

"But what about the rumor that he raped a girl at your other school?"

"He started that rumor. Apparently, he'd rather be called a rapist than a faggot."

"Wow," I said. "That is so messed up."

"Tell me about it. Welcome to Lifestyles of the Rich and Pathetic."

I knew all about that world. I wished I could tell him just how much we had in common, and how ironic was it that if Belinda knew the pretentious family I really came from, I'd probably have her blessing.

"Okay," I said, "I understand your problems with

Matt and your mother, and I'm guessing you quit football to spite her, but why do you want everybody to think you're some kind of nerd?"

He didn't say anything for several seconds, then he sighed again. "Drew and I were different in a lot of ways, but we were a lot alike too. We both loved to play chess—I was the only one who could beat him—and we were on the math team together in sixth grade. Then I started playing football in seventh grade and we seemed to move in different directions after that. When he died, I felt like I'd abandoned him. Maybe if I'd stuck with some of the things we both liked, he wouldn't have felt so alone. Maybe he wouldn't have killed himself if—"

"No, don't say it." I turned around in the swing and put my arms around his neck. "It *wasn't* your fault. When somebody gets to the point that they truly want to kill themselves, nothing anybody says or does can change their mind. Trust me, I know."

"How do you know?"

"Because I tried it a few years ago. Cut my wrists and everything, just didn't bleed out fast enough before somebody found me."

It was too dark for him to see the scars on my wrists, so I put his fingers over the raised tissue. He moved his thumbs across them for a second then lifted both wrists to his lips.

"I'm glad you failed."

And I'm glad I got myself killed later so I can be here with you now.

"Yeah, me too," I said. "But nobody could've talked me out of it back then."

"Why'd you do it?"

I turned around and leaned against him again. "My

205

life just sucked in general, and I didn't think I could take it anymore. Turns out it got a lot more sucktastic before it got better, but I don't want to talk about all that. You still haven't told me why you basically wear a disguise all the time."

"No, it's not a disguise," he said. "It's my tribute to Drew. He was the one on the chess team, and this is how he dressed and combed his hair. When I look in the mirror, I see him looking back at me. Almost like he's still here."

I nodded. "And your mother has to see him every day too."

"Yeah, this way she lost her Golden Boy instead of the son she was so ashamed of." His arms tightened around me. "I knew you'd understand."

He was right—I understood it all too well. I even envied him for getting the chance to punish his mother daily and witness how much it bothered her. It was a crappy thing for us to have in common, but it drew me to him even more.

"I can see why you do it, Triple C. And it doesn't make any difference to me how you dress or what people think about you anyway. I liked you before—crazy math watch and all."

He held up his left arm. "This was Drew's too. I gave it to him on our fourteenth birthday. And that reminds me." He reached into his pocket and pulled out a small box. "This is for you. Go open it under the light so you can see."

We both went to stand under the bulb. Inside the box was a silver ring that featured a black stone in the center with grey swirls running through it. All around it were smaller stones that I suspected were diamonds from the way they sparkled in the dim light.

"The big stone is like yours, isn't it?" I turned

206

around to examine the ring on his left hand.

He nodded. "It's called Apache Tears, and there's a story behind it. In the 1800s, seventy-five Apaches were outnumbered by the cavalry on a mountain in Arizona, but rather than be slaughtered or surrender, the warriors rode their horses off the cliff that's now called Apache Leap. Legend says that when the Apache women heard what their men had done, their tears turned into these stones when they fell to the ground. When you give it to someone, it's supposed to take away their tears for a lost loved one, because the Apache women already cried enough tears for everyone."

I looked up at him. "Who gave you yours?"

"My dad's grandmother, Julia Stanton. She told me the story behind it too. After Drew died, I stayed with her in Tampa until I could bear to come back home." He took the ring from the box and slipped it onto my finger. "I hope it helps heal your heart from losing your friend Jada."

I kissed him before I could start blubbering like an idiot. When I trusted myself to speak, I said, "I love it, Triple C. But where did you get it in a day's time?"

He smiled. "I went to my mother's favorite jewelry store and told them what I wanted, then I threw some money at them to rush it. Being loaded pays off sometimes."

Chapter Twenty-seven

Lew came over for a few hours on Sunday afternoon so Nathan could show him that he'd solved the chess problem, but he couldn't stay long because he had to attend a family dinner with his grandfather. He suggested that I go with him as his date, but I told him I didn't think it would make a good first impression on his grandfather if his mother and I came to blows in the middle of dinner.

I checked the newspaper Sunday night and spotted a paragraph on page six of the metro section that said an unidentified man's body had been found in a vacant lot on Flagler Street with an apparent self-inflicted gunshot wound to the head. No arrests were expected in the case.

I logged onto the Transdead Trustee blog and added a toned-down version of what I'd done to Rufus. I halfway expected to get a reprimand from Flo because of it, but all I got was another snippy message that my e-mail address still wasn't appropriate. I figured I got away with it because he'd shot himself and it wasn't actually me who'd killed him.

Monday morning on the school bus, I squeezed Annalee's hand as soon as she sat down beside me. "Hey, how you holding up?"

"Fine," she said, but her smile looked a little shaky at the corners. "I saw a couple of police cars across the street Saturday morning. I could tell they were questioning the employees at the gas station, but they never came around to our apartments."

I told her what I'd read in the newspaper. "They're probably glad to have one less junkie on the street and happy to close the case as a suicide." I touched her ponytail with a frown. "Why didn't you do your hair and makeup this morning?"

She studied her cuticles. "I decided that wasn't me. Rufus wouldn't have noticed me if I'd looked like myself."

"That's not true and you know it," I said. "Besides, there's no telling how many other women he'd already done that to or would've hurt later on. We did the world a favor by getting rid of him."

"I know. I'm not sorry he's gone." She still wouldn't look at me. "But I'd rather stay invisible from now on."

"Listen, there's nothing wrong with the way you look either way." I took her hand again. "I just wanted you to know you had options if you ever want to use them. Okay?"

"Okay." She suddenly caught her breath. "Oh my gosh. Where did you get that beautiful ring?"

I couldn't keep the goofy grin off my face. "Lew gave it to me Saturday night."

"It's like the one he wears, isn't it?"

I nodded. "His great-grandmother gave it to him after—"

I stopped when I realized I couldn't talk about anything he'd told me until I asked him if it was okay. I'd have to clear it with him soon, because a girl had to be able to talk to her best friend. Surely he knew that.

"After what?" Annalee asked.

I turned to look into her eyes. "I can't say anything about it until I ask him first. Please don't be mad at me."

"Why would I be mad?"

"For keeping secrets from you."

She sighed. "Gwen, you saved my life. I'm not gonna get mad at you for anything, and especially not because Lew likes you. Besides, you have to keep secrets from him too since we can't tell anybody what we did to Rufus. And he must really like you a lot to give you a ring after one date."

I held up my hand and touched the ring. "The stone is called Apache Tears, and there's a legend behind it. I guess I can tell you that much at least." I told her the story and said, "Isn't that cool?"

"Yeah, it is," she said. "But there's something else I want to know, and you don't have to get Lew's permission to tell me."

"What?"

"Is he a good kisser?"

I slung an arm around her shoulders. "He's even better at that than he is at chess."

When we got off the bus at school, I saw Lew standing with Sidney and the guys. My stomach did a little flip just at the sight of him. He smiled and took my hand as soon as we walked up to the group.

"Might as well bite the bullet and let everybody know about us," he whispered in my ear. "Hope you're okay with it."

"Sure," I said.

Justin and Leonard were staring at us in obvious surprise, but Sidney looked like he was almost about to cry.

"Sorry, guys," Lew said. "I fought her off as long as I could, but she wore me down."

"Yeah, right," I said. "He thinks this means I'll do his chemistry homework for him, but he's wrong."

When the bell rang, Lew walked me to my locker

and said he'd see me at lunch. I wanted to ask him about how much I could tell Annalee, so I said, "Hey, can we skip lunch and go somewhere to talk?"

"Why, what's wrong?"

"Nothing, I just need to ask you about something in private."

"Can it wait until after school? Eating's kind of a habit with me." He rubbed his stomach and gave me a doleful look.

I laughed. "It's overrated if you ask me, but I guess we can talk after school so you won't die of starvation."

After Lew left, I hurried to catch up with Sidney. "Hey, I hope you're not mad at me for going out with Lew."

He kept walking without looking at me. "Why should it matter to me?"

"Aw, don't be like that, Sid." I linked my arm with his. "You know it never works out when good friends date each other. I didn't want to risk losing your friendship."

His expression softened a little. "I guess I know what you mean."

"Great," I said. "Besides, I can tell you don't want to be tied down to one girl anyway. You're too much of a player for that, right?"

He struggled not to smile. "Yeah, there's a couple of girls on the DerpWar forum who always flirt with me. It drives Leonard crazy."

Typical of high school grapevines, everyone had heard about me and Lew by lunchtime. Judging by the comments I got from several girls throughout the morning, I could tell that his nerdy persona had shielded him from their radar only slightly, especially considering the car he drove and his family's money. They had probably assumed he must be gay when he wasn't interested in any of them, so it brought out their claws to find out he'd passed them over for street trash. Made my morning fun at least.

When Lew and I walked into Mr. Forrester's classroom together sixth period, Matt said, "Damn, Stanton. You go from trust fund babies to a streetwalker. Bet your mama's thrilled."

"She is," I said. "We're getting a mani-pedi together after school today, then she's taking me shoe shopping. Streetwalking's hell on the Manolo Blahniks."

Lew laughed and Matt looked surprised that neither of us got mad at his insult. Now that I knew the reason behind their feud, I understood why Lew usually ignored his comments, but I had to wonder how much they really bothered him. It couldn't have been easy to lose his brother and his best friend at the same time.

"Don't forget our talk after school," I told Lew when we sat down.

"I won't, but I have chess practice," he said. "Mr. Weston told us he'd be late because there's a faculty meeting, so I can slip away for a little while after I get everybody started."

"Okay, where do you want me to wait for you?"

He thought for a few seconds. "Mr. Weston's room is on the back hall by the football field. Meet me behind the bleachers on the gym side."

I gave him a sideways look. "Slipping back into your old jock ways, huh?"

He winked at me. "Hey, do you want to be a chess team groupie or not?"

* * *

I called Karen from the office after school to let her know I'd be home a little later than usual, then I went to sit in the bleachers and wait for Lew.

Football practice was going on out on the field, and one of the coaches—a tall blond man with bulging muscles—was yelling at a group of players on the near sideline about how they needed to read the other team's offense from the way they lined up. When he finished his profanity-laced rant, all the players started to run back onto the field, but the coach grabbed one of them by the facemask and pulled him back.

"Get your ass in my office, Winston!"

Matt took off his helmet and tried to protest. "Coach Morton said I could take some snaps at quarterback since Scott—"

"I don't give a damn what he told you!" The coach shoved him toward the gym. "You'll be lucky if I let you dress out Friday at all!"

"But I been working extra hard, Coach." Matt's voice had a pleading note to it. "I knocked a quarter second off my forty time and beat all my maxes in weight training."

"Yeah, I know how you did it too," the coach said. "And we don't need no juicers on this team!"

As they passed the bleachers where I was sitting, the man glanced up in my direction. I gasped when I saw solid black eyes looking back at me. I knew he'd noticed mine too when he stopped.

"Come see me in my office when I'm done with this moron, young lady." He pushed Matt forward again. "We can talk about that eye problem of yours then."

He walked away before I recovered enough to respond. I was still thinking about all of it when Lew arrived a minute later.

"Okay, what's up?" he said as he sat beside me.

213

"Hey, what are juicers?"

"Steroid users." He looked confused. "That's what you wanted to ask me about?"

"No, I just heard one of the coaches call Matt one."

His expression went rapidly from surprise to concern to anger.

"Damn it, I can't believe he'd do something so stupid!" He kicked the bench in front of us. "I guess he figured he'd never make it in college ball unless he got bigger."

Uh-huh. So he *did* still care about Matt as a friend. I realized we needed more time to talk than he had right now, so I made a quick decision.

"Look, I didn't think about it before, but I'm gonna need a ride home now since I missed the bus. Why don't I hang out here until you're done with practice, then you can take me home and we'll talk in the car."

He seemed relieved at my suggestion, probably because he needed time to process the news about Matt. "Okay, I'll meet you here in an hour." He jumped down then turned and motioned for me to lean over. "Sure you don't want to go under the bleachers with me for a few minutes like a good little groupie?"

I shoved him. "Watch it, Triple C."

Ten minutes after Lew left, Matt stormed out of the gym, his face as red as his practice jersey. He rejoined the players on the field, but I didn't know enough about football to tell if it was the offense or defense. I looked at the gym and saw the coach with the black eyes standing in the doorway. He crooked a finger to summon me, so I walked over and followed him inside to his office.

"Close the door and have a seat," he said, sitting behind the desk. He leaned back in his chair and folded the

214

biggest arms I'd ever seen outside of Hollywood. "How long have you been a Transdead Trustee?"

I pulled a chair in front of the desk and sat down. "Just a few weeks. How 'bout you?"

"Way too long—since I was your age. What's your name?"

He didn't look much older than eighteen, so I had no idea how long he meant.

"My real name's Jada, but I go by Gwen now. I'm supposed to be a foster kid who used to live on the streets."

He nodded. "What's your assignment?"

"It's kinda complicated." I wasn't eager to tell him how I'd messed around with online predators. "Let's just say I'm an advocate for girls who need somebody to stand up for them."

He stared at me a moment, then a smile spread slowly across his face. "You broke my quarterback's arm, didn't you?"

"What makes you say that?" Despite his smile, I wasn't sure he'd be okay with everything I'd done to Scott.

"Yeah, you did it." He laughed outright. "No wonder he made up that crazy shit about getting jumped. Couldn't let everybody know he got his ass kicked by a girl. What'd he do to piss you off?"

I told him about the roofie parties and how I'd put the fear of Zombie Girl into Scott. He seemed to get such a kick out of it all that I decided to trust him with a little bit more inside information.

"Hey, just so you know, Matt Winston wasn't part of it. In fact, he was the only guy who stood up for Caitlin—the girl who told me what they did. He got her out of there and made sure she got home safe."

His face sobered as he considered that a few

215

seconds. "Might be because he couldn't get it up. Juicers have that problem sometimes."

"Okay, TMI." I held up my hand. "But that's not why he helped her. I just thought you should know he's not a total asshole."

He shrugged. "I know he's not the first kid stupid enough to think football is worth risking your life over. I think I knocked some sense into him today, so maybe he'll stay off the juice from now on."

I looked from his huge arms back to his face. "That's your assignment, isn't it?" He nodded and I said, "Is that how you died?"

"No, but it played a big part in how I screwed up my life so bad that I ended up with my car wrapped around a tree." He stared at his clenched fists a second then sighed. "But that's a long story you don't want to hear. Trust me."

"Okay, but I do have a question for you," I said. "You said before that you've been a Trustee for a long time. If you're doing what you're supposed to do and helping guys like Matt, why are you still here? Is there another part to your assignment?"

"Not that I know of. I'm still here because I broke the rules." He sighed again, and the look on his face was filled with the deepest sadness I'd ever seen. "See, there was this girl I loved when I was alive. I lost her because I was stupid for a long time before I ever did any drugs, but I never stopped loving her. Still haven't."

"You tried to contact her?"

"No, but I keep tabs on her. You know, to be sure she's happy. The Internet makes that easy to do even when I'm nowhere near her." He looked up with a little smile. "And I might've sent her a few anonymous birthday gifts."

I shook my head in amazement. "You gave up

216

forever to stay here with her, and you can't even talk to her."

"It's worth it." He seemed to be looking at something in the distance that only he could see. "I always knew she was the closest I was ever gonna get to Heaven."

I could tell he truly had no regrets about the choices he'd made. I couldn't help envying him for knowing his own heart so well and having the courage to follow it. And I also wished I'd had the chance to love somebody as much as he loved that girl.

"Anyway," he said, "just because I screwed up my own assignment doesn't mean I can't help you with yours if you need it." He wrote down a number on a slip of paper and held it out to me. "Call or come see me anytime you need to talk to somebody who knows what you're going through."

"Thanks, Coach." I took the paper and stood up to go.

He held out one of his huge hands for me to shake. "You can call me Wade."

When I left the gym a few minutes later and walked back to the bleachers to wait for Lew, I saw Matt watching me from the field.

* * *

Annalee was with Lew when he met me after chess practice.

"He took my backpack and won't give it back," she said. "I told him I didn't need a ride home but he won't listen. I can take the bus like I always do."

"Oh, let him play chauffeur," I said. "It makes him feel like he's in touch with the common people."

Lew laughed and picked up my bag too. "I told her you wouldn't mind, but she's kinda hardheaded."

217

"Yeah, I know." I linked my arm with hers as we walked to the parking lot. "It's one of the things we have in common."

After we dropped off Annalee at her house, I told Lew to go somewhere we could talk. He suggested one of the outdoor cafés in CocoWalk, the ritzy shopping village inside Coconut Grove. When we were seated outside the Cheesecake Factory with a huge slice of *dulce de leche* caramel between us that looked so delicious it made me wish I still had taste buds, I asked him how much I could tell Annalee.

"She noticed my ring on the bus this morning and remembered that you wear one like it. I told her the Apache legend but not how it applies to you."

He took a bite of cheesecake then fed one to me. "You can tell her anything you want. I'm sure she won't say anything to anyone."

"I know she won't," I said, "but I had to ask you first. Don't worry, I'll make sure she knows not to let on that you're Superman underneath those Oxfords."

"Yeah, well . . ." He took another bite. "She kinda knows that already."

"What are you talking about?"

He sighed. "Remember I told you about the time I took her home and her mother and some creep were both wasted? The guy said something to Annalee on their way out the door, and I guess he didn't like what she said back because he shoved her inside the apartment and made her fall down." He rubbed the knuckles of his right hand. "I got out of my car and told him not to put his hands on her again. When he told me to fuck off, I broke his jaw."

And that was when Annalee had fallen in love with him. I knew it as surely as I knew that Rufus was sporting a

218

stylish new toe tag.

"Wow, I'm impressed that you only broke his jaw," I said. "I would've broken every bone in that ugly face of his."

He frowned. "You've seen him there? I told Annalee to let me know if he came back."

I made a disgusted noise. "Yeah, her mom can't seem to stay away from him. I'm sure Annalee didn't want you to know that."

The crease between his brows deepened. "Did he try anything with you?"

"Hey, I thought you told me you solved your problems without resorting to . . . what did you call them? Barbarian tactics."

"This is different. You don't have to put up with anybody mistreating you ever again."

I covered his hand with mine and leaned across the table to kiss him. "Thanks, but I can take care of myself, especially with a scrawny maggot like him. Trust me, I convinced him that if he wanted to keep his balls attached to his body, he'd stay away from Annalee for good. I'd be willing to bet you that hot rod you drive that he won't be back."

"Remind me not to ever make you mad at me," he said.

I grazed his chin with my fist. "You're wicked smart, Triple C."

He got quiet while we finished the cheesecake, and I wondered if he was thinking about Matt.

"So are you gonna say anything to your boy about the steroids?"

His surprised look told me I'd guessed right. "No, I'm sure that would only make things worse."

"Might be worth a shot," I said. "Have you tried to talk to him at all since everything happened?"

He shook his head. "He made it clear he doesn't want to talk to me about anything."

"Male ego much?" I sighed. "Guys are such tools."

"You know, maybe you're right," he said. "I should invite him over for a slumber party. We can talk while I do his hair and makeup."

I reached across the table and shoved him. "Yeah, just remember not to take him around your girlfriend or she might flirt with him all night and totally ignore you."

He laughed and shoved me back. "Hey, I'm okay with that as long as I'm the one who gets kissed at the end of the night.

Chapter Twenty-eight

Julian was so charged with adrenaline when he left McCarthy's office that he had to duck into the executive washroom before someone noticed his inappropriate state. He was finally getting the respect and recognition he deserved, and the exhilaration was like an aphrodisiac. For the first time in his life, he had an erection that had nothing to do with young girls.

McCarthy was considering a land purchase for a new resort development, and he was sending Julian to evaluate the property and meet with the principals, then report back to him on the deal. Never mind that all his usual purchasing agents were tied up with a big merger they were negotiating and that McCarthy himself couldn't go because he had another of his phantom illnesses. He clearly felt that Julian was the best man for the job.

This was the first step up the corporate ladder that Julian had been waiting for. He was sick of being McCarthy's lapdog and pandering to him and his bitch of a wife. Her condescending attitude and frequent insults at Julian's expense almost made him wish he could add her to his list of conquests. If her aging body hadn't repulsed him completely, he'd wipe that mocking look off her Botoxed face for good.

But he didn't have time to dwell on any of that now. He had to go home and pack, and he couldn't leave without making sure everything was safely hidden away from prying eyes. The one other time he'd gone away overnight with McCarthy on business, he'd felt certain his mother had been snooping around in his apartment while he was gone. Of course, his laptop and box of souvenirs had been with him, and the items he used to kill the girls were hidden under the spare tire in his car. But she could have found the collection of magazines he still had from his adolescence, before he'd discovered the wealth of material available on the Internet. Fortunately, she was way too large to fit inside his closet where they were hidden.

On the drive home, he entertained himself with fantasies of tightening the fishing line from his kill kit around his mother's neck, although he wasn't sure it would strangle her through all those disgusting rolls of fat. He might have to break out the scalpel he liked to use on the girls' perky young breasts. He imagined the blade slicing through his mother's jugular, and his erection returned with a vengeance.

It had definitely been too long since he'd had any fun. He still had to stay out of the Sugar Daddy chatrooms where he'd met WETNWILD16, and the one prospect he had in the FaceSpace group hadn't responded to his message offering jewelry. The little whore probably thought she was too good for him. Even with the online anonymity, some of them still saw through his charade and dismissed him like every other female he'd ever known.

He felt himself slipping into the dark place and slid his hand into his pants to pinch the tender skin, but he stopped when a thought occurred to him. To hell with Cherry Licious and all the others like her. Soon he wouldn't have to pretend to be a wealthy corporate magnate. He'd be one for real. Then he'd have ambitious tramps falling all over themselves to win his favor, just like they did to McCarthy. Sure, they were all a bit older than

Julian preferred, but he could always make them dress like the adolescent sluts he loved to put in their places.

He parked his car in the driveway and hurried to the stairs leading up to his apartment, but his mother's voice called out to him before he got halfway up.

"You're home early, Julie. What's wrong?"

Julian stopped but didn't turn around. "Mr. McCarthy's sending me away on business for him, Mumsy. My flight leaves tonight, so I have to pack."

"When will you be back?" The disapproving note in her voice made him grip the stair rail so tight that it hurt his hands. "You know I need you to take me to the outpatient center Friday morning. Dr. Coleman's doing my colonoscopy then."

"I'll be back on Thursday," he said, continuing up the stairs. "Don't worry, Mumsy."

"Do you want me to help you pack?"

"No, I can do it!" He scrambled to get his key in the lock and open the door.

"Well, make sure you take plenty of underwear so you won't have to get them laundered while you're gone. You know you're allergic to everything except Mumsy's special soap. And don't forget to pack the cream I bought you for that stubborn eczema on your peepee."

Julian slammed the door shut behind him and leaned against it, his fingers twisting his nipples as hard as he could. Who was he kidding? There was no way he'd ever be anything other than a pathetic freak as long as that mountain of sweaty, smothering flesh still drew a breath. The only hope he had of escaping her clutches was to finally kill her the way he'd dreamed of doing since he was twelve years old. Ever since she'd started using the catheters and nightly enemas to "cleanse" him after she caught him masturbating with his yearbook open to the cheerleader pictures.

He unzipped his pants and administered the punishment he deserved, but he promised himself that as soon as he got back from this trip, he'd fulfill his ultimate fantasy. He'd drive her to a remote spot in the woods nearby and slice her throat so he'd never have to hear that screechy, chastising voice of hers ever again. Then he could do whatever he wanted to do, anytime he wanted to do it. Then he could finally be a man instead of Mumsy's little Julie.

Yes, he'd do it as soon as he got back from the meeting in Miami.

Chapter Twenty-nine

I couldn't wait to talk to Annalee now that I had Lew's permission, so Zombie Girl hit the streets again after Karen and Brad went to bed. When I got to Annalee's apartment, I punched out the newly taped window pane and made a note to tell her it wasn't safe to leave it that way. Once her heart rate returned to normal after I woke her up, we had a long talk about everything Lew had told me.

"He must really trust you," she said. "I'm glad, but it's a little surprising since he's only known you for such a short time."

"I guess it's because he knows I lost somebody too." I told her the story I'd given him about how Gwen had met Jada at the group home and lost her to a predator. "I know all of it was a lie, but I really do know how he feels because I lost Cassie."

"Have you thought about what it will do to him when he loses you?"

"Of course I have. I'd never hurt him on purpose." I didn't like her suggestion that I wasn't considering his feelings, mostly because I'd worried about the same thing myself and didn't want to think about it.

Annalee must've heard the defensiveness in my tone, because her eyes filled with tears. "I didn't mean it that way, Gwen. I know you wouldn't hurt him intentionally. I just know how hard it's gonna be on him when you leave, because it's gonna kill me."

God, I was so stupid for not knowing that's what

she'd meant. I should've known her heart was always in the right place.

"Don't worry, I'm not going anywhere for a long time," I said, pulling her into a hug. "Even if I was ready to go, I haven't gotten anywhere on finding the scumbag."

She hugged me back then wiped her eyes. "You never heard back from that guy you messaged on FaceSpace?"

"No, nothing." I didn't tell her I hadn't bothered to check Cherry Licious's account in almost a week.

She looked relieved. "Well, I'd be lying if I said I wasn't glad. I don't want you to find him. And I'm really glad Lew has you to talk to. It must have been so hard for him to lose his brother like that."

It was almost three o'clock when I left, and the streets were as close to deserted as they ever got in that part of town. My Zombie Girl outfit helped me blend in with the shadows, so I was surprised when I heard somebody calling Gwen's name just before I got to the end of Annalee's block. I turned and saw Javier at the bus stop where Lew had picked me up the week before.

"What you doing here this time of night, *mami*?" He eyed my outfit and laughed as I walked back to the stop. "And what the hell you wearing?"

I sat beside him on the bench. "Okay, you caught me. I'm a member of a secret sorority called . . . the Zodiac Girls. We meet at Annalee's house, and this is what we all wear."

He folded his arms and looked at me. "I know I ain't smart like *mi socio* Lew, but I ain't stupid neither. Don't bullshit me, *chica*."

"Didn't Lew tell you I was a street kid? Old habits are hard to break."

226

He still looked skeptical. "What habits?"

I sighed. "I've got a nice foster family now, but sometimes it feels like I can't breathe in their house. They're great and all, but sometimes I have to get out and run the streets before I suffocate. Me and Annalee needed some girl talk, and I didn't want to wait 'til tomorrow."

He seemed to swallow that for the most part. "So what's with the clothes?"

"I learned a long time ago that black makes it easier to stay out of sight when you need to keep it on the down-low."

"*Si*, I know that's right." He leaned back and rolled his neck.

"You just getting off work or going home from a date?"

"I closed tonight." He winked at me. "And the *niñas* don't let me go home after a date. Sometimes for many days."

I laughed. "So I hear from Lew."

"I hear some things too." He put his arm behind me on the bench. "I hear you and him got something going on now. Make sure you do him right, *mami*. He is *mi hermano* always."

"Don't worry," I said. "But don't tell him you saw me here, okay? I know he'd freak out if he knew I was running the streets at night by myself."

He nodded. "His world is not ours. Most times, I'm glad I don't live in his."

"You mean because of his mother?"

He spat on the sidewalk then unleashed a stream of Spanish I was glad I couldn't understand.

"I don't know what you said, but I'm sure I agree. And you'll be glad to know she totally hates me."

227

His sneer faded into a smile. "Let me know the next time you go there. I think I have to visit Mama then so I can see the look on that *puta's* face."

* * *

The chess tournament the next day was held at Vizcaya Academy in Coral Way. Since it didn't start until four and the chess team was supposed to meet in Mr. Weston's room for one last practice session before they left, I waited for Lew and Annalee on the bleachers again. The football field was empty this afternoon, so I passed the time reading *Flowers for Algernon* for my English class.

"Why were you talking to my coach yesterday?"

I looked up to see Matt standing in front of me. "Can't you guess? I'm banging him for lunch money."

"Bullshit. You got rich boy's money now. What were you talking to him about?"

I knew he was trying to find out if I knew about the steroids. Underneath his usual hostility, I could tell how worried he was, but I didn't know which one he was more worried about—getting to play football or everyone finding out he wasn't who they thought he was.

"Relax, Matt. Your secrets are safe with me."

"What're you talking about? What secrets?"

His fingers were fidgeting noticeably at his sides, and he kept wiping his hands on his jeans. Maybe it was because I knew he and Lew used to be friends and that Lew still cared about him, but I couldn't help feeling a little sorry for him.

"Look, you can stop pretending, Matt. I know what you did for Caitlin, I know about you and Lew, and I know why your coach was yelling at you yesterday. I'm not gonna open my mouth about any of it. I swear."

He tried to maintain his threatening posture and was

228

still glaring at me, but I could almost see the relief wash over him. And he also didn't deny anything I'd said.

"Why? What do you want in return?"

I laughed. "Hadn't thought about asking for anything until now. Let me think about it and get back to you."

He looked like he was trying to decide whether or not I was serious, then he turned to walk away. "Yeah, whatever."

"Hey, wait," I said. "I thought of something."

He turned around and eyed me suspiciously. "What?"

"I want you to talk to Lew."

"I got nothing to say to him."

"Yeah, we both know that's not true. Looks to me like the two of you have a helluva lot in common. You're both pretending to be somebody you're not, and it's because neither of you have dealt with his brother's death."

He looked around to see if anyone was nearby, then he ran up the bleachers until he was standing on the one just below me. "Shut your mouth about that." His voice was a furious whisper. "You don't know anything about it, and it's none of your business."

I looked at him unfazed. "I know it's not fair for him to lose both his brother and his best friend all because of that bitch he has for a mother."

"He didn't have to quit football, did he? He didn't have to stop being himself and turn into some weirdass copy of Drew!" He slammed his fists against the bench on either side of my feet, tears streaming down his cheeks. "He didn't have to go away too!"

I leaned forward so my face was right in front of his. "You need to say those things to Lew. Try acting like

229

his friend instead of trying so hard to prove you're a man."

"You don't know what you're talking about! Just shut the hell up!" He turned away and stomped down the bleachers.

I let him go without saying anything else. I hadn't expected him to admit as much as he had, so I actually thought it had gone pretty well. At least I'd planted a seed of reconciliation in his mind. I went back to my reading, and Lew got there about ten minutes later.

"Annalee's riding with Sidney," he said. "She told me he needed the ego boost after you broke his heart."

I laughed as I walked down the bleachers. "Okay, let's go. I want to be sure I get a good seat in case there's a crowd."

It took us only fifteen minutes to get to Vizcaya Academy. Lew parked beside the same black Jaguar I'd seen at his house on Sunday night.

"Your grandfather's here?"

He nodded and took my hand as we walked toward the gym. "He and my aunt and uncle always try to make it to at least one of my matches. Granddad plays chess himself, but Uncle Bud and Aunt Jaycee only come because they love me."

"That reminds me," I said. "Nathan wanted to come, but his science project won for the county, and the award ceremony was this afternoon."

"Tell him congratulations for me. What'd he do his project on?"

I shrugged. "Something about swamp water and mango trees. I'm clueless about that stuff."

He stopped and looked at me funny. "You're a genius at chemistry but clueless about biology?"

"Hey, don't judge me." I pulled him forward again.

230

"I can't help how my brain works."

When we entered the gym, he led me over to a handsome older gentleman standing with a blond man who looked so much like Lew that he had to be his dad, a good-looking man with dark hair, and a blonde woman with a figure that had to be a major distraction for a gym full of teenage boys. Everyone in the group turned to look at us with unmasked interest as we approached.

"Here he is." The older man held out his hand to Lew. "Ready to crush the competition, my boy?"

"Absolutely, Granddad." Lew turned to me. "This is my girlfriend, Gwen Stewart. Gwen, this is my grandfather, my dad, my Uncle Bud and my Aunt Jaycee."

"Nice to meet all of you," I said, surprised when Lew's grandfather took my hand and lifted it to his lips.

"Mack Stanton at your service," he said with a smile that made Lew's seem almost dull in comparison. "I'm always proud of my grandson, but I must say I'm extra pleased with him today for bringing such a lovely young lady to keep on old man company during the tournament."

I shot Lew a questioning look and he shrugged. "I told you he was twice as charming. Granddad, she's only been my girlfriend for a couple of days. Cut me some slack and don't steal her, okay?"

Mr. Stanton continued to smile at me. "You know how it works, my boy. Every man for himself."

I elbowed Lew. "Too bad for you, Triple C."

Lew's dad rescued my hand and shook it. "Please excuse my father, Gwen. He can't seem to help himself around beautiful women. I'm glad you were able to come today. Lew's told us a lot of nice things about you."

"Good," I said, "because I'm sure your wife wasn't

too complimentary." Might as well get it out there to start with.

"Not a problem." He patted my hand without so much as a blink. "My wife and I agree on very few things these days."

"Talk about déjà vu," Lew's uncle said to his wife. "Jaycee, does this remind you of the first time I brought you home to meet Dad and my brothers?"

She nodded and held out her hand. "Hi, Gwen. I'm Jaycee and this is Bud. If Belinda hates you, I'm sure you and I are gonna get along great."

Lew had to go check in with the tournament officials, so his family and I went to sit in the bleachers near the tables set up for the matches. The talk was mostly polite questions about school and my foster family. I was a little surprised that Lew had told them I was a foster kid, but none of them seemed to have a problem with it. They weren't anything like I'd expected from people as wealthy as I knew them to be. Nothing like my parents, that was for sure.

After the first round of matches was over, I went down to congratulate Lew on his win and to speak to Annalee, whose match had ended in a stalemate. Lew told me there was one more round of qualifying matches, then the finals would be held Thursday at Bay Harbor.

"How're things going with the relatives?" he asked.

"Fine," I said. "Your grandfather's a total trip, and your dad and your uncle are both nice. I see what you mean about your aunt. I can tell she's a smartass like me. Guess that's why I like her so much."

"I knew you would." He looked around to see if anyone was watching and bent to give me a quick kiss. "Wish me luck. The guy I'm playing next is supposed to be

Brickell's big gun."

"You can take him," I said. "And if you get into trouble, you can always break his jaw."

"Ha-ha. Very funny."

He left to take his seat for the next match, and when I turned to go back and sit with his family, I saw his Aunt Jaycee coming toward me.

"Why don't we sit by ourselves this round?" she said. "We can talk without the men interrupting."

"Okay, sure." I followed her to the far side of the bleachers where only a few people were sitting, wondering what was coming.

When we sat down, she said, "I've never been one for playing games, so I'm gonna cut to the chase, okay?"

"Sounds good to me."

"This is the first time I've seen my nephew smile in almost a year. I know I have you to thank for that, Gwen, so I want to be sure you don't let that pretentious bitch he has for a mother scare you off."

I didn't know what I'd been expecting from her, but it definitely hadn't been an offer of backup. "You don't have to worry about that," I said with a laugh. "I don't scare easily."

"Good, because I've decked her before and wouldn't hesitate to do it again if you need it. I love that boy like my own, and I'd do anything to see him happy."

"Thanks, but I've got a pretty good right hook myself."

She put an arm around my shoulders and grinned. "A girl after my own heart."

"What'd she do to make you hit her?" I asked.

"Let's just say I was setting a precedent. She learned not to mess with me anymore."

"Lew's dad seems like such a nice guy," I said. "Why'd he marry such a bitch?"

Jaycee sighed. "That's a story that'll have to wait until we have more time to talk." She snapped her fingers and pointed at me. "Hey, why don't you come over tomorrow afternoon and keep me company? Bud's got meetings all day with his dad and his brother, and the last one is at Lew's house. If we're lucky, Belinda's head will explode when she sees the two of us there together."

I laughed. "I can probably do that. I'll ask my foster mom when I get home tonight."

We rejoined the men just in time to see Lew take his opponent's queen and clinch the match, putting him in the finals on Thursday. He and the rest of the Bay Harbor team stayed on the floor to watch the end of Annalee's match with an Asian boy from Vizcaya. Their game was still going on after all the others finished, so everyone in the gym was soon watching.

I didn't know if I had any zombie vibes I could transmit telepathically, but I did my best to send some down to Annalee so she wouldn't panic from all the scrutiny, and it appeared to be working. She was so focused that she didn't seem to realize everyone was watching. In fact, the Asian kid looked a lot more bothered by it than she was.

The pressure must've finally gotten to him because he made a bad move and tried to take it back, but the judges wouldn't allow it. Annalee moved in for the kill and got a big round of applause when she announced *checkmate*.

I ran down the bleachers to congratulate her. "Way to go, Annalee. You totally out-finessed that guy. Like the Chuck Norris of chess."

"Gwen's right." Lew put an arm across her

234

shoulders. "Your concentration was amazing, Annalee. I want you to talk to the team tomorrow at practice about how to keep your focus, okay?"

"Sure, if you want me to." Her face blazed a deep purple when she looked up at him.

Nah, she didn't love him. She freaking adored him.

Chapter Thirty

Lew took Annalee and me to the Medianoche Mezzanine to celebrate after the tournament. The food was still tasteless, but I enjoyed it a lot more than our first time there, and this time I didn't mind their chess talk at all. After Lew dropped Annalee off at her apartment, he wanted me to go back to his house with him, but I told him I needed to get home early.

"Your aunt wants me to keep her company tomorrow after school while your uncle's at his meeting," I said. "Karen and Brad have been good about letting me do so much stuff with you, but I don't want to push it."

"Okay," he said with a sigh. "I guess I can go home and play chess with Granddad tonight."

I laughed. "You're a real party animal, Triple C."

When we got to my house, he walked me to the door and didn't let go after he kissed me. "Thanks for coming to watch me today. I know you must've been bored to death."

"No, it was fun," I said and actually meant it. "That killer look you get when you win is kinda sexy."

He smiled. "Wait 'til you see me wearing the championship medal. You won't be able to restrain yourself."

I pretended to shiver. "Ooh, just thinking about it gets me excited. Maybe I need to sneak out tonight and meet you."

"Can you do it without getting caught?" he said. "I

can park at the end of the street and wait for you."

I'd only been joking, but I could tell he was serious when he pulled me closer. I was about to tell him yes when the look in his eyes told me he had a lot more than kissing in mind. I shivered for real despite the heat that spread instantly through my body when his hands slipped under my shirt and drifted up my back to my ribs. And I didn't know if I wanted them to stop or keep going.

Wait, what? How was I supposed to handle this?

"I was just kidding," I said. "You don't want me to get grounded, do you?"

"No, but I don't know if I can wait until tomorrow night to see you again."

His thumbs teased the lace at the bottom of my bra as his lips brushed my neck. While my body was willing his hands to continue their explorations, my brain was screaming at me that I needed to push him away. Before I could decide which one to listen to, the porch light came on and decided for me. Lew backed away just as Nathan threw open the door.

"Did you win, Lew? Did Gwen tell you why I couldn't come to watch?"

Karen appeared in the doorway and grabbed Nathan by the collar. "I'm sorry. He saw Lew's car outside and took off before I could stop him."

"No problem," Lew said. "I won both my matches, Nathan. How'd you do in the science fair?"

"Honorable mention." He turned to look at Karen expectantly. "Can I go watch Lew in the finals, Mom? Please!"

"Only if Lew and Gwen don't mind." She looked at us apologetically.

"Sure, Nateman," I said. "Maybe we can start a

wave in the stands when Lew wins the whole thing."

Up in my bedroom, after I'd gotten the okay from Karen to go to Lew's house the next day after school, I lay on my bed and tried to figure out what I was gonna do the next time I was alone with him. He was clearly ready for things to get a lot more serious between us. That didn't really surprise me—he was a normal teenage boy after all. The surprising thing was that he'd kept things so innocent this long. The problem, of course, was that I wasn't anything close to being a normal teenage girl, and in more ways than one. Besides the whole being dead thing, I didn't know what the crap I was doing when it came to making out with a boy.

My smartass attitude had always led everyone to think I was worldly and experienced, but I was actually clueless in the heavy breathing department. I didn't know if it had been my emotional numbness or what, but the guys I'd dated when I was Jada hadn't stirred so much as a feather's tickle in me. I'd always cut them off quick anytime they'd gone past kissing or even hinted at groping me. And I definitely hadn't slept with any of them.

But Lew had stirred something in me I'd never felt before—even more confusing since I didn't feel pain or other sensations anymore. That couldn't be an accident, so did it mean it was okay for me to act on it? I couldn't really imagine that being allowed. Were they testing me?

If I'd ever needed a friend to talk to, it was now. But no matter how I tried to justify it or convince myself that Annalee would understand, there was no way I could talk to her about the pros and cons of making out with Lew. Not when I knew how she really felt about him.

I thought about talking to Karen, but how was I supposed to explain my complete lack of information, considering Gwen's history? *Yes, Karen, I know I used to be a hooker, but I'm still a virgin. Can you tell me what it's like to go to second base?*

I rolled over and covered my head with the pillow. What would the consequences be from Upstairs if I let Lew round any bases? I still wasn't sure Flo's department knew about everything I did, but surely Transdead Trustees were monitored somehow. Maybe I needed to ask Wade about that.

I got up and found the slip of paper with his phone number on it and decided to call him after Karen and Brad went to bed. It shouldn't matter how late it was since I knew he didn't sleep either. After I took my shower, I checked my e-mail and Gwen's FaceSpace account, but there was nothing interesting on either one. Lew hadn't posted anything on his wall or sent me any messages. Probably playing chess with his grandfather.

I thought briefly about checking the account for Cherry Licious, but I closed the browser without logging in. Might as well admit that I didn't *want* to find BOSSMAN. I wasn't ready to go yet, and I was starting to wonder if I would ever be ready.

I waited until eleven o'clock then got the cordless phone from the hall and took it to my room. Wade answered after the first ring.

"Hey, this is Jada. You said I could call if I needed to talk to you."

"No problem," he said. "What's up?"

"How'd they find out you broke the rules? Are they monitoring everything we do?"

"Probably, but I told 'em what I did."

"Why?"

"I wanted to stay here. I told you why."

239

"Okay, so after you broke the rules, they said you had to stay here forever?"

"No, they said if I went a year without breaking the rules again, my account would be cleared."

"I don't get it," I said. "Why don't they do anything to stop you from contacting her? Like send you to the jungles of Africa or somewhere like that?"

"Not many juicers in Africa," he said, then he sighed. "They told me it had something to do with free will, whatever the hell that means."

"Huh. No kidding."

"Why all these questions, Jada? What are you thinking about doing that you don't want them to know about?"

"Nothing. I was just curious."

"Cut the bullshit. Does this have anything to do with that guy I saw you getting into the Corvette with today? Nice car by the way."

"No, I just wanted to know if they're monitoring us, that's all."

"Look, I got no right to lecture you about anything, but just be careful, okay? You won't have to live with whatever you do, but *he* will."

* * *

I thought about Wade's warning all day at school on Wednesday. Should I get back to my search for BOSSMAN before things went too far with Lew and I ended up breaking his heart? Or should I follow *my* heart like Wade did and stay until I was ready to go?

Annalee and Lew must've noticed my distraction because they both asked me about it. I obviously couldn't talk it over with either of them, so I passed it off as thinking about the paper I had to write on *Flowers for Algernon*.

240

They seemed to buy that.

I hadn't decided squat when I got off the school bus and was still distracted enough that I didn't notice Dougie getting off after me until the bus was gone. I hadn't seen him on the bus since the day I'd kicked his ass and figured he'd been avoiding me, which suited me just fine. After the bus pulled away from the stop, I walked east toward Lew's house but stopped when I heard him call out from behind me.

"Hey, bitch!"

I turned around and laughed when I saw the baseball bat in his hands. "No, I can't play ball with you today, Dougie. I got somewhere to be."

"I don't know what kinda karate shit you used on us, but it ain't gonna do you no good this time." He held the bat in his right hand and slapped the barrel of it with his left. "Time for a little batting practice."

Oh, jeez. He must like cheesy action flicks too.

"Fine. Let's get it over with," I said. "I told you I got somewhere to be."

I walked toward him and deflected the bat with my right arm when he swung it at me. It felt like somebody grabbing me, but that's all. Dougie sneered when my upper arm bent almost in half and the bone cracked loudly, but his smile disappeared fast when I held up my arm so he could watch it straighten out again before his eyes. While he was still gaping at me, I took the bat from him and broke it across my knee.

"Batting practice fail," I said. "Find a new hobby, dipshit. You suck at being a badass."

I dropped the broken bat and grabbed him by the shirt, then I tossed him into a nearby yard, far enough to make an impression on him without breaking any bones. I guess he got the message because he scrambled to his feet and took off running down the sidewalk.

I started to walk off then stopped and went back to pick up the broken bat shards and put them in one of the garbage cans on the street. Zombie Girl didn't litter.

Chapter Thirty-one

I pushed the intercom button on the gate at Lew's house and gave my name and reason for being there. When I reached the driveway around the fountain, Jaycee came out the front door to greet me.

"I'm so glad you're here," she said. "Belinda's entertaining a gaggle of her country club friends, and I couldn't stand it another second." She motioned for me to follow her. "Let's go down to the beach. I asked Yelina to send out some drinks and snacks for us."

"Yelina, is that Javier's mom?" I asked as we started down the walkway.

"You know Javi?" She looked surprised. "Is he back in school?"

I told her about meeting him at the library while Lew was tutoring him. We'd reached the end of the steps but turned left instead of right toward the pier. After a few seconds, I could see we were headed toward two Adirondack chairs set up under an umbrella about fifty yards away.

"Javi's a good kid," Jaycee said. "He just got lost after Drew died."

I sat in the chair on the left and dropped my backpack on the ground beside it. "Lew told me they've been friends since they were little."

She put on a pair of sunglasses and leaned back in her chair. "The three of them were like brothers until they were about fourteen, then they all seemed to go off in different directions. I'm glad Javi and Lew found their way back to each other."

"How'd you know Lew had told me about his brother?"

She looked at me over the top of her glasses. "I saw that ring on your finger. He wouldn't have given you that without telling you what it meant. I'm guessing you must've lost somebody too. I'm sorry, sweetie."

I fingered the ring. "You wouldn't think we'd have much in common, but we do."

"Doesn't surprise me a bit. Bud and I came from different planets, but we're like two sides of the same damaged coin."

"You think that's why you were drawn to each other?"

She laughed. "No, it was nothing but lust to start with, but we figured out pretty quick that there was a lot more to it than sex. How about you and Lew?"

"Oh . . . no." I couldn't believe I felt a blush spreading over my face, especially in front of Jaycee. "Nothing like that yet."

"Good for you," she said. "Glad you're not screwed up like we were."

"Screwed up how?"

She took off her sunglasses and stared out at the bay. "Bud was the world's biggest playboy until he met me, and I was convinced that nobody could ever care about me for anything but sex. We were both clueless about love, but we managed to figure it out together." She turned to look at me. "Everything happens for a reason, and I know we were meant to save each other."

Once again, I found myself wishing I'd had the chance to know what it felt like to love somebody that way.

244

"I'm clueless about it too," I said. "In more ways than one."

"Sounds like that needs some elaboration," she said. "Want to talk about it? No judgment, I promise."

My embarrassment from a minute earlier vanished in the face of her frankness. Maybe she was the one to answer my questions.

"How much has Lew told you about my past?"

She shrugged. "He said you're a foster kid and used to live on the street for a while. That's all I had to hear to know you and I are probably cut from the same cloth. I didn't need any details."

"Then it might surprise you to know that Lew and I haven't done anything but kiss."

Her expression remained neutral. "Maybe a little, but if that's all you're comfortable with, then I think it's great."

"That's just it," I said. "I don't know what I'm comfortable with, and I'm pretty sure it's gonna be put to the test tonight. I don't have a clue how I'm gonna react."

She turned around sideways on her chair. "Well, I'd be willing to bet that Lew will be okay with whatever you decide. Even when he used to date all those country club princesses that Belinda was always throwing at him, he never played their games. That boy's got his head and his heart in the right places."

I suddenly felt guilty for doubting him. "I guess I really should've known that about him already. He's been great to me about everything."

A uniformed young man arrived with a cooler of drinks and a tray of snacks that included crab puffs and shrimp cocktail. Jaycee thanked him by name and asked how his sister was doing at Florida State. I wondered if

Lew's mother even knew her driver's name, and that reminded me to ask Jaycee about her as soon as we were alone again.

"You said you'd tell me about Lew's parents today. Is his mom just a trophy wife, or did she get pregnant to trap his dad?"

Jaycee scoffed. "Belinda didn't want kids at all. It took Luke years to talk her into it, which is why Lew's so much younger than all his cousins."

"So why'd he marry her?"

"Bud told me Luke's been in love with her since kindergarten, but even with all his money, she never paid attention to him until he got to be a big football star in high school. None of the Stantons have ever been able to understand why Luke loves her, but he obviously does."

"Even after what she did to Lew's brother?"

She sighed. "That was the closest they've ever come to splitting up. Everybody took it hard, even Belinda in her own warped way. She ran off to Europe for two months and ended up hospitalized for anorexia. Luke either stayed at work or stayed wasted the whole time she was gone, and Lew shut down completely. He was a little better when he came back from his great-grandmother's in Tampa, but he still wasn't himself—literally. It was like he was trying to turn into Drew or something."

I told her what Lew had said about why he did it.

"Gwen, do you have any idea what a big deal it is that he opened up to you about that? None of us could get him to talk about it at all. He must feel a connection with you that he doesn't have with anybody else."

"You really think I helped him? That I'm good for him?"

"There's life in his eyes again and his smile is back.

That's because of you." She reached across the space between our chairs and took my hand. "You saved my nephew, Gwen."

Could that be true? Lew and I did have a connection because of the similarities in our lives. That couldn't be just a coincidence, could it? Was it part of why I was here?

"I'm glad he can talk to me," I said. "We both have a hard time trusting people."

"I'm glad too." She squeezed my hand before letting it go. "Especially right now. Friday's gonna be really hard for him."

I started to ask what she meant, then it hit me. Friday was the anniversary of his brother's death. Was that why things between us had suddenly gotten more intense?

During the next hour, I heard stories about how Jaycee and Bud had met each other in college and how she had come to write a popular series of children's books. I was surprised by that until she told me the spunky heroine was based on herself as a child and got into trouble in every book. I was happy to let her talk while I thought about Lew and tried to figure out what the crap I was gonna do.

"Well, Bud should be done with his meeting soon, and I guess I've run my mouth enough for one day." Jaycee stood up and began gathering her things. "We're gonna go get a medianoche before we leave tonight. Ever had one?"

I picked up my backpack and nodded. "Lew took me to the Medianoche Mezzanine where Javi works on our first date, and we went back yesterday when we took my friend Annalee home after the chess tournament. She lives a couple blocks down from it on West Flagler."

"I make Bud take me there at least once whenever we're in Miami," she said. "Aren't they to die for?"

"Yeah, they're awesome." I didn't really miss food,

but the way everybody drooled over those sandwiches made me wish I could find out what all the fuss was about.

When we got back to the house, Lew's Corvette was just coming down the driveway. Jaycee hugged him when he got out of the car.

"Thanks for loaning me your girl today," she said. "We had a great time and soaked up some nice rays."

"You're welcome," he said. "Aunt Jaycee, this is our friend Annalee. She's on the chess team with me."

Jaycee turned to look at her. "You're the one who kicked that guy's butt in the last match yesterday. Way to go." She slapped her a high five.

Annalee blushed, but I could tell she liked the praise. "Thanks, but Lew's the chess master. The rest of us just try not to embarrass him too bad."

I saw Jaycee's eyebrows go up slightly at the adoration on Annalee's face when she looked at Lew. She threw me a questioning look, and I gave her an I-know-but-what-can-I-do shrug in reply. Luckily, the front door opened just then and Lew's father, grandfather and uncle came out with two other men. Bud shook hands with the group, then he hurried over to us.

"Free at last, free at last," he said, wrapping Jaycee in a bear hug. "I'm all yours and I'm starving. They're bringing the cars around in a minute so we can go stuff our faces."

"We're going to the Mezzanine," Jaycee told Lew. "You kids want to join us?"

"We were just there yesterday," he said. "Besides, Gwen and I have plans after we take Annalee home." He put his arm around me, and I felt it tighten around my waist meaningfully.

"Bud and I can run Annalee home," Jaycee said.

"Gwen said you live over by the sandwich shop, right?"

I could tell Annalee was about to protest, but Lew jumped at the offer before she could say anything.

"Thanks, Aunt Jaycee. Is that okay with you, Annalee?"

"Oh . . . sure," she said. "I'll see you and Gwen tomorrow."

I got hit with another tidal wave of emotions—guilt over Annalee's feelings, excitement that Lew couldn't wait to be alone with me, and fear for the same reason. It wasn't like him to do anything that might hurt Annalee's feelings, so I knew something big was definitely going on with him and wondered again if it was the anniversary of his brother's death. It looked like I'd be hitting the streets again later that night so I could talk to her and make sure we were okay.

Jaycee and Bud went back to join the group of men while they waited for their car to be brought around. Lew put my backpack in his car, then he said, "Let me go say something to Dad and Granddad real quick, then we can go."

"Sure, take your time," I said. "I'll be over in a second to say hello." I waited for him to walk away then I turned to Annalee. "I need to talk to you about what's going on. I'll come over to your house after I get home tonight, okay?"

"Why, what's the matter?" she said.

"Nothing, I just need to talk some things over with my bestie."

She smiled. "Okay, but remember that some of us still need sleep in order to function."

"Oh, crap. I forgot about your tournament tomorrow. Never mind. I can wait 'til later to talk to you.

No biggie."

She seemed pretty okay with everything, so I didn't feel quite so guilty. We joined the group by the fountain just as Lew's grandfather was saying something about a Ferrari to one of the other men. I had to fight the urge to shudder at just the mention of the car's name. From the weird look I got from one of the men—a short guy wearing a bad Armani knockoff—I wasn't sure if I'd succeeded. I suddenly couldn't wait to get out of there with Lew and was glad when the cars arrived. And I was glad there was no Ferrari among them.

"What's wrong?" Lew asked after we'd said our goodbyes. "You had a funny look on your face back there."

I tried to shrug it off. "I was afraid Annalee's feelings would be hurt if we ran off on her, but when Jaycee started talking to her about her books, I knew she'd be okay."

"I felt kinda bad about it too," he said, "but I couldn't wait to tell you what happened after school today, and I couldn't tell you in front of her." We'd reached the steps at the end of the walkway, and he stopped and put his arms around my waist. "I've got a surprise for you too."

"Let me guess." I looked up at him and smiled. "You bought me the house next door and had it completely furnished in one day."

"No, but that's a good idea." He brushed my lips with his. "How would you like to watch the sunset from the deck of my dad's boat?"

"Are you sure that's okay with him?"

He nodded. "I asked first. And it's just the pontoon boat, not the yacht."

"Oh, well in that case you can forget it." I backed away and pretended to be offended. "I wouldn't be caught dead on anything under thirty feet."

"We're good then." He took my hand and pulled me in the direction of the boathouse. "The Sun Tracker's a forty footer."

A half hour later, we were moored out in the bay off the northern seawall of the Stanton property, watching the sunset from an oversized chaise on the deck above the cabin. The water looked as if someone had strung it with strands of lights in every shade of red and gold.

"You did good, Triple C. Thanks for ordering the cool light show."

"You're welcome," he said. "What's the use of being loaded if I can't show off for hot girls?"

I sat up and looked at him. "Girls?"

"Girl—definitely singular." He held up his hands in defense.

I smiled and leaned back, pulling his arm around me again. "Okay, so tell me what happened after school."

"Matt stopped me on my way to Mr. Weston's room and said he needed to ask me something."

"Really? What did he want?"

"He asked me if I was going to the cemetery on Friday and wanted to know if he could go with me." His hand closed a little tighter around my elbow. "Friday will be a year."

"Jaycee told me," I said. "What'd you say to him?"

"I told him I thought Drew would like it if we went there together."

"Did you talk about anything else?"

"No, I could tell he's still mad as hell at me, but he did say we had some stuff we needed to talk about. This is the first time since Drew died that he's said *anything* to me that wasn't an insult or a threat. At least it's a start."

I turned and put my arms around his neck. "I'm really happy for you, Triple C."

"I don't know what you said, but I know you talked to him, Gwen." He cupped my face in his hands and looked into my eyes. "Thank you for giving me back my best friend."

He pushed me back on the chaise with his upper body covering mine and his knee between my thighs, his eyes never leaving my face. I swear it felt like I couldn't breathe even though I didn't need to anymore.

"When Drew died, it was like half of me died with him. I didn't feel alive again until the first time I kissed you. Do you have any idea how much you've done for me?"

If it's possible for dead hearts to swell with happiness, mine did then to know I'd made a difference in his life.

"Maybe that's why I'm here," I said. "Remember when you said it was like we were destined to meet? I think maybe we were. I think whoever writes this crazy script we all have to act out wrote me into your life so we could save each other."

His eyes moved over my face like he was searching for something. "But I haven't done anything for you."

"Yes you have, Lew. If I've helped bring you back to the people who love you, then I know I did at least one worthwhile thing in my whole wasted life." I put my hands on his cheeks. "You make me feel like I matter."

"Don't talk about yourself like that," he said. "You matter more than you know."

He kissed me with an intensity that I felt too, and I forgot about everything except the way his fingers sent little shocks through me everywhere he touched and how I loved the way I felt his body react when I ran my hands over the muscles in his arms and chest. All my worries about what to do or not to do disappeared, because everything felt right. I wouldn't be feeling any of it if I wasn't meant to be with him.

And everything seemed amplified by a growing anger inside me at all the things I'd been cheated out of. It was all so damn unfair. Yeah, I'd been stupid to do the things I'd done, but stupidity wasn't a sin, was it? Why did I have to die for it? If this was my only chance to know what it felt like to love somebody and have them love me back, then I was going for it with everything I had.

I deserved to know what it felt like to live at least once before I had to die.

So when Lew pulled away from me and sat up, I almost cried out in protest. "What's wrong?"

"Absolutely nothing," he said. "I just need to catch my breath a second. Before we go too far."

An hour earlier, I would've been relieved to be let off the hook like that, but everything was different now. "I thought that's what you wanted."

He turned and touched my face again. "I do, but not yet. I've got a lot more planned for us tonight."

"Like what?"

"Dinner for starters. There's a seafood tray in the galley that Yelina made for us. Then I thought we'd go for a swim after it gets dark."

"But I didn't bring a suit."

He smiled. "That's why we need to wait until dark."

Chapter Thirty-two

We stayed on the upper deck until the sun's last rays surrendered to the horizon, then Lew took me to the cabin and made me lie on another chaise while he set out the food in the dining area, complete with candles and a vase of roses.

"You're gonna make somebody a great little wife someday," I said when he was done.

He took my hand and led me to the table. "As long as I can still have my career."

It occurred to me that we'd never talked about anything to do with the future—for obvious reasons on my part at least—so while I pretended to enjoy my cardboard crustaceans, I asked him about his college plans and what he wanted to do afterward.

"I haven't made up my mind about college yet." He cracked open a lobster leg. "But I know I want to do something in software development. The problem is Granddad wants me to work in the company and eventually take over for Dad. I don't want to disappoint him and will probably end up doing it someday, but I want to do something I enjoy for a while at least."

"How does your dad feel about it?" I peeled a few more boiled shrimp without eating any.

"He's okay with whatever I do. I think he secretly wanted me to play pro football, even though there wasn't much chance of me making it that far. I was pretty good for a high school player, but I'm not even sure I could've played in college like Dad. He played at Florida on scholarship."

"Why didn't he keep playing?"

He shrugged. "He's the oldest of his three brothers, so Granddad always expected him to follow him in the company. Besides, he had to be sure he made a lot of money if he wanted to keep Belinda." He put down his fork with a disgusted look.

"Your aunt said everybody in the family believes he really loves her, even though none of them understands why."

"He does. I don't understand it either." He took a drink from the bottle of Chimay he'd surprised me by drinking. "Sure you don't want one of these?"

I arched an eyebrow at him. "Trying to get me drunk, Triple C?"

"Do I need to?"

"No, and it wouldn't work anyway. I'd drink you under the table."

"You're probably right." He finished the bottle and tossed it into the trash. "I don't usually drink anyway."

"Then why tonight?"

"Liquid confidence I guess." The look in his eyes became intent. "I didn't want to disappoint you."

"Not possible," I said.

His smile turned a little wistful. "I'd be lying if I said I wasn't worried about getting through the next few days with my sanity intact. I guess I just wanted tonight to be special."

"It is. Everything's perfect."

He gestured at my plate. "You haven't eaten much. Don't you like the food?"

"It's great. I just don't want to get a cramp if we go

for that swim you mentioned."

"Yeah, I may need you to rescue me since I stuffed my face." He took my hand and pulled me to my feet, then he put his arms around me.

"No worries." I put my arms around his neck and smiled up at him. "I was the star pupil in the country club lifeguard course when I was twelve."

His brows met in confusion. "Country club?"

Crap, how did I let that slip out? It must be because the more we talked, the more I could see how perfectly matched we would've been if I'd known him when I was Jada. So damn unfair.

"Did I say country club? I meant court-mandated community service for juvie kids." I laughed and he totally bought it.

"Well, that's good to know," he said, "because I'm definitely gonna need some mouth-to-mouth."

I was both relieved and disappointed to find out he'd only been teasing earlier when he made me think we were gonna skinny dip. There were assorted swimsuits in one of the storage bins, and he lowered the privacy curtains over the cabin windows so I could change. I picked a black bikini I hoped would get a major reaction from him, and it worked.

"Put your eyes back in your head and go put on your trunks," I said. "My turn to check you out."

When he emerged from the cabin a minute later, I felt sure my face looked exactly like his when he saw me in the bikini. I knew he'd been hiding muscles under those Oxfords and khakis, but I wasn't prepared for the sculpted curves and planes of his arms and chest, and his legs were downright incredible. The boy was freaking gorgeous.

"Come on, let's go." He smiled and took my hand

without pointing out that I needed to be careful not to trip over my tongue.

I had always loved swimming, and it was even better now that I wasn't bothered by the annoying need to breathe. I was also relieved to find out I could still float and didn't sink like a dead rock. After twenty minutes or so, Lew asked me if I was getting cold, and I realized I had no idea if the water was warm or freezing.

"It's a little chilly," I said, trying to play it safe.

"Want to go back aboard?" He put his arms around me with a funny little smile. "I can try to warm you up some."

The butterflies were back to remind me I was about to move into uncharted territory without a compass. The dinner break had interrupted my earlier determination to go for it, and I wasn't sure it would come back even though I wanted it to.

I can do this. I trust him completely, and I know he'd never hurt me.

"I'm okay," I said, "but we can get out if you're ready."

"Oh, I'm definitely ready." He pulled me closer and I felt how ready he was.

This was it. If I was gonna back out, it was now or never. When his lips trailed kisses down my neck, the decision became easy.

"Let's go get warm, Triple C."

We climbed the ladder on the side of the boat and went into the cabin where he turned off everything except a recessed light over the door leading to the aft deck. When he flipped a switch on the instrument panel, Bruno Mars serenaded us from hidden speakers.

"Do you have any idea how beautiful you are?" He

pulled me into his arms and swayed slowly to the music.

"I could ask you the same thing." I ran my hands over his chest and smiled up at him.

His fingers brushed my cheek, then they drifted down my neck and trailed lightly across my collarbone. "Such artistic lines. Makes me wish I could paint."

My own fingers were busy admiring the artistry of his biceps. "It really should be a crime to keep these hidden under sleeves all the time. I'm glad I finally got to see the real you."

"I want to see you too," he said, bending down to kiss me. "All of you."

I felt his fingers slide the straps of the bikini top off my shoulders, then his hands moved to undo the clasp in the front and take it off. When his hands returned to my bare skin, my body reminded me instantly of how much I'd wanted him earlier. I gasped and covered his hands with mine to keep them there, but he misunderstood my reaction.

"Gwen, I'm sorry . . ." He pulled his hands away and backed up. "I shouldn't have rushed you like this."

"No . . ." That was all I got out before he grabbed his shirt from the table beside us and wrapped it around me.

"I should've known this would be hard for you because of everything you've been through. I'm sorry for being so selfish. I just wanted us to be as close as possible."

"No, but you . . . I didn't mean . . ." All of a sudden I couldn't seem to form a coherent sentence.

"It's okay." He put his arms around me and rested his chin on top of my head. "We can take it as slow as you need to. We've got all the time in the world. The rest of our lives."

And there it was. Because only one of us had a life

anymore.

What was it Wade had said? *You won't have to live with what you do, but* he *will.* I knew he was right, and I also knew that Lew wouldn't be talking about the rest of our lives if he didn't already think he loved me. I had no idea if he really did or not, but I knew that if I let him make love to me now, it would break his heart when I left. I couldn't do that to him just to satisfy my selfish desire to know what love felt like. I couldn't let him lose his smile again after me.

I'd been trying to convince myself that I could stay as long as I wanted to. Maybe I could, but I couldn't stay with Lew. He deserved to be with someone who could give him a family and grow old with him, and I couldn't do either one. I had to finish my assignment and leave before he fell any harder for me, because I wasn't gonna cheat him out of the life he deserved just because I'd been cheated out of mine.

So I let him go on thinking I'd freaked out because of the way I'd been used by men in the past. I'd been lying to him the whole time I'd known him, so what was one more lie?

"I'm sorry, Triple C. I thought I could do it, but I can't."

He tilted up my face and made me look at him. "You don't have to apologize to me for anything. Nobody's gonna make you do anything you don't want to do ever again."

I tiptoed to kiss him. "Thank you for understanding."

After we were both dressed, he untied the boat and moved it to the end of the pier so we could sit in the swing before he took me home. I leaned against his chest with his arms wrapped around me and asked him to tell me some stories about his brother so I wouldn't have to talk. I needed to plan out what I had to do over the next few days.

As soon as I got home, I had to rev up my search for BOSSMAN, even if it meant going back to the Sugar Daddy chatrooms where I'd met him the first time. Once I found him, I'd set up a meeting no matter where he wanted it to be. I'd find some way to get there even if it meant taking Karen and Brad's car to do it.

I also had to distance myself from Lew as much and as gently as possible. I'd find some excuse not to see him so much—God knows I was good at coming up with lies. Maybe I could start hinting to him that I might have to change foster homes. But whatever I did, I couldn't do any of it until after Friday. He needed me to get through that, and no way was I gonna let him down.

When he took me home and I kissed him goodbye at the door, I couldn't help holding on to him a little tighter since I knew I wouldn't be able to do it much longer. I guess he noticed because he asked me if I was okay.

"Yeah, I just had such a great time tonight that I don't want it to end."

"Me either. But we'll have plenty more nights like this, I promise."

"I know. And you need to get some sleep anyway so you can kick ass in your tournament tomorrow." I gave him one last kiss and started to open the door, but he turned me back around and held my face in his hands.

"I love you, Gwen. I hope you know that."

Oh, shit. I'd hoped I could do what I needed to do and get the hell out of his life before he said those words to me. What was I supposed to tell him now? I couldn't bear to hurt him, but if I told him I loved him too, it would only

260

hurt him more later on.

I looked into his eyes and couldn't stop the tears that slid down my cheeks. "I don't know anything about love, Triple C. I just know I'm glad we found each other."

I could tell it wasn't what he'd been hoping to hear, but at least he didn't look like I'd just ripped out his heart. He brushed the tears from my cheeks with his thumbs and kissed me again.

"We'll figure it out together. I'm wicked smart, remember? And like I said before, we've got all the time we need."

I would've given anything for that to be true.

* * *

My anger swelled with each step I took as I climbed the stairs to my room. I couldn't wait to find BOSSMAN and make him pay for all the things he'd stolen from me. While I booted up my computer and logged in to FaceSpace, I amused myself by picturing what I'd do when I found him, and it made Rufus's last moments look like a peaceful death in comparison.

But all my rage was replaced with absolute terror when I clicked on the red notification and saw the subject line of the new message.

I HAVE YOUR FRIEND

Chapter Thirty-three

I couldn't do anything but stare at the monitor for several seconds, every muscle in my body paralyzed by fear.

BOSSMAN had Annalee.

There was no reason for me to think so, but I knew it was him. Somehow he'd managed to find me, and now he had my best friend. Without realizing how I got there, I found myself on my knees with my face turned heavenward. It had worked for me once before. Maybe it would work again.

"Please let her still be alive. Please, *please* hear me. I'll do anything!"

I had no idea if anybody was listening, but at least I'd tried. I got up and sat at the computer again, my hand shaking so bad that I could barely hold the cursor still to open the message.

> WE HAVE UNFINISHED
> BUSINESS. IF YOU WANT
> YOUR FRIEND TO GO ON
> LIVING, COME TO ROOM 347
> AT THE PALM WINDS HOTEL.
> CALL THE COPS AND I'LL
> SLICE HER THROAT.

Okay, it sounded like he was using Annalee as a lure. Maybe he hadn't hurt her and would let her go if I did as he said. My fear receded for a few seconds until I realized that the only way he could have found out how to contact me was from Annalee, and she wouldn't have told him anything unless he'd forced her by doing something terrible to her.

The only thing I could do was go there and hope Annalee was still alive. But once I'd made sure she was out of harm's way, I'd show him who had unfinished business. That was for damn sure.

My ability to think rationally returned along with my rage. As desperate as I was to get to Annalee, I had some things to figure out before I left since I'd never be coming back. I'd wanted to stay long enough to let Lew down gently, but all bets were off now. BOSSMAN would be drawing his last breath tonight no matter what, and that meant Gwen would have to disappear forever. I didn't have a choice about what I had to do, but there was one thing I had to make sure of before I left. I e-mailed my request to Flo and got a reply within two minutes.

According to Google Maps, the Palm Winds was only a few miles away, so I wouldn't need to take Karen or Brad's car. I put on my Zombie Girl outfit one last time and jumped out the window. I didn't know if I'd been able to run super fast all along since I'd never tried to do it, but I definitely could do it now. It took me less than fifteen minutes to get to the hotel, just long enough to work out a few final details in my head on the way.

The hotel had seen better days. All the units were accessed from the outside, but there was one wing of rooms with balconies that looked out on Biscayne Bay. The room I was looking for was one of the bay view units on the end of the third level. Perfect for what I had planned.

I listened at the door and heard a television playing inside, but that was all I could hear. I knocked and took a step back. The TV went silent and I heard locks being undone, then nothing for a few seconds.

"Open the door and come in! Try anything funny and your friend dies!"

The red curtain descended over my vision instantly at the sound of the voice that had been the last thing I heard before I died. It took all my self control not to kick in the door and rush the sonofabitch, but I knew I had to play it smart until Annalee was safe. I opened the door slowly and saw him standing across the room behind Annalee. He had her gagged and tied to a chair, a knife to her throat.

I froze for a second when I recognized him as one of the men who'd been at Lew's house for the meeting— the short guy in the bad suit who'd been looking at me funny. I'd thought it was the mention of a Ferrari that had made my skin crawl, but now I knew it was because I'd been standing three feet away from my murderer.

I went in and pushed the door shut behind me. My vision was still draped in red fury, but this time it made it easier for me to see the things I needed to see, almost as if they were highlighted. The hand holding the knife to Annalee's throat was shaking badly, and his eyes reminded me of an animal caught in a trap. The whites were visible all the way around the irises, and they darted around the room as though he expected someone to jump out at him any second.

The bastard was scared shitless and holding on to his sanity by a thread.

"I don't know how the hell you're still here," he said, "but you won't be getting away this time, bitch. Do what I say and maybe I'll let your friend die quickly. Give me any shit and I'll make you watch while I take my time with her."

"Please don't hurt her!" I used every drop of

deceptive skill in me to make my voice sound terrified. I had to make him think he was in control until I could get him away from Annalee. "I swear I'll do whatever you say."

He gave me a reptilian smile and motioned to a coil of twine on the bed. "Lie down and tie your feet with that rope. Roll over and put your hands behind your back when you're done."

I did as he said and tied my feet, making a point to show him how tight I made the knot. While I worked, I noted a few more details about the room. Annalee was crying and scared, but she didn't seem to be bleeding anywhere. She was tied to the chair with the same thin twine I was using, and the knife in his hand looked like a steak knife. He obviously hadn't come prepared for murder, so running into me at Lew's house had been a freak accident. Once he'd recognized me, he must've followed Jaycee and Bud to Annalee's house so he could snatch her and make her lead him to me.

"Turn over like I told you!" He pressed the knife harder against Annalee's throat and made her whimper.

"I will, just don't hurt her!" I turned over and added, "You're the boss, okay?"

I heard him laugh and knew I'd said the right thing. "You're damn right, you little bitch. Nobody's gonna tell me what to do ever again. I'm calling the shots!"

He planted a knee in the small of my back and grabbed my hands to tie them. I didn't know what he'd done with the knife and couldn't take the chance that he might lunge at Annalee with it during a struggle, so I decided not to do anything until he turned me over and thought I was bound and helpless.

When he finished tying my hands behind me, he

265

yanked my head back by my hair and put his mouth close to my ear. "You stupid tramp. Now you're gonna watch while I have some fun with your little friend. And when I get tired of her, the three of us are gonna play some games together. You'll be begging me to kill you both before the night's over, but it won't do you any good. I'm gonna take my time and enjoy it."

I forced myself to wait until he took his knee from my back to roll me over. As soon as he did, I snapped the rope around my hands and ankles like pieces of thread.

"Change of plans," I said. "I'm in charge now."

I grabbed the knife in his hand by the blade and tossed it aside, then I kicked him in the chest hard enough to send him flying across the room. His back struck the television and knocked it against the mirror on the wall behind it. He ended up sprawled on the floor in front of the dresser, covered in shards of glass.

I landed on top of him before he had time to moan. After wrapping a long piece of the twine around his neck several times, I lifted him by it and his belt and threw him against the bed's headboard hard enough to make his eyeballs rattle.

"Having fun yet, asshole?"

I knotted the ends of the rope around one of the bedposts, tight enough that he couldn't move but not tight enough to choke him. He was barely conscious, but his hands still clawed at the rope around his neck. I had to see about Annalee before I finished with him, but I indulged myself by kneeing him in the nuts as a parting shot.

I broke the ropes holding Annalee to the chair and pulled the gag from her mouth, then I threw my arms around her. We clung to each other while we both sobbed.

"I'm so sorry, Annalee. Did he hurt you?"

"I'll be okay." Her lips were cut and swollen, and she seemed to be holding one of her arms against her chest at a funny angle.

"What did he do to you?"

She shook her head. "It doesn't matter now. What are we gonna do?"

"He's the sicko who murdered me," I said. "I have to kill him."

"But you'll go away if you do." Her eyes were huge with fear. "Can't you just call the police? Or we could just leave him here like this and—"

"No." I put my hands on her cheeks and looked into her eyes. "I can't take the chance that he'll get away. I have to make sure he doesn't kill anybody else."

She hung her head and cried silently a few seconds before she looked up at me again. "He already has. Before you got here, he was bragging about the other girls he's killed. He's even got souvenirs from all of them." She pointed at the table by the bed.

I went to the nightstand and looked in the wooden box sitting beside a MacBook. The felt-lined box held an assortment of jewelry and tokens that would be easy to find on teenaged girls at any high school campus, and my anger returned at the thought of the dead girls they represented. Mostly there were rings and bracelets, but there were some odd things like a grubby rabbit's foot, a dime with a hole in it on a chain, and a St. Jude medal.

And lying on the very top was the Best Friends pendant that Cassie and I had bought at the mall for my birthday on the night she died. The other half of the split heart had been on a chain around her neck when they buried her. I picked it up and stared at it a second, then I closed my hand around it and turned to hit him in the gut with the fist holding my necklace.

"Your sick hobby ends tonight, you maggot. And I'm gonna make you pay dearly for all the things you stole."

The rope around his neck kept him from making more than a strangled grunt, but his eyes looked as if they were about to pop out and shoot across the room. His mouth started moving and at first I thought he was trying to beg for his life, then he raised one of his hands between us with his middle finger extended, his eyes bright with an insane gleam.

Well, okay then. If he was too far gone to be sufficiently scared, I'd have to crank up the volume. I picked up the knife then walked back over where he could see me.

"I don't think you realize what deep shit you're in, Cupcake. But maybe this will give you a hint." I plunged the knife into my chest three times in rapid succession. "You're about to find out what happens when you piss off a dead girl."

His eyes lost some of their defiance and fluttered as if he were about to pass out, so I slapped him a few times until they opened wide again.

"Uh-uh. No fair running out on the party. I don't want you to miss a second of all that fun you said you wanted to have with us."

"Gwen," Annalee said from behind me, "can't you just castrate him? Would you get to stay then?"

If my poor dead heart hadn't already been breaking because I had to go, I would have laughed at her suggestion. I turned and hugged her a second before leading her back to the chair and kneeling in front of her.

"That wouldn't work because he could still go on

268

killing girls even if he couldn't rape them. I have to send him to Hell where he belongs."

"Will you just disappear when he's dead?" Tears streamed down her face again.

"That's how it's supposed to work, but I fixed it so it'll be a little different for me. And I'm gonna need your help to make it work."

"What do you mean?"

"We'd be able to keep you out of it if I could just kill him and let the gators in the Everglades eat the scraps, but then everybody would think I ran away when I disappeared, and I can't do that to Lew. He can't think I deserted him."

She shook her head. "I don't understand. What are you gonna do?"

"This is the story I want you to tell everybody." I squeezed her hands. "Tell them I snuck out and went to your place after Lew took me home tonight. Javier saw me on the street after I left your house the other night, so he can back you up that I did it all the time. While I was there talking to you, sleazebag over there broke in and tied us up, then he brought us here to rape and kill us. I managed to get untied when he left for a few minutes, but he came back while I was untying you. I ran to the balcony and he ended up going over the rail in the struggle, but he stabbed me while we were fighting over the knife. Can you remember all that?"

She still looked confused. "Yes, but how will that change anything?"

"Before I left Karen and Brad's tonight, I made a deal with Flo that my body will stay here so it looks like he killed me. That way Lew will at least know I didn't want to leave. That it wasn't my choice."

269

Understanding finally registered on Annalee's face. "You mean I'll have to watch you die for real once he's gone?"

I nodded and hugged her. "I'm so sorry to put you through this, but it's the only way. We have to do it for Lew." I pulled away to look at her again. "And I need you to tell him something for me, okay?"

It was several seconds before she could say, "What?"

"Tell him I should've said I loved him when he said it to me tonight. I told him I didn't know anything about love, but I was wrong." I took the ring off my finger and put it on hers. "Tell him I gave you this before I died to remind both of you not to cry for me, because you and Lew are the reason I know what love is."

"Oh, Gwen." She put her good arm around my neck. "I'm gonna miss you so much. You're the only real friend I've ever had."

"That's not true," I said. "Lew's your friend too, and he's gonna need you to be there for him. You're gonna need each other, and I hope someday you'll tell him how much you love him, because I know you do."

We held each other and cried until a noise made us turn toward the bed. The bastard was clapping slowly, as if to say he enjoyed our touching scene.

I sniffed and looked at Annalee. "I think it's time for this rat-faced fucker to meet Zombie Girl. What about you?"

She wiped away her tears and nodded. "Make him suffer."

I broke the rope around his neck and replaced it with my hand, lifting him off the bed to hold him in the air like the world's ugliest rag doll. "Since the fall's gonna break most of your bones, it won't look suspicious if I break a few before I toss you off the balcony."

His voice was choked and garbled, but he managed to say, "Fuck you, bitch!"

I'd heard somewhere that a broken femur was supposed to be the worst pain ever, so I gave him a zomjitsu chop to the right thigh. From the sound of the crack, it broke completely in half, and from the sound that came out of his mouth, what I'd heard was true. He screamed for a good five seconds then continued to moan and cry, but even in all that agony, he still tried to spit on me.

I threw him to the floor and stood on his arms. "Dude, I don't know if you're just stupid or you're too insane to think anymore, but you don't seem to get that you're about to die an excruciatingly painful death."

He forced out a laugh through his tearful grimace. "No, you're the one who doesn't get it, you stupid bitch! I don't care if you kill me. At least the whole world will finally know everything I've done!"

Hold on a second. This was a way to torture him even more.

"Not if we get rid of that box of souvenirs and your laptop," I said. "Nobody will know you did anything except fail big time tonight."

Before my words had time to register with him, I felt Annalee's hand on my shoulder.

"We can't do that, Gwen."

I turned to look at her. "Why not?"

"The families of those girls he killed deserve to know what happened to them. You can't take that away from them just to punish this piece of shit. You have to leave those things for the police to find."

She was right as usual. I might not be able to save the other girls he'd killed, but I could save their families a little bit of suffering. And there was something else I needed to do too.

"You're right," I said. "Even Vanessa deserves to know the truth. Even after everything she did, I don't want her to think I just ran away." I held up the necklace from Cassie that was still in my hand. "Put this back in the box for me before the cops get here."

She took it and squeezed my hand. "I'm proud of you for doing this for her."

"Oh, how *sweet*." Scornful laughter floated up to us from the floor. "Go ahead and kill me, you stupid little slut. I can't wait for my fat cow of a mother to find out everything I did so she'll know how much I hate her. I hope it makes her choke on her Little Debbies!"

Suddenly, all the things he'd said earlier about calling the shots and nobody telling him what to do made sense. A smile spread slowly across my face as I thought of an even more perfect way to make him pay.

"Aw, but that's not the way it's gonna go down, dickhead. See, you don't get to control *anything,* just like the night I died. I played you for a chump and made you kill me before you got to have any fun, didn't I?" I laughed at the look of dismay growing on his face. "The whole world's gonna find out you're nothing but a pathetic loser who needs a gun to get laid, because my best friend here is gonna tell everyone how you were crying for your mommy when you fell to your death."

"NO!"

Annalee bent over and laughed in his face along with me. "Yeah, that's right. I'm gonna tell them that after you went over the rail and couldn't hold on any longer, your last words were *I love you, Mommy! Please forgive me!*"

"No . . . I *hate* her . . ." His face was a sniveling child's, and his words became incoherent babbling.

I jerked him up by the collar and walked to the balcony. "Annalee, wipe off the knife and bring it to me, please. I'm sick of his whining."

She wrapped the knife in a towel and followed me outside.

"Wait a second." Her tears spilled over again as she kissed my cheek. "I love you, Gwen. I'll never forget you."

I blinked away my own tears. "I love you too. Tell Lew I wish I could've told him goodbye."

I took the knife and jammed it into my stomach up to the hilt, then I grabbed the scumbag's hand and forced his fingers around the handle to put his fingerprints on it. He didn't even try to resist, tears and snot running into his blubbering mouth. I lifted him over the rail and held him dangling in midair.

"Any last words, Mama's Boy?"

He squeezed his eyes shut, and a dark stain spread slowly outward from his crotch.

I clucked my tongue. "Oops, looks like you peed your cheap pants. Worst. Sugar Daddy. Ever."

I let go of his neck and watched him splatter onto the rocks below.

Then everything went dark.

Chapter Thirty-four

I was in Afterlife Admissions again, alone in Flo's cubicle. I looked around but didn't see anyone, and the only thing I heard was the horrific elevator music coming from the speakers, this time featuring the soundtrack from *Mamma Mia*. Kinda appropriate when you thought about it.

I was about to get up and go look for somebody when Flo appeared on the other side of the counter. "Hello, Miss Gayle. Congratulations on completing your assignment."

"Yeah, you can hold off on the party and balloons," I said. "Not really in the mood for celebrating right now."

Her eyebrows rose in surprise. "I would think you'd be happy about your success. You've accomplished a great deal."

I slouched in my chair. "I got rid of two scumbags and taught a few more a lesson. Big freaking deal."

"I don't think you quite understand, Miss Gayle. Eliminating the man who murdered you was indeed your prime directive, but you had another objective to discover on your own. We're very pleased that you succeeded."

I frowned at her a second, then I got it. "Oh, you mean learning to deal with emotions. Yeah, I had loads of fun with that. Thanks a lot for tacking it on."

"That was only part of it. You had to discern your true goal completely of your own free will, and the solution had to come from within your heart."

What the hell was she talking about? Did she mean

274

the stuff that happened with Lew?

"Can you stop with the Hallmark Channel crap and just tell me what I did?"

She sighed. "You forgave your mother, Miss Gayle. When you told your friend to put back your necklace so your mother would know your fate, you finally let go of your hatred for her."

"But I didn't . . ."

I stopped because I realized it was true. When I'd found out that Lew dressed and acted like his brother to punish his mom, I'd really thought I would've jumped at the chance to do the same thing to Vanessa. Making her wonder forever what had happened to her daughter would've been the perfect revenge, but that's not what I wanted.

No, the truth was that when I'd read the articles online about Vanessa's search and seen the reports of how distraught she was over my disappearance, it had secretly made me hope she'd loved me after all. I hadn't been able to admit it to Annalee, but I had wanted it to be true. And I still did.

"Okay, fine," I said. "I guess you're right. So what do I get for it—a special parking space for Transdead Trustee of the Month?"

Flo typed something on her keyboard that prompted printing sounds. "No, you get something much more significant. I'm afraid this changes everything."

"What does that mean?"

"So much additional paperwork." She retrieved several papers from the printer and put them on the counter with another sigh. "You'll need to sign these forms in triplicate before you go back."

I jerked upright. "Go back? Are you telling me I

275

have to keep being a Trustee because I sent that message to my mother with the necklace?"

She turned the papers around and pointed to the top. "No, Miss Gayle. You get to go back to your life."

I read the heading on the top of the page: DISCHARGE OF LIEN.

"But . . ." I looked up at her in confusion. "I thought the whole point of clearing my account was to go on to the Afterlife. That's what you told me before."

"As I explained to you when you first arrived here, Miss Gayle, every Transdead Trustee has a contract with us that must be honored by resolving what was left unfinished in their life, but your prime directive is only part of it. If you're able to discern your underlying objective and complete it before your mission is over, your obligation is fulfilled *in toto*. And, as I said before, that changes everything." She pointed to a dotted line on the paper. "Please sign here and initial here and here."

I scribbled on the papers without really seeing them. "But why didn't you tell me I had some secret goal to figure out from the start? That would've made it a lot easier, you know."

She sighed again. "Must I get out the dictionary and read you the definition of the word *secret*, Miss Gayle?"

I was still too confused to let her sarcasm bother me. "Wait, so does this mean I'm going back to Gwen's life?"

Flo took out an ink pad and rubber stamp. "Please pay attention, Miss Gayle. You get to go back to *your* life, as Jada Celeste Gayle. Since your murder was never confirmed, you will be able to resume your life as though you've been a runaway all this time, just as the authorities believed. This is where your talent for—shall we call it *fiction?*—will come in handy."

She paused to stamp ACCOUNT CLEARED on all the documents and secure them with a golden paper clip.

"The story you invented for the young man about how Gwen Stewart met Jada Gayle at the group home for runaways will allow you to tell everyone that you took her place after *she* was the one who disappeared. You did it to keep your mother from finding you."

I knew all of it was true then because my heart was pounding wildly in my chest, and the sudden need to breathe reintroduced itself with a vengeance.

"But what about the deal we made that my body would stay there so everyone would think he killed me?"

"That is why we had to bring you back here for further instructions before we could proceed. When you return in a few moments, you will once again be on the balcony with your friend."

"What's been going on while I was gone?"

"This entire meeting has taken place in the blink of an eye. It really shouldn't come as a surprise to you that we are not bound by Earthly time constraints here, Miss Gayle."

I had to consciously slow my breathing and was afraid I was about to hyperventilate.

"Lean over and put your head between your knees," Flo said. "As you can see, you are once again subject to bodily functions. Unfortunately, that means you will be in considerable discomfort when you return because of your injuries."

I raised up too quickly and had to duck my head again before I passed out. "You mean I could still die from the knife wound?"

"That wouldn't make much sense, now would it?"

277

Her voice was tinged with exasperation. "Your injury will be serious but not fatal. You will have to recover in the usual manner."

I finally got my breathing under control and raised up to look at her. "Okay, I think I understand it all now. But I have one more question before I go."

"And what is that?"

"I met a guy named Wade who's been a Transdead Trustee for a long time, supposedly because he broke the rules. Does he have a Double Secret Objective that he doesn't know about?"

She gave me an impatient look. "You know I can't discuss someone else's account with you."

"Oh, come on, Flo." I slapped the counter with my hand. "I know you don't have a sense of humor, but don't you have a heart?"

She arched an eyebrow. "I see you've become well-acquainted with compassion, Miss Gayle."

"You're right," I said. "I beat both levels of your Transdead game like a boss, so I deserve an answer to my question."

She stared at me a moment, then she straightened the already neat papers in front of her. "I obviously can't tell you any specifics, but usually when someone remains a Transdead Trustee from their own choosing, it's because they haven't forgiven themselves for something they did in life. Unless he can do that, his regrets will keep him forever in debt."

I thought about that for a second. "And it wouldn't do any good if I tipped him off, because he still wouldn't forgive himself."

"Quite insightful." She typed on the keyboard again. "Now if you'll just sign this new promissory note,

278

you can be on your way."

"Promissory note for what? I thought you said my account was cleared."

She bent to take a sheet of paper from the printer. "Your Afterlife Account was cleared of your previous obligation. This is for the new promise you made."

"What new promise?"

She sighed again and typed something before turning the monitor around so I could see it. The screen went black for a second, then an image appeared of me on my knees earlier that night, saying I would do anything if Annalee was still alive.

I scowled at her. "So what do I have to do now?"

She slid the form over in front of me. "You must promise that you will live a life that means something, Miss Gayle."

I tried to wipe away my tears, but I wasn't fast enough.

Flo handed me a tissue from under the counter. "Despite your reluctance for candor in your blog updates, I think you already know what I mean. You've earned a second chance at life that most people don't get, so I hope you'll make the most of it." She hesitated a second, then she put a hand on my arm. "I know you will."

I picked up the pen and signed my name in big, bold letters.

"Good, now if you'll also initial here"—she pointed to a yellow box of text at the bottom, all business again— "everything will be documented properly."

I struggled to read the extremely fine print in the box, then I looked up at her.

"I have to serve as a Post-Mordem Peer Partner on a PRN basis? What does that mean?"

"PRN stands for *pro re nata*, which is Latin for *as the circumstance arises*. It's most commonly used in the medical profession, but it applies in this case as well."

I looked up at the ceiling. "Well, thanks for the vocabulary lesson, but that's not what I meant. What's a Post-Mordem Peer Partner? And what's with all the P's?"

"It means you must be available in the future to counsel other Transdead Trustees if you are needed. We may not ever need your services, but you must help if you're called upon. The P's are merely a result of our Administrator's fondness for alliteration. Personally, I don't approve of such frivolity."

I laughed as I initialed the box, then I handed the form back to her. "You know, I'm really gonna miss you, Flo. Can I still e-mail you sometimes?"

She arched an eyebrow again, but I thought I saw the tiniest hint of a smile.

"It's not expressly forbidden, so I suppose it would be okay. Just make certain that you change your e-mail address to something appropriate."

* * *

When I opened my eyes, I was on the floor of the hotel balcony with Annalee clutching my hand to her lips, my necklace still dangling between her fingers. I knew for sure I was mortal again, because my stomach felt like somebody had filled it with red-hot coals from a barbeque grill. It was an effort just to breathe, but I managed to squeeze Annalee's hand hard enough to get her attention.

"Gwen, I thought you were gone . . . oh my God, you're *bleeding*."

"Call 911 . . ." I took the necklace and tried to smile but couldn't swing it. "I'll give that to . . . my mom myself."

280

Her forehead wrinkled, then her eyes widened with dawning joy. She ran to the phone and I heard her telling the 911 operator to send an ambulance and the police. I was having a hard time keeping my eyes open, so I didn't know she'd come back until I felt her take my hand again.

"They're coming. Oh, Gwen, I don't know why you're still here, but please hold on!"

I knew I was about to lose consciousness and needed to tell her what to say to the cops. I mustered every bit of strength I had left and forced my eyes open.

"Stick to story . . . for now . . ."

* * *

Sirens approaching. Voices shouting instructions with more sirens in the background. Annalee crying. Tubes and needles invading my body, and still the fire pit in my stomach.

Welcome darkness.

Sirens again. I'm in a vehicle moving at high speed. Voices relaying numbers and readings in dire tones. Somebody telling me to hold on, then something covering my mouth. Brief escape from the pain when the darkness comes again.

Hospital noises and new voices, all of them shouting instructions. People poking and prodding me everywhere. More tubes and needles. Bright lights, beeps and whooshing sounds, then the slow descent into darkness for what I pray won't be forever, despite what Flo told me.

Finally, I really do want to live.

* * *

I heard Lew's voice before I opened my eyes, but he wasn't talking to me.

281

"Please let her wake up, God. I know I swore I'd never believe in you again after Drew died, but I take it all back. I'll do anything if you let her come back to me."

My eyes fluttered a few times before I could get them to stay open. Lew had my hand in both of his with his forehead pressed to them, so he didn't see me open my eyes.

"Careful with those promises, Triple C. He'll hold you to them no matter what."

His head jerked up and he gasped, then he leaned over to kiss me. "I thought I'd lost you. Oh, Gwen . . ." His voice broke as he started to cry.

"Jada," I said, brushing away his tears. "My name is Jada."

~~~

About the Author

JOYCE SCARBROUGH is a Southern woman weary of seeing herself and her peers portrayed in books and movies as either post-antebellum debutantes or barefoot hillbillies á la Daisy Duke, so all her heroines are smart, unpretentious women who refuse to be anyone but themselves. Joyce has three published novels and also has short stories featured in several anthologies. She writes both adult and YA fiction and is active in her regional chapter of SCBWI. Joyce has lived all her life in beautiful LA (lower Alabama), she's the mother of three gifted children, and she's been married for 31 years to the love of her life—a superhero who disguises himself during the day as a high school math teacher and coach.

Web site — http://joycescarbrough.com
Blog — http://joycescarbrough.blogspot.com
Facebook — https://www.facebook.com/pages/Joyce-Scarbrough-Books/225355834210672
Twitter — @JoyceScarbrough

Also by Joyce Scarbrough

True Blue Forever

Different Roads

Symmetry

CPSIA information can be obtained at www.ICGtesting.com
Printed in the USA
LVOW10s1734210715

447055LV00007B/1026/P